Come the King

On Dragon Wing

With Eagle spread

Of Lion bred.

Seed once spurned,

The stones returned.

From his back, the Dragon torn,

Two of Blood and Three of Bed--one day born.

Sons, One of Each and One More--

One More and The Tribal Four.

But come again the Dragon Sign

White Dragon draws the final line.

Glory upon Glory and Woven In.

> --the last verse of Kaul-Leb, Poet and
> Prophet of the Dragon

Found by his bedside the morning of his death.

Kaul-Leb went to the Dragon almost twenty-five years after his beloved wife, Steela. After her crossing, the Poet of the Dragon wrote primarily lines of prophecy studied by the Elders of the Conclave, People of the Dragon. Much of his later works were archived in Conclave as being too frightening for the general population. But his last work, the one written on what was to be his last night of life, was studied by Dragon young as a prophecy of hope. It fueled many debates among the People as to its meaning.

He had been found that morning by one of his grandsons, a boy of eighteen, one of Lart's children.

The boy immediately went to his mother, the youngest daughter of Stahl, to tell that Grandfather had crossed over.

Chapter One
The Wanting

It was at the yearly remembering for the poet Kaul-Leb in their village that Stell first noticed among the extended family of the Great Poet a young girl with striking light green eyes. Out of the corner of his own blue ones, he had felt himself being watched. When he turned his head, he barely caught a glimpse of the teasing look as she turned back, being chastised by her mother to show respect.

Two years.

For two years the young man had been in love. There were times he could not continue with his work for thinking of the sweetness of her soft, tender, passionate lips and her gentle touch on his arm as they walked together in the evenings. But at twenty-three he would have to wait another two years before they could marry. Another two years. He sighed. Two more years. But at the end of those two years—Always and Forever, she would be his.

Stell had been in love with Slia for two years.

Everyone knew, everyone was pleased, and everyone loved the sweetness between them.

He had stolen a few quick kisses but would no more try to be with her before their marriage than he would try to live underwater. In two years more...Until then, he would love his beautiful girl, the oldest child of the Black Dragon Chieftain, and the only daughter, and dream of their lives after he covered her in his marriage cape.

Slia had noticed Stell, quietly flirted, and won his heart just after she reached puberty. She would be seventeen when they married, he would be twenty-five. Perfect ages for a young couple of the People.

"Slia," her mother warned. "Pay attention to your stitch length."

The girl dropped her eyes down to the bed linens under her hand and sighed.

She began picking out the errant stitches in her pattern.

"Keep your mind on your work, child."

"Soos, Mother."

Slia had rather keep her mind on the man she had promised to wed. Stell was tall, but not too tall. She could feel how muscular his arms were when they walked together, hers through his. His back was straight and strong, his stride quick and with purpose. Unless she was on his arm, then he slowed to savor her being beside him.

His blue eyes! Oh, his eyes! They looked at her with passion and gentle love. His coarse black beard and mustache were already as full as any grown man's. His hair gleamed with good health, pulled back with his temple braids—no wonder she couldn't concentrate on mere stitching. She imagined the day he would sleep under her linens—maybe that would help her watch her stitches. But it didn't, for she only imagined what those linens would witness between them when she and Stell were at last joined.

She worried over her young man, though. It seemed there was always rumor of war. No longer did the People of the Dragon fear the Song-hee to the southern plains, for their fearsome armies had been devastated by inferior leadership of two successive kings. The Song-hee had been led by the Poet's spirit to join with the Dragon and become one people. Her own father, and thus she and her brothers, carried Song-hee blood. Father's Blood Great-Grandfather had been one of the last of the mighty Black Lions, betrayed and surrendered and enslaved.

The new worry came from the west. There had been skirmishes for a generation, but with the Chief Elder Salar becoming old, it was feared the Torbraugh would feel he was also weak.

A time of war came.

The day that Stell went to war with the other young men, Slia was certain her heart would break. He and the other young men of their village and surrounds rode out mounted atop nearly every horse in the area. They rode under the banner of the Black Dragon, the tribal symbol of almost all families living nearby, even the Song-hee who had joined their people and lived in the nearby area.

Before he mounted his steed, Stell had said his farewells to his mother, and grandmother, and neighbors. Then he turned to Slia's family.

Slia's brothers were too young to go to war. Sadly, though, her father was not too old. He had already held his family close and kissed them each many times before Stell appeared beside them.

For the sake of good manners, he first addressed her mother and at last, Slia.

"I'll be back soon; you know I will."

From within his tunic folds, Stell pulled a Dragon Eye stone attached to a leather cord.

"Wear this for me," he said, slipping the cord over her head and placing the stone over her heart. She grasped the red stone in her hand, it was warm, as if alive. The warmth of it came from Stell's body, and it made her feel it was part of him.

It didn't matter that they were in public, for their parting, the two embraced and kissed passionately.

When a young man goes off to war, it is best he carries within him the reason to return. Those who did not avert their eyes gave mute approval.

The warriors pulled themselves up into the decorated leather saddles and trotted their horses away, shields and swords shining in the strong sunlight. They and their horses were protected with metal and leather armor. A few sported the new weapon introduced to them years ago when the Torbraugh had made their previous, futile attempt at taking down the Conclave—they wore quivers full of lethal arrows across their backs, bows strapped to their saddles. Sprinkled among the dark-haired People of the Dragon were the Song-hee Dragons, mostly fair in coloring. Being one people had made their force stronger, and had fueled their belief that they would live in peace. None looked back, it being considered an act of doubt against the Dragon. All those left behind, though, watched until the last rider was out of sight, most with tears tracking down their cheeks. Slia was no different.

Her hand returned to the stone and lifted it to her lips, kissing it softly and letting it drop. Like many others, she went home to weep even more. Not only for her beloved, but for her father, as well. Every home in the village and surrounding countryside felt the emptiness. If not for a son, husband, brother, or love, at least for a friend. The community was suddenly almost fifty men and older boys lighter.

Chapter Two
The Battles

The warriors of the People from Stell's village joined with others, first with other Black Dragon villages, then with the men and boys of the other districts. So ominous was the threat against the People that Apprentices and Junior Elders from the Conclave mixed in with the village militias. These Servants of the Law of the Dragon had continued the training they began as children even though they were now dedicated to the study of the Law. Their robes of office had been abbreviated from the usual long length and shortened to the size of a regular tunic to allow for ease of movement in battle.

Conclave Custodians remained guarding the Conclave. It had taken their Chief Elder Salar over a year, when he was young, to recover from an arrow to his gut from the previous attack. It was known that he had survived only because the Spirit Warrior of his grandfather Kaul-Leb had counseled him to return to life. If he were to be wounded again, they feared he would have no choice but to cross over into death.

A generation of training with their Song-hee brothers had hardened the People of the Dragon in warfare. The Song-hee among them had learned how to fight on horseback instead of always on foot.

Each had learned from the other and discovered new skills together. Through experimentation with captured weapons and Torbraugh archers as forced coaches, the new generation of warriors copied this deadly, long-ranged killing device.

Stell found himself assigned to a company of fighters with Dragons and Song-hee Dragons of two districts, Black and Red. He knew nearly all the citizens he rode among, having vied with them at various war games throughout his upbringing. The Chief Commander was a direct descendant of the revered Kaul-Leb, a grandson of his son Lart, known as Sekale.

Although more of Dragon blood now than Song-hee, Sekale harkened back to his great-grandfather Kaul-Leb as a young man. His hair was the color of spring honey, and his eyes were the same emerald green as his famous ancestor, or so said those who had seen Kaul-Leb as a youth. But he sported the heavier bone structure of the Dragon men and a full, blonde beard and mustache. His braids of citizenship were thick pulled back with his coarse, wavy hair.

On his right shoulder blade was a Red Dragon, the line of Kaul-Leb apparent with the dual headed beast, one head a dragon, and one a black lion. On his left shoulder blade was his marriage dragon, but it was red with a lion's head. He had married a Song-hee woman whose family had affiliated with the Red Dragon District.

All the warriors in the company knew Sekale's back well as he usually practiced without his tunic, preferring to feel the sun on his broad, muscular shoulders.

Never one for the study of words, Sekale was not like his great-grandfather, he preferred the warrior life and was known as a premier fighter. Stell expected that Sekale's company would enjoy the thick of the coming battles. Their sub-commander was Slia's father, himself a blood descendant of the poet Kaul-Leb. Sekale had chosen his distant cousin partly because of their shared heritage and partly because he believed the Black Dragon Tribal Chieftain had a steady head on his shoulders and gave good advice.

Stell had fought, briefly, one time against Sekale at war games and been knocked quickly down in the dirt on his behind. He had barely earned his Dragon then and knew he wouldn't last long when the draw had placed him opposite the older warrior. Stell had been embarrassed at being taken down so early, but Sekale smiled graciously and extended his hand to help the boy Stell up from the ground.

"You have good form," he had said. "You are just young and inexperienced."

Sekale had spent the rest of the afternoon schooling the young Stell in battle strategy until Stell had actually landed a couple of good blows. Sekale had laughed and grasped him about the shoulders declaring Stell would be a mighty warrior one day.

He always acknowledged Stell when they saw one another at games, which always impressed Stell's peers, and now had chosen him for his company.

Ten days after leaving home, Stell saw his first battle with the Torbraugh White Eagles.
Sekale, mindful that half his company were untried youngsters like Stell, placed them at the rear and middle.

"Let them see war before they have to feel it," he said to his officers. "Never put the young in front. They will never have the opportunity to learn and grow in skills if they are killed outright."

Sekale had led in many border skirmishes before the full war declaration and thrived on the atmosphere of fighting. A third of the company were Sekale's Song-hee veterans, trusting him not only because he was a proven leader, but unlike many of Dragon heritage, he resembled them and married one of their daughters. And they knew that the Song-hee he resembled had been one of the last of the legendary Black Lions.

"Ready your shields," he ordered. They had all practiced fending off arrows, spears, and swords. Sekale took it personally if any of his troops received even a glancing blow.

"Archers, pull and release."

From the middle of his company, behind the shields of those in front, his archers let fly the first barrage of long-range arrows.

The Torbraugh Eagles, who still mostly fought on foot, knelt down under their upturned shields and accepted the first hits from the Dragons. Several over eager Eagle archers, preparing an answering barrage were premature in standing to shoot and caught the last of the Dragon arrows in tender flesh.

"Archers, again. And charge."

Sekale had trained his chosen archers to pull and release with their horses' reins held in their teeth.

The other riders were tasked with protecting not only themselves but their brothers with bows. Stell and a Red Dragon he had met before at war games were assigned one of the veteran Song-hee Dragon archers to protect, one on either side of him.

In the few days of preparation, Stell's horse had been trained to match strides with the horse alongside him whenever Stell called, "Match." His stallion was to stay by that horse until reined in or kicked in the flank to go elsewhere. That freed his rider to watch the sky for arrows. For the rider was protecting not only himself and his archer, but the horse, as well.

"Archers!"

The archers let fly once more. This would be the last volley of this battle, almost immediately they would be too close to their targets. After the last flight of arrows, bows were shouldered, and swords drawn. Sekale did not have to order this, his men were trained to know.

Stell reined his horse, signaling it to abandon its matching stride. The sword in his hand had been his father's. Sekale had given his approval of its keen edge just the night before.

For a bare moment, Stell thought of his father, dying in a stream swollen by spring rains trying to rescue a drowning calf when Stell was only nine. He had asked his mother once why she never remarried.

"If I ever find another as good as your father, I might," had been her reply. Evidently, she had never found one. Stell and his little sister, Sisten, had grown up watched over by their father's friends. Three years ago, Sisten had married a young man of their village now in the Conclave. He had risen to Senior Elder just months before the war and would not be in the fighting.

Sekale's horse was the first of the company to make contact. Sekale and his big brute of an animal landed in the middle of a pile of men and shields and swords. Sekale's battle cry was nearly as intimidating as having his large, vicious stallion purposefully stomping with his enormous hooves directly on a man's chest.

Man and steed thrived on the sounds, sights, and smells of close battle. It had been said that Sekale took the strain of Blood Fever he inherited from his Song-hee ancestors and tamed the Beast to his own will.

Even though Stell's body held not a drop of Song-hee blood, he found himself catching Sekale's enthusiasm and plunged into the fray beside the more seasoned warriors. The sound and feel of his blade clashing against the metal of others sent a thrill through him he could not later explain. Stell found himself enraged at an Eagle who had the audacity to aim a blow at his mount's front right ankle.

The man's blade slid off Stell's as the young Dragon countered the blow then jerked his sword back up to slice through the man's chin, nose, and forehead as if the tough leather face armor were not in place. The man went to his knees screaming and Stell obliged by countering with a blow to the back of his neck, relieving the man's pain.

They had engaged just before the sun was at its apex and by mid-afternoon, the warriors were gathering firewood to send the killed on to the Dragon when the sun went down. It was to be a large pyre for the People of the Dragon would not leave a warrior uncared for in his death, no matter what flag flew above his head in life.

Almost half the Eagles had fallen outright. Those too wounded to survive were dispatched with as little pain and as much dignity as possible. Battle wagons were loaded with the badly wounded Dragons and the less severely wounded of both sides and dispatched to healing stations behind Dragon lines. Surrendered Torbraugh had their sword hands tied behind them and were led away surrounded by mounted troops.

Sekale had his warriors fed before sunset to properly attend to the sending. Brush and quick burning grasses were used to kindle the bottom layer of the wood that served as the laid fire's base. Logs and limbs were loosely piled to allow good air circulation to keep the fire burning hot.

Then a laying on of the fallen bodies of the enemy. More wood was laid down over them building up the setting of the fire. Two horses were lost in battle and their bodies came next. Another layer of wood and the men tenderly laid the bodies of the fallen People of the Dragon. Three Red Dragons had fallen, as well as four Black Dragons, two of those being Song-hee Dragons. There were twenty-three fallen Eagles.

As the sun set, Sekale took a burning branch from a cooking fire and lit the sending pyre. To show deep respect, all stood until the last coals winked out.

Any flesh or bone left was considered the Dragon's gift to his wild children and not to be disturbed by man's hands. In the morning all would take a handful of ash and rub it on their saddles to carry the dead into battle again, unforgotten.

The number of dead Torbraugh varied from battle to battle but was usually much higher than suffered by the People of the Dragon. Stell became a seasoned warrior and was moved up in the company formation as new men joined.

The Torbraugh generals were growing weary of Sekale's victories. Any White Eagle survivors that were able to make it back behind their lines were closely questioned and spies were sent to observe, but not engage.

Stell still rode beside the same Song-hee Dragon archer, but they had lost the man who first guarded the other side. A tried and found worthy replacement from a Blue Dragon village was discovered and joined them.

Sekale's company had grown to over a hundred men strong.

The coming engagement with a Torbraugh company of similar strength was expected to go as the others had.

"Men," Sekale admonished them just before leaving their place of overnighting. "Do NOT become complacent that we will always win."
His high-spirited mount was ready to go and pranced around.

"Victory is likely to become harder to win as we encounter more and more experienced fighters. Keep your head about you—and keep your life."
"Victory to the People," he called and allowed his horse its head as he brandished his sword in the air.

The company roared behind him and all fell into their assigned position behind Sekale. His pulled back hair bounced as it fell down the middle of his back.

Stell could see all his leader's movements now from his forward place in the company. His Song-hee Dragon archer had his bow in his hand. He and Stell had become friends over the weeks they rode together. His name was Sturl, having been born among the Dragons, his parents gave him a Dragon name.

Sturl had straight sandy-red hair and was a full citizen with braids falling down from his temples and pulled back behind his neck with the rest of his hair. He was married and had three small sons. His wife, he told Stell, was of pure Dragon descent. He missed his little family greatly and spoke of them often when the company was not fighting or training. Sturl had most likely heard enough about Slia to find her in a crowd, as well.

Sekale raised his sword to stop their advance.
In the valley below the small rise they were on, was a company of White Eagles, ready for the Dragons.

"Archers, ready.

From all over the spread of the company was heard, "Match."

Horse ears twitched listening each to his own rider.

"Archers, release and charge."

Arrows flew and horses ran three abreast in the ranks of the archers and their protectors. As soon as one arrow was released, another flew from each bow, Sekale having ordered earlier in the day to fire as often as they could. He expected a hard fight.

They were quickly too close for further releases and swords replaced bows, protectors signaled their horses to break off matching.

As usual, Sekale and his big stallion plunged into the middle of the front of the enemy line, but the usual ended then.

The whole front line of Eagles raised their shields high while those right behind them dropped theirs and pulled hidden spears from the ground at their feet. Sekale and his horse were alone, surrounded by spears thrusting at them alone. The horse went down and Sekale with it. None of the Dragon warriors could get near him to help defend him. At least twenty spears found their mark and Sekale's body lost its fight to hold his spirit.

For a stunned moment, the Dragons could not react, but then Sekale's training took hold and Slia's father's orders began to be heard and obeyed. Several Dragon mounts fell to the spears, taking their riders to the ground. One of those was Stell's horse, falling so fast and so hard that Stell did not react quickly enough to get clear of the beast's weight and his left foot was trapped.

As he struggled, an Eagle warrior fought his way to him and caught the calf of Stell's right leg with the edge of his sword, slicing through the strong leather leggings protecting it and down to the bone, severing the muscle nearly in half. Then the man raised his sword up out of the bloody mess of Stell's leg and aimed at the young Dragon's side where his armor laced. The tough cords binding his armor together cut apart as though made of spider webs and the sword point hit rib bone and soft tissue. He prepared to raise his arms for another gouge when his brown eyes opened wide in surprise and he fell across his victim, a Dragon arrow sticking from his back.

Sturl did not have time in battle to check on his friend's condition, but feared his own strike had come too late. He turned to other targets. He was on foot, but had avoided being trapped by his falling animal.

Stell entered the blackness.

He was walking down a long, dark hallway that echoed with every step he took. A very great distance away he could barely discern a weak glimmer of pale light. Slowly, an awareness of others nearby came to him. He could see no one, but was aware that they walked near him. He could only hear his own footfalls. Only his own breathing. On he walked. He didn't know where, only that he must keep walking toward that pale light.

After what seemed like an instant and forever both, he was aware of someone up ahead in his path. It must be a warrior, for the tall man balanced a sword tip at his own feet, the hilt in his large hand, standing casually, waiting for Stell.
Stell could not see the warrior's face until the man spoke, then an inner light shone from it, as though reflecting moonlight.

"This path is not for you, my young friend, not today."

It was Sekale, his voice warm and friendly, but firm.

"Sekale? What is this?"

"It is the path to forever, the crossing over, to death."

"Are you? Am I dead? The battle, what happened?"

"Soos, my boy, I have crossed over. I am dead. I was too badly wounded."

He laughed.

"I warned all of you about arrogance, but did not heed my own words. You are hurt, but you will live. You will not go into battle again, for your leg will not heal completely, you will always limp and walk with some difficulty, but you will live. The battle? There were heavy, heavy losses on both sides."

Sekale looked to his left. Vague forms passed by them and went on.

"So many lost," he said sadly.
"Before you turn and go back, will you do something for me when you are healed?"

"Certainly, Sekale, what?"

"Go to my wife and children and tell them my last living thoughts were of them. Now, go."
Sekale's spirit was gone. The dim light ahead was fading. Awareness of others around him was no more.

Stell turned around and faced the way he had come.

Total darkness. Deep nothingness. He took a tentative step.

His leg! The pain, the wrenching pain! His right leg felt like it was on fire. And his side—he groaned at the pain. Never had he felt pain before in his life like his leg and his side. A deep, low moan escaped him. Something was pulling at his hand—his sword—his father's sword—someone was trying to take it from him. He grasped it harder, with all his waning strength.

"Esoos!" he managed to say only slightly above a whisper. No!

Gentle hands pried his fingers from the hilt of his father's sword.

"Easy, son, we're not taking it from you, you'll still have it. We just need to get you in the wagon."

He lost his grip on the hilt and it was lifted away.

Carefully, very carefully, he was lifted by many sets of hands and gently placed on a softness. He was on his left side. He couldn't focus his eyes. He could barely breathe for the pain.

The hilt of a sword. His sword? Was placed in his left palm and his right hand carefully lifted and placed atop it.

"See? You've got it back now, son. Just lie still and let us take care of you."

A warm cloth was draped over him and the wagon slowly began to move. Several sets of hands held to him slightly to keep him steady on his side.

He closed his eyes, he couldn't really see, they wouldn't focus.

A light hand pressed at his neck.

"He's just resting, his heart still beats, but weakly."

"How did they find him? I thought they had all the living out this morning."

"They were getting all the dead ready for the fire when they pulled that Eagle sword out of his side and he groaned. He had been checked earlier. My guess is he was almost crossed over, but the Dragon sent him back."

"He's so pale, he's lost so much blood. Do you think he'll live?"

"He will have the best chance he can be given. This battle was so bad that I've heard Tay himself is coming to see to the wounded."

"The Chief Elder's son?"

"Soos."

Stell lost consciousness completely.

Chapter Three
The Healing

Stell had vague impressions of more pain, especially in his leg. Voices. Blurred faces. He couldn't find his sword. When he managed to ask about it, in hoarse whispers, voices without faces assured him it was nearby. More pain. Vile, nasty tasting liquids were put in his mouth and he was too weak to expel them. They slid down his throat, burning.

He felt himself being washed and felt a mild, disjointed embarrassment at being cleansed by others. His leg hurt so badly tears slid out of his eyes and pooled in his ears. They were gently swabbed dry and soft cloths placed around his face to catch any other tears.

Sometimes gentle, but knowing hands pressed on his body feeling of his insides through his skin, or felt of his leg.

At times, the hands touching him were small and soft, or large and toughened from use.

Finally, one day he opened his eyes and could actually focus. Someone was washing his torso, then a strong-smelling salve was spread on his side. His leg wound was left alone.

His mind brought to his attention the recollection of who was treating him.

"Sisten..." he whispered. His sister was caring for him.

"Stell!" she said softly and smiled at him. She leaned down and kissed his forehead.

"How? Where?"

"After you were first treated, you were brought here to the Conclave. You are in our family quarters in the Senior Elder Corridor of the Conclave."
She kissed him again.

"Everyone is tending to someone. Either in family quarters or in the Great Hall."

Sisten carefully sat beside him on the edge of his bed.

"When they brought you in, I had you brought here to me. We had the room since Stilk still sleeps in our room."

"The baby, how old is he now?" Stell whispered. It still hurt too much to pull in enough air to use his voice. "Can I see him soon?"

"He is almost six months, and soos, you may see him. Lie still and I'll go get him, he's with Sailk in his study."

She rose and left. In a moment, a tall, lean, gangly man in Elder robes entered, Sailk, Sisten's husband.

He was smiling as he came toward the bed and placed his hand on Stell's forehead.

"No fever, that's good. Stilk needed changing and Sisten doesn't want me doing it, she's certain I would forget and leave him bare bottomed. They will be here in a moment. It's good to see you doing better."

Stell smiled. He liked his bookish brother-in-law.

That he treated his little sister with worshipful awe made it easy.

"My sword?" he asked.

"Sisten put it up where the baby couldn't reach it, don't worry, it's here and it's safe. It was your father's, wasn't it?"

"Soos," Stell whispered.

Sisten entered with the baby in her arms. He was a well-fed little bundle of constant action, slobbering over cutting new teeth. His pure blue eyes were framed by large black eyelashes and his dark hair was getting long enough to fall into curls.

"So big," Stell whispered.

"You haven't seen him since he was first born," Sisten said, leaning low to give Stell a good look at his nephew. Stilk reached for him.

"Not yet, dear boy, Uncle Stell needs to heal a little more before you maul over him," Sailk said and took Stilk from his mother.

"I think we should send word to Tay that Stell is awake, don't you, Sisten?"

"Soos," she answered.

"You stay with your brother while my helper and I go find a Custodian to get him."

Sailk and the baby left the room. The front door to their quarters opened but did not close. It wasn't long before they were back with an older man with graying red hair and beard.

"I was just down the corridor coming this way when your two men told me the good news," he said to Sisten.

He squatted down beside Stell.

"Well, young man, you certainly look much better than you did the first time we met," he said softly. Stell smiled. The little talking he had done had tired him.

Tay, the leading medical authority of the People of the Dragon and the younger of the Chief Elder's twin firstborn sons, felt first the pulse in Stell's neck, then expertly examined the wound in his side and recovered it.

"I'm going to poke around on your leg a little bit to see how well that muscle is healing, it may hurt quite a lot, but it's the only way I can tell how its doing. If it hurts too much, tell me and we'll let it rest a little before I keep going."

"Soos," Stell whispered.

"Sisten, you may want to take the baby out, he doesn't need to see."

"Soos," she answered and took the baby from Sailk and left the room.

Tay moved the soft, warm covers off Stell's leg and then the loose bandage was removed. Cool air touching the healing wound made his leg twitch.

"Did you feel it move just then?"

"A little," Stell whispered.

"Good."

Tay dipped his fingers in the pot of salve by the bedside.

"When I put the honey salve on my fingers before touching a wound, there tends to be less chance of infection later," Tay explained.

He lightly touched the site of the mutilated calf muscle. Hot streaks of pain shot through the still raw, partially open wound.

Stell felt sick to his stomach. He was afraid he might vomit and hurt his side. Cold sweat broke out on his forehead and his breathing became harder.

The pain became more intense as Tay pressed harder, and Stell lost consciousness.

He awoke not too long after as Tay was loosely wrapping his leg, a satisfied look on his face.

"It is healing well, Stell. For as badly as you were wounded, it is healing well. It will take a long while, but you will probably be able to walk again, with a bad limp."

"That's what Sekale told me."

"Sekale?"

"Soos, in the dark corridor, Sekale told me before I came back."

Tay could not doubt him, he had heard too often of his great-grandfather's appearances as a Spirit Warrior. Even though not close in age, Tay and the warrior Sekale were both great-grandsons of the poet Kaul-Leb. And Tay's father, Kaul-Leb's grandson, the Chief Elder of the Conclave, Salar, had walked that dark corridor when he nearly died.

"Slia?" Stell asked. "Will I be able to see Slia soon?"

"Here, drink this," Tay said and put a mug to Stell's lips, one hand holding the wounded warrior up high enough so he would not choke.

"We will talk of other visitors when you are a little stronger."

The elixir in the mug soon had Stell in a restful sleep.

Tay did not want to speak of Slia with Stell just yet. He wanted the youngster to want to heal. Speaking of Slia would not help. It was Tay that advised Sisten to hide the sword, not for the baby's sake, but for Stell's.

Chapter Four
Slia

Shortly after the battle that cost so many lives on both sides, including Sekale and one of the Torbraugh king's favorite cousins, emissaries from the Conclave of the People and the White Eagles met and began negotiations for a treaty to end the war.

Concessions were made on both sides. In deference to the Chief Elder Salar's advantaged age, the Torbraugh king decided he would be gracious and go to the Conclave itself to personally sign the treaty for peace. In truth, he was consumed with curiosity over the Conclave, its buildings, and the old Chief Elder.

In late autumn, the king, his personal guard, and a division of Eagle warriors with assorted dignitaries rode through the Black Dragon central village accompanied by an escort of seasoned Dragon fighters.

"Keep the children in the house," the Black Dragon Chieftain admonished his wife. "There will too much excitement and too many strangers moving through the village today."

He had returned home several days after the battle that had claimed Sekale and so badly wounded his daughter's betrothed, Stell. He had seen Stell being attended by the Chief Elder's own son and been assured that the boy would most likely live before he made his own way home.

Slia wept bitterly to hear of her beloved's wounds and wanted to go to him. She wept again being told he could have no visitors for now. The Conclave buildings were overrun with the healing wounded; there was no room for young sweethearts.

By the time the king's convoy was scheduled to cross through the village, she had learned that Stell's own sister was taking care of him under the supervision of Tay and was satisfied of his treatment. She was relieved that no young daughter of an Elder was seeing to him. She considered him far too handsome to be attended by an unattached female surrounded by no one but men interested in their boring law manuscripts.

The White Eagle Torbraugh king was only a reported short march away from the village when a frantic knock came to the Chieftain's family's door.

His wife opened their door to find a boy from an outlying farm standing waiting for her answer.

His eyes were wide and his breath coming in hard gasps.

"Please come, Mother sent me for you. She says the baby is coming soon!"

The boy's father was among the wounded being treated at the Conclave. He had had to shoulder far too much in his father's absence and was doing his best to work their farm with the help of two younger brothers. Delivering his young brother or sister was beyond him as he had only received his citizenship braids in mid-summer.

"Have you and your brothers eaten today?"

"Soos, Mother had us eat earlier this morning—she thought the baby would wait until tonight or tomorrow, but just a bit ago said it is coming sooner."

"Slia," she called into the house. "Wrap one of the new loaves in a cloth and bring it while I get my baby things!"

"Soos, Mother," the boy heard.

Slia arrived at the door with the fresh aromatic bread loosely wrapped as her mother returned with the basket of her birthing supplies.

"Slia, you and your brothers stay in the house. You know what your father said. He has to be at the square to greet that king."

"Soos, Mother."

Mother turned to look Slia in the eye.

"I mean it—stay in the house."

"Soos, Mother, I heard."

"Do more than hear, Girl—obey!"

"Soos, Mother."

Mother knew how headstrong her daughter could be. Slia pushed the door shut as her mother and the anxious boy hurried away.

She wanted to see what a king looked like. She wanted to see how Torbraugh warriors were. She just wanted to see.

Father and Mother both said to stay in the house.

They did not say she could not have the door open and watch. She would still be obeying what they both said. She knew that Mother would not want the door to be open, neither would Father. But they had not SAID so.

Sure that her mother was well out of the village, Slia opened the door again. There were some villagers on the street, but not a crowd. Most would be at the square who wanted to set eyes on the king and those around him.

"Why is the door open?" Salmar asked. He was the oldest of her brothers, but younger than Slia by almost two years.

"Mother said to stay in the house."

"I am staying in," Slia answered.

"But the door is open."

"I know, but I am IN the house."

"She had the door shut, though."

"Mother is not here, is she?"

"Esoos, she is not," he said and looked around.

The other two brothers came to the open door.

"Are we going to see the king?" asked one.

"What will Father say?" asked the other.

"If you are so worried," Slia snapped, "go hide under your bed!"

She nervously fingered the Dragon Eye stone pendant through her clothes. She had hoped to watch without her parents finding out. But with all three of the boys questioning her, she was sure there would be no keeping it a secret. She had about decided to push the door shut when in the distance came the muffled sounds of many footfalls, both of horses and men.

Slia knew that there would be a short welcoming ceremony in the square. She had heard her father, as Black Dragon Chieftain, practicing what he would say to the king. He was nervous, but not all that excited to have the king who had waged war passing through his village.

Slia had heard him explain that the bad feelings must be buried, or at least not given vent to, for diplomatic reasons. After the ceremony, Father would join the entourage accompanying the king to the Conclave for the signing of the treaty. The Black Dragon District was the last one he was to go through before reaching the Conclave. The other Chieftains would already be with the assemblage.

She knew the coach belonging to the Red Dragon Chieftain. Old Lart, recognized son of the poet Kaul-Leb no longer traveled on horseback, but used the coach given to his mother as a wedding present by her beloved back when Slia's own great-grandfather was a small child.

For a while, the sounds of movement were quiet.

She could distantly hear her father speaking, but could not quite understand what he said. Having heard his practicing, she could say it word for word.

"Your Majesty, fellow Chieftains, men of the Torbraugh, White Eagle Warriors, and Citizens of the People of the Dragon, it is my pleasure to welcome you to the Black Dragon Central Village for this momentous occasion. We ask of the Dragon that there be peace from this day forward between our peoples and that we nevermore seek hostilities toward one another. We appreciate your kind consideration and respect for our elderly Chief Elder Salar in meeting with him at the Conclave of the People. If there is anything we may do to make your visit within our borders more pleasant, please do not hesitate to ask."

Slia knew that her father did not feel the kindness nor respect of his words, but that he wanted the fighting to be over and done with. The war had cost a terrible price in blood.

She could hear other voices, one voice with foreign words and another in Dragon. The king speaking and another translating, she guessed. Then the voices were done and slowly, the footfalls and other sounds of movement as the march toward the Conclave resumed.

Slia stood on tiptoe to see as a huge white horse rounded the main road through the village. It was a magnificent beast with gold and precious jewels worked into its forelock and mane. The reins coming from the bit and the gleaming bridle were worked in fine stitching of golden threads with jeweled beadings. A fine cloth also cunningly stitched covered the saddle on its back.

Riding the horse was a man, must be the king, a man with such bearing and self-assurance, he seemed to take up almost twice as much space as any other man. On his head was a golden crown worked in jewels of many colors. Under the crown was a high forehead framed in hair so silver it could have been refined by a jeweler. The thick, heavy mass of wavy hair was mirrored in his full, but well-trimmed beard and mustache. His eyes were blue, but not the icy blue of most of the People of the Dragon, but a blue so deep to be almost black. His face, where not covered in beard, was well-tanned and radiant.

Slia noted that his shoulders were even broader than Stell's and that under his tight white leather leggings were well muscled thighs. Down his back hung a beautiful cape of red in a cloth Slia did not recognize. His tunic was of a supple white leather that rose and fell gently with each breath. White leather gloves graced his hands. One hand was raised, waving to the people while the other lightly held the reins. His horse obeyed without nervous prancing about. It, too, seemed to realize just who was on its back and took pleasure in being the royal mount.

She took no notice of anyone else in the parade before her home, not even of her own father and his wide-eyed look at seeing his children in display framed by the doorway of the family home.

The Torbraugh king saw them as well and halted his horse. For a brief moment his eyes locked with Slia's. Flushed and embarrassed, she dropped her gaze down to her feet and backed away from the door. Too late, for the king's interest had been aroused.

The Torbraugh king was twice a widower. He had a grown son, his heir, as well as two other grown princes from his first queen. From the second queen he had gained another two sons and two daughters. They were all grown. His second wife had been gone almost five years and he had been actively seeking a young, comely maiden to enliven him for the remainder of his years.

The king knew that the Dragons had no royalty—no true aristocrats, such a strange people. But the girl must be of a good family as the home she graced was one of the largest he had seen among these people, and she looked quite intelligent for one so young. The young males with her must only be brothers for they looked too near her age to be her sons. But they were handsome boys—he could see himself fathering a remarkable child through her.

Yes, he would have this beautiful Dragon girl as his third queen—how fortunate for her.

He dropped the reins and pulled his right leg over the top of the saddle to slide down to the ground beside his horse. Walking under the horse's neck he advanced toward the open door of the home, smiling. Villagers parted in front of him as he walked through them, his hand extending as he guided himself toward the home.

Slia had backed away from the door, her brothers now in front of her. They, too, parted from his path as the king approached and held out his hand to Slia. She looked up, flustered, not knowing what to do. It seemed rude to ignore the king's gesture. She brought her hand up and forward and soon found it enclosed within the grasp of soft leather.

The king talked softly to her as he led her forward, toward his horse. She understood none of it.

"Whose beautiful child is this?" he asked as he reached his animal. A man in tan leather livery translated.

"She is my daughter," the Black Dragon Chieftain replied. The man translated.

"I will make her my queen," the king said and put her hand to his lips, planting a light kiss. He could not understand it himself, but was instantly besotted by the shy girl in front of him. Younger than all of his own children, when he recalled that gaze that caught his attention, her soul seemed older than the ages, a soul meant to join with his.

He wanted her more than his next breath, more than the next beat of his own heart. She had to be his.

Slia was frightened and breathing rapidly and hard.

She wasn't sure about what was happening but realized that it had nothing to do with her own plans for the future.

"Forgive me, Your Majesty, but my daughter is betrothed to another, a young man of our village, and has been for some time now."

"Where is this tardy young man that he has not already claimed this lovely girl?"

"He lies wounded, recovering from battle, Your Majesty."

The king was vexed at being challenged for what he wanted, but understood that these people were ignorant of rank by birth.

"Then it will most likely be some time before he could marry."

He smiled.

"I make marriage to this maiden a prerequisite for signing of the treaty. Surely, disappointing one wounded man is not worth continuing the war?"

After all had been translated back and forth, gasps were heard here and there throughout those gathered around.

Slia looked to her father with tears in her eyes.

Why, why, why had she not been obedient and stayed hidden within her home? Stell, oh, Stell! I will never even get to see him again! But how could I face him? Stell!

Within moments, it seemed to her, the Dragon wedding ceremony was performed with a borrowed wedding cape, though the king had no Dragon mark to display. A man from the king's group said a few words as well and Slia was informed she was now a married woman. Stell was lost to her forever.

Slia's few items of clothing were gathered up by village women and packed in a travel bag taken by one of the king's attendants. Slia was lifted into the king's arms atop his huge horse and the procession continued on to the meeting at the Conclave.

By the time Slia's mother returned to the village with news of the successful birth of the farmer's wife's son, her own child was gone without a good-bye and her sons were in tears for their sister. Her own husband was travelling with the foreign king who now possessed their daughter. There was no comforting the bereft mother. She could not comfort her sons. Her heart was broken.

That evening, within sight of the Conclave buildings where her love lay still unconscious in his long recovery, in the king's huge travel tent, in his arms,

Slia yielded herself to her husband. He paid little attention to the red stone on a cord around her slender neck but worshipped her supple body with his own.

It was then that Tay, hearing of his patient's loss to the king, ordered the sword be hidden away and forbade any talk of Slia's loss within the confines of Sisten's family's quarters. If the young Dragon warrior were to have a chance to live, he must not know until his body was out of danger. He must not lose hope for the future or he would lose the will to live.

Chapter Five
The Truth is Told

Slia had been gone from the Dragon Territories into the land of the Torbraugh almost a month before Stell's body healed well enough to allow him to regain a hold on consciousness. Tay had tended to him daily, using the skills he had perfected under the Song-hee healer Mido when Salar had been so badly wounded many years ago. Mido had taught him how to carefully get fluids and a small bit of nourishment into a healing body without choking.

Tay decided that Stell need not know about Slia's marriage until it was absolutely necessary to reveal the truth. He had heard that the girl's own mother was wasting away in her grief, and had offered advice, but he knew that he had no cure for a wounded soul. He knew that when Stell became conscious and started asking for Slia that it would not be much longer before he must be told. Tay wanted to wait as long as possible to allow the wounded body strength to combat the pain that would grip him.

He continued to tell Stell there could be no other visitors for the present. Everyone must be kept away to give credence to withholding the devastation that was to come. But there was one he could not command to stay away from Stell. One who could tell him whatever he wished to say.

As Stell lay in his sister's quarters, asleep in his dreams, Sekale came to him.

"Stell, my boy, listen to me."

In his dream, Stell turned from working in the pleasant fields of his home to see his fallen commander. They were dressed the same, both wearing only their britches and boots, upper bodies tanning in the bright sunlight.

Sekale inhaled deeply, taking in the sweet aroma of the fertile crops—or so it seemed.

"Child, there is something you must do."

"What, Sekale?"

"Remember what I told you before about my family?"

"Soos, as soon as I am healed enough, I must go them and tell them your last thoughts were of them. I remember. But I am not healed. I am not allowed to see anyone but my sister's family and Tay. I am not allowed to even see my betrothed, Slia."

Sekale gave Stell a look of deep pity.

"Slia is no longer your betrothed, Stell," he said softly.

"What do you mean?"

"The king of the Torbraugh saw her and demanded her in marriage. She is gone with him. She is his wife, now, his queen."

On his bed, in his sleep, Stell's mouth fell open. He mouthed what he said in his dream.

"Esoos! She would never....Slia loves me, we are betrothed!"

"She had no choice, Child. The king demanded her or he would not sign the treaty to end the war. She gave of herself for her people. Believe me when I tell you, she did not want to marry the Torbraugh king. She wanted only you."

"Then let me die."

"Esoos, Stell. You must go on. You will be able to help her later on in life in a way you cannot imagine now, and I cannot tell you. But know that she will need you."

Tears fell from Stell's eyes in his dream and in his bed.

"Slia," he whispered.

"She loves you still and always will, but she is married to another. She has no claim on you and you have none on her. You must learn to live without her just as she must learn to live without you."

"Let me die."

"You must not, your future is tied with the future of the People—and with hers."

"Do you mean she will come back to me?"

"Esoos, Child, you will never see her again in this life, but she will need you just the same."

"Why haven't they told me?"

"They pitied you, Child. They feared for your life and they had no hope to offer you. But I do. You will love again, perhaps not with the same fever, but you will find a contentment in it. Trust me, Stell, I know."

Sekale was gone.

Stell woke, sobs wracked his body, but he stifled them. He didn't want to wake his sister or her husband and child.

Slia was gone from him, but yet he could help her.

His beautiful girl was gone. Long gone. He knew the treaty had been signed while he had been teetering between dying and living, his mind buried in the recesses of a wounded body. He lay in misery, awake until nearly dawn. He wished he could get up and go off somewhere to think, but he couldn't stand yet, couldn't even sit up without help.

Up in the morning he perceived a cool, wet cloth being lightly placed on his face and someone sitting beside him on his bed. He opened his eyes to see Tay right by him with Sisten hovering nearby.

"Did you have a rough night, Stell?" the healer asked. "Sisten was concerned when you slept so late and looked so pale."

"I know."

"You know what?"

"I know about Slia and the king."

Tay did not deny, but frowned.

"Who?" he asked. "Who told you?"

"Sekale, my battle commander, he came to me in the night and told me while I slept. He died in the same battle I was wounded. He spoke to me before, while I was...was barely alive before I woke."

"Are you saying he came as a Spirit Warrior?"

"Soos."

Tay did not doubt. He had heard too frequently about his great-grandfather, Kaul-Leb, coming to his own father, Salar, years ago when the Song-hee were getting ready to join in with the People of the Dragon. And how he convinced his father to come back to them when he nearly died by a Torbraugh arrow.

He heard Sisten lightly gasp behind him.

Tay also knew that he and Sekale were both descendants of the old Song-hee, though they had barely met. Sekale had been but a very young boy and Tay already a grown man. He knew his distant cousin resembled their common ancestor—evidently in more ways than the mere physical.

"What else did he tell you—or can you tell me?"

He continued wiping around Stell's eyes with his damp cloth. No wonder his eyes were swollen, the vision during his dreams had broken his heart.

"I wanted to die, but Sekale told me that Slia would need my help someday—I will never get to see her again, but she will need me. And that she will always love me."

Tears tried to well in his eyes, but he blinked them away.

Tay gently propped Stell up in his bed.

"Sisten, do you have the broth?"

"Soos, Tay," she answered, handing the mug to the older man.

Tay helped Stell slowly drink from the mug until the contents were consumed.

Sisten stood watching it all, letting Stell's information take hold in her very practical mind.

"Sisten, I believe our young man is ready for another serving of broth, and this time bring us a slice of that fresh bread I smelled as I came in. We'll soak it in the broth and then let him try putting that in his stomach."

In a few moments she was back with the mug refilled and a small plate with warm from the oven fresh bread on it.

Tay took the food from her and set it carefully on the bed between himself and Stell. He picked up the slice of bread and tore it in half. One part he put back on the plate and the other piece he dipped down into the broth. Holding the mug under it to catch the drips he brought it to Stell's mouth and supervised as the young man took the first bite of solid food in more than three months.

Stell rolled it around in his mouth, enjoying the texture and taste to the fullest before carefully swallowing.

"Take another sip to make sure it goes down well."

Tay held the mug back to Stell's mouth. Once he was again on solid food for real, Stell would have the strength to feed himself, but not yet. Being so badly wounded and nearly bleeding to death coupled with so many weeks of inactivity had drained his limbs of their usefulness. Tay doubted Stell could hold the half piece of bread by himself, let alone the mug and contents. Carefully, Tay fed him the rest of his moderate feast.

"Are you ready to settle back into bed, or would you like to stay sitting up for a while?"

Sisten had left to answer a cry from her baby elsewhere in their quarters.

"Tay," Stell said lowly. "What I would really like to do is make a trip to the privy. All that broth is, well, wanting out."

Tay smiled and gently patted Stell's leg, well away from the wound in his calf.

"I know, but you would have to be carried and held."

Stell closed his eyes for a moment, then reopened them.

"Hardly worth the trouble."

"Soon, though, you are healing. Soon."

Tay pulled a shallow earthen pot from under the bed and slid it under the covers, positioning it for Stell's use. After Stell was finished relieving himself into it, the pot was taken away by a young Apprentice stationed outside the door.

Having eased Stell back down into the bed, Tay left.

The healer was satisfied with his patient's progress. Controlling bodily functions again was a big improvement. He was less anxious for the youngster's recovery now that the Spirit Warrior had broken the painful news in a manner that no mere mortal could have done.

A few weeks later Tay had to tell him, though, of the loss of Slia's mother. The bereft woman had grieved herself to death over her daughter, her being a queen had not mattered. Stell was deeply saddened. But he was still too weak to attempt attending her sending to the Dragon. Tay sent a rider to obtain a small pinch of her ashes wrapped in cloth for Stell to show his respect over. Stell had been gently aided to walk to an outside door with an Apprentice under each arm. He rubbed the ashes between his fingers and allowed them to blow away in the breeze.

A week later, he was allowed to walk by himself to the privy using two sturdy canes shadowed by a stout young Apprentice, should he fall. He didn't fall and was soon granted permission to make the trip slowly, but completely alone with only his canes. Two weeks after, he was on his way home in a Conclave wagon with a ream of instructions from Tay to his village executioner—the only healer available so far from Conclave.

Halfway home from the Conclave, one of his four Conclave Custodians rode ahead to give word to his mother he would be there before sunset. Stell carried with him a long missive from Sisten to their mother as well as a lock of the baby's hair. He already knew that his sister was sending word of another grandchild to be born. Happy tidings, he enjoyed being the barer of happy tidings.

Although he was still saddened over the loss of Slia, Stell did his best not to dwell on his empty heart.

Tay had counseled with him that he could worry himself enough to weaken his already weakened body. If he were to be able to come to Slia's aid someday in the future, he would need to regain as much strength as he could. Plus, he had a promise to Sekale to fulfill.

He dozed in the wagon, confident in the Conclave Custodians to deliver him to his mother's house. He was exhausted from the day's travel, even though he had only sat. But it was good to be going home. He missed his mother and his grandmother. He was the last wounded soul to leave Tay's care, he had been the most seriously wounded to survive.

Tay would have accompanied him home but for concern over the elderly Chief Elder Salar. Salar's mind was still as sharp as the knife he kept hidden in his boot, but his physical appearance was growing more fragile. And Tay was very protective of his father.

By the time Stell's wagon rolled into the Black Dragon village, everyone he knew, and many he did not, had gathered to welcome him home. Many offered to help him from the wagon, but the Conclave Custodians gently declined on his behalf.

"The Healer Tay has taught us how to get Stell out of the wagon without hurting him," the ranking Custodian said. "After that, you may help him all you wish."

The Custodians had practiced for two days with Tay as their mock patient until he was satisfied of their competence.

Watching with a heavy sadness were Slia's father and brothers. For so long they had loved Stell as a member of their family. Her father had imagined the fine grandchildren he would hold in his arms and the boys had looked forward to calling him their older brother. Now that was gone. He would be their friend, but their bloodlines would never cross.

He had lost his love, but they had lost their daughter, sister—and a wife and mother weeks later.

As the Custodians tenderly extracted him from the wagon, his mother and grandmother waited anxiously to hold him in their arms. He had barely been set on his feet, with both canes firmly planted in the soil, when his mother took his face in her hands and kissed his cheeks and forehead.

"My boy, home at last!"

"Let me get my hands on that boy, too!" his grandmother said and smothered him in kisses.

After greetings from his friends and neighbors, the Custodians settled their charge within his home. He was thrilled to be home, even though he had enjoyed visiting with his sister and her family after he had healed some, he was tired of Conclave life and preferred to be back to his own village.

Slia's father, the Black Dragon Chieftain, insisted the Custodians stay with him and his sons for overnight. His boys could use the diversion of these men, and so could he.

"Stell, did you know Sisten is having another baby?" his mother asked after she greedily read the soft skin covered in her daughter's writing.

"Soos, Mother, she told me just last week."

"And you didn't say a word!"

"I promised my sister not to, Mother. She wanted you to find out from her."

"When is the baby to come?" asked Grandmother.

"Sisten didn't say," Mother said, looking back over the skin, the little lock of hair from her first grandson in her lap.

"From the way she talked, less than half a year more," Stell announced. "See I did get to tell you something." He laughed. It was the first time since Sekale broke the news about Slia. Actually, the first time since Stell had been wounded.

He reached into his tunic and brought out a leathern pouch, tied at the top with leather cords.

"Mother, can you take care of this for me? The Conclave allowed me a compensation for being so badly wounded."

"How much is it, Son?"

"This is fifty gold coins. They said every month for the next two years, I will receive the same. It is meant to help support my family since I cannot just yet."

"Fifty in gold?" Grandmother exclaimed.

"Soos, Grandmother. They told me they want no one to suffer because of my service to the Dragon."

Stell didn't know that Tay had campaigned for Stell's compensation to be fifty instead of the usual twenty-five due to his loss of Slia. He knew Stell would not have accepted the full amount had he known. He was correct.

Stell's mother took the pouch of coins from her son and secreted it away. They had not suffered with his being gone—except in worry over him. Friends and neighbors had been generous to a fault.

Their fields just outside the village had not wanted for the working. They had been tilled, seeded, and the crops managed by volunteers. After it became known around the village just how badly he had been wounded, suddenly everyone had too much of all kinds of food stuffs that they had insisted the two women share in. Their larder was now full to overflowing after it had become known Stell was on his way home.

Showing great restraint, none of the families with daughters soon old enough to wed had begun sending them yet on errands to the little household.

In little less than a year, Stell would reach the age of full manhood, he would be twenty-five. They all knew how his heart must still ache over Slia—they had all seen the pair together in the past. But they knew that the day would come, when his heart had had time to finish its grieving and his young body had recovered as far as possible, that someone's daughter would have a chance to make a good life with him.

By the time Stell reached his full adulthood, he had managed to put away one cane when walking about outside their home. Inside, moving slowly, he could manage without any. He pushed himself to regain his strength. He hated being an invalid.

He was thrilled to be working his fields again and thought soon he must travel to the Red Dragon village where Sekale's family lived. It began to weigh on his mind until one night Sekale came to him again.

"It is time, Child. My family needs to hear from me through you."

"Where will I find them, Sekale? Are they in the village proper or outside it somewhere?"

"They were invited to live in the old family home after my death."

"The home of Kaul-Leb?"

"Soos, my great-grandfather's home. The home where my grandfather still lives, although he is very old now, very old. He will cross over before another year is out. I was the youngest of his grandsons, it pained him deeply to hear of my death. He doesn't remember it now, but I have gone to him in his sleep to ease his pain."

"Does your family expect me, Sekale, or do I need to send word first of my coming?"

"Tinka, my wife, has been thinking you might come. She knows you were with me when we both fell. But she knows you were badly wounded. She has been wondering of late how you have healed. She is a very good woman. I think you will like my sons. And my daughter, she barely remembers me now. She needs to hear of me. My father, too, will welcome you. He lives close to Grandfather. He would also like to hear of that day. My wife's brother will insist you stay there with them for your visit."

"My visit? Am I not to just go and tell what you want and then come back home?"

"Esoos, Child, even yet that would be too much for you to endure. You would be exhausted for days. Go, visit, see all the things my grandfather has accumulated and all Kaul-Leb's writings—or some of them. I swear the man tried to write every word that there is a thousand times."

Sekale laughed the way Stell remembered his doing and joined him. In the room next to his, Stell's mother heard him laughing in his sleep and was comforted over her son. He did not laugh enough since returning home.

Chapter Six
The Red Dragon Village

Strella, Stell's mother was not overjoyed when he informed her that he would be travelling to the Red Dragon village. He told her of Sekale's visits and how he had promised to take the message to the grieving family. She conceded that he should go.

She would have insisted on going as well, but Grandmother was too old to leave all alone. And Grandmother hated to travel away from home.

Stell did not ride his horse, which would have made for a quicker trip. He was not yet comfortable with being on horseback for so long, it made his leg ache to stay atop a horse for more than a ride to his fields and back. Maybe someday.

So at dawn, he climbed up into the driving seat of his wagon after kissing his mother and grandmother good-bye and set off for the Red Dragon village where Kaul-Leb the Poet had come as an adolescent.

It pricked Stell's heart because thoughts of Kaul-Leb always brought thoughts of his lost Slia, one of the old poet's Blood Descendants. He mused as he drove the single horse wagon with the sun at his back that Slia had wanted to name a son after not the poet, whose blood flowed in her veins, but after the man who had not been able to father a child and had asked for Seed Rights of Kaul-Leb, Steela's young Second Husband, then a slave in her home.

Steela's first husband had been kinsman to the man Saan, which had given him the right to ask, or rather demand, the Ritual which had produced Slia's great-grandfather. She had always felt Saan had been neglected, so wanted to name a child for him.

"I wonder if the king will let her give a Dragon name to his son, should they have one," he said out loud to his uninterested horse.

He drove on, passing through two other villages before reaching the one he sought. He remembered it from that time in his youth when he met Sekale in war games and was trounced by him. It made him smile to remember how kind Sekale, only about ten years older, had been to him, both then and when they fought together against the Torbraugh.

Torbraugh brought his thoughts again to Slia and he pushed her from his mind. She was gone forever, there was no good to come from pitying himself over her loss again and again.

He remembered correctly where the old home of Kaul-Leb was and went right to it. As he drove into the stone courtyard, he was seen by two boys of obvious Song-hee parentage who ducked away, presumably to tell a stranger had come to their home.

He carefully climbed down, the muscles in his bad leg threatening to start cramping from sitting in the wagon for so long. He leaned heavily on his cane once he was on the ground.

An old man, very old, came from the house.

"You are Stell, are you not? I am Lart, Chieftain of the Red Dragon—and you are wondering how I know you, soos?" the old man said and laughed.

"Soos, Sir," Stell said. "I don't remember meeting you."

Lart laughed, his emerald green eyes sparkling. He was old, but still spry as far as Stell could tell. Lart stood tall, his countenance alert and radiant. His shoulders were not stooped and his walk steady. It was well known that his father Kaul-Leb had been in excellent health until one day he had just died.

Some were sure his beloved had come for him, tired of waiting for him to join her, and she had taken him away. Stell wondered if the same would be for Lart—no sickness, no pain, just crossing over. All this raced through Stell's mind in an instant.

"I saw you, young man, the day Sekale sat you on your behind at war games. I knew he liked you when he took time to work with you later. And then he chose you to fight under him. My grandson liked you, so I bullied Tay into letting me look at you in your sister's home at Conclave before you ever woke up."

He smiled.

"Being a Chieftain gives me a little bit of leverage at Conclave—especially with some of Father's other children."

"So, did Sekale send you here?"

"You know?"

"Soos, I don't remember exactly what he has said in my dreams, but I know he has been there, just as Father did long ago. I've had the feeling you would be coming to us before long."

Lart put his hand on Stell's shoulder.

"Come in, Child, come meet the family and make yourself comfortable."

As they went through the door, Lart called out. "Steela, my love, we have a guest. Tinka, come see who has come to see us."

Two women came from the kitchen. One was a white-haired woman, she would be Steela, granddaughter of Kaul-Leb's love and named for her. Grandmother Steela had been of no actual blood relation to Lart, but had been the only mother he had ever known. The other woman was pure Song-hee.

She was tall and slender with light brown hair and dark brown eyes. For a woman, her shoulders were broad, a trait bred into the warrior caste of Song-hee for generations. She stood erect and carried herself with self-assurance. Even with the sadness around her eyes, Stell thought she was beautiful. No wonder Sekale had been such a happy man.

Stell saw both women glance at his cane. At first, he had felt ashamed when others noted his affliction, but had come to realize that at least he could walk. And he could still work—a fact he was proud of. He could have died, or been permanently bedridden.

"This is Stell."

Stell bowed slightly.

"Stell, my wife Steela, and our granddaughter Tinka, Sekale's dear wife."

Stell noticed that Lart did not distinguish between people born into the family and those who married in.

The women acknowledged him and insisted he sit at their table for refreshment.

While they sat and visited over a strong, sweet tea, a little blonde girl wandered in. She climbed up into Lart's lap and played with the buttons of his tunic.

She called him Ganfader.

Stell thought of what Sekale had told him, that his little one barely remembered him. It was time to tell Tinka and the little one what Sekale had said.

"If you wondered why I have come," he said. "It was to fulfill a promise I made to Sekale. He came to me, when I was wounded, before...before I awoke." He paused. Would they believe him?

"After you were wounded?" Lart asked.

"Soos, Sir. As I was balancing between living and dying. He came to me and convinced me to live. And he wanted me to tell his family... to tell you, Tinka that his last thoughts before he died in that battle, were of you and your children."

Tears welled in her eyes, but did not spill.

"Thank you, Stell. For coming all this way to tell me. Did he—do you know, did he suffer before he died?"

"Esoos," Stell said. "I saw. It was quick, he did not suffer."

She smiled.

"He always said that when his time came, he wanted to die well. He had a warrior's heart."

"Soos, he did. He was a good leader. He cared for his men. And he enjoyed battle. He really did. I was honored to serve under his command."

"Soos," Tinka said and smiled. "He always told me that he felt his Song-hee ancestors racing through his veins. He was disappointed he couldn't go into full Blood Fever."

"That boy," Lart said and wiped a tear from his cheek.

"Enough!" he said then. "Sekale lived the life he wanted. That cannot be said of every man."

"Esoos," Stell said, "it cannot."

"True, Child, your life has not gone the way you thought, has it?"

"Esoos, it has not, Sir. But it has not been all bad. I have had good, I have been blessed in many ways. I was allowed to know Sekale, and he gave me the strength to continue on. Even though it was lost, I have known love. I have held my sister's child in my arms and have many friends, friends that cared for my mother and grandmother when I could not. And I lived when it was thought I was dead."

Lart reached out and patted Stell's knee. As he did, a knock sounded at the door.

The visitor's face appeared.

"I hear you have a guest."

It was Sturl, the Song-hee archer Stell rode beside in battle.

"Sturl, how did you know I was here? I didn't know you lived in this village!" Stell said excitedly and stood slowly using his cane and the table to rise.

Sturl hurried to Stell to keep his friend from trying to walk to him. They embraced as only comrades in arms can, fully aware that each had saved the other countless times.

"When I shot your attacker, I thought he had killed you and was just dishonoring your body. After you were found alive, I saw you only briefly before they rushed you to the Conclave. You don't know how excited I was when my nephews came to me to tell me you were here visiting my sister."

"Your sister?" Stell asked and turned to look at Tinka. "I didn't know Tinka was your sister."

She smiled back at Stell.

"Soos, Sekale was never one to play favorites, but he didn't want anyone in our company to know," Sturl explained.

"Sekale sent Stell to me," Tinka told her brother.

Sturl look back and forth at the two of them with a quizzical look on his face.

"Sekale has been coming to Stell, he is Stell's Spirit Warrior."

Sturl pulled Stell into another embrace then let him go.

"Sturl, please sit with us," Lart said, patting an empty seat beside himself.

Steela was already up and preparing another mug of strong tea.

Sturl sat after taking the mug from Steela and thanking her.

"Please, Stell, you will stay with my family while you are here—my wife has threatened my life if you do not," he laughed and then sipped his tea.

As he spoke the little girl left Lart's lap and went to Sturl's.

"Uncle Sturl?"

"Soos, Sar?"

"Me come stay wif you?"

"Not today, my love."

"Just Stell?"

"Just Stell. Soos."

"His horse and wagon can stay here, though," Lart said. "We have more stable room than you do."

"Thank you, Grandfather," Sturl said, smiling at Stell. "Looks like we've got you planned out."

"Soos, it does," Stell said, a little overwhelmed.

"While we're at it, Stell," Lart said, "you should call me Grandfather, as well. Makes everything simpler, I have two grandsons in the area named Lart."

"If you prefer it, certainly, L...Grandfather," Stell said, correcting himself.

"Soos, I do."

They talked a bit more then Stell and Sturl, with little Sar sitting between them on the wagon seat, drove Stell's wagon to Sturl's home to unload his things. He met Sturl's Dragon wife and their four children.

Sturl's wife was shorter than his sister. More than a head shorter, small even for a Dragon woman. But she was quick and busy and bossed everyone around, especially her adoring husband. Stell could feel the love contained in their home. Sica might scold, but never harshly, and usually with a quick smile. Their children were tall, like their father, but obeyed their mother as if she cracked a whip.

His wagon was unloaded quickly and his things carefully taken to the room they were giving him for his stay. Then all four boys climbed into the wagon with their little cousin to take it back to Grandfather's house. Stell wondered what everyone would do if Sekale's prediction about their beloved elder came true. He feared the whole community would be in a state of deep mourning for ages.

"Grandmother expects everyone at her house tonight to eat," the boys announced when they returned.

Sica had been baking and shooed her children away from the fresh breads and sweet things.

"Seown, get my big basket and we'll take some of these things with us when we go," she said. If Grandmother said to come, they went, but Sica would not go empty-handed.

"Soos, Mother," the oldest boy answered and disappeared to the rear of the home, returning with a large basket over his arm. "Shall I pack them up?"

"Esoos, let them cool a bit more first."
She shooed men and boys to the main room of the house to allow Stell to sit a bit and talk with her husband.

"Children, I expect to hear nothing from any of you unless you are asked to speak, understand?"

"Soos, Mother," a chorus of four answered and followed their father and his guest. They had heard of this man since their father returned from the war and were anxious to be allowed to listen to the conversation. They would have promised their mother to stand on their heads to do so if she had made it a condition of staying in the room.

They had heard of his prowess in battle and how well he had shielded their father when he was shooting his arrows, they had heard about how badly he had been wounded, and about his losing his beloved to the Torbraugh king.

Now they listened eagerly to talk about their Uncle Sekale and how much both men sorrowed when he crossed over in battle. The war stories filled them with wonder and would fuel their active imaginations for ages.

Stell told of the months of recovery within the walls of the Conclave and the tender care given him by the Healer Tay, the Chief Elder's own son. Then their father asked about Sekale as a Spirit Warrior.

He told of Salar himself coming to visit with him, treating him kindly and putting him at ease. Stell candidly told of walking the dark corridor and the things Sekale had told him. Then of how deeply he had hurt when he learned that Slia had sacrificed their future together to ensure the end of the conflict. The youngest, Salpir, could not help himself, but went to Stell and climbed up in his lap, tears rolling down his small cheeks. He made no sounds other than an occasional sniff, but put his arms around the man's neck and hugged him. Stell snuggled the child against his chest and patted the small back.

"It's alright, Little One, it is not so bad, now. I can walk again, and I can work my fields. And there is no more war."

Salpir said nothing, but sucked his thumb. He popped it back out of his mouth when Sica came into the room.

She gave him a stern look, but said nothing about it.

"I see you have met our lap-sitter, Stell," she said.

"Soos," he said and hugged the child to himself.

"Salpir, since you have laid claim to our guest, why don't you show him where his room is and where the privy is. Then boys, hands and faces washed before we go to Grandmother's—I'll not have everyone see dirt on you coming from my house. That goes for the big boys, too," she said and smiled and returned to her kitchen to pack her basket.

"We all have our orders, boys," Sturl said and stood. Seown jumped up and retrieved Stell's cane for him from where it had fallen to the floor beside his chair. Salpir climbed down and waited for Stell to stand, then took his left hand and led him to the rooms.

Everyone polished to Sica's satisfaction, they started the walk, cutting through between buildings in the village to shorten the way. No one appeared to mind that their guest did not have a quick stride, but seemed proud to have him with them. The two men walked in front of the group, with Sica and Salpir then the other boys, Seown carrying the laden basket proudly.

The house of Lart and Steela was near capacity with family, all come to see and meet Stell. He thought that the whole of the Red Dragon Tribe must be related to Lart—and a good many of it were, by blood or marriage.

All of the People of the Dragon knew of his loss of his love to appease the Torbraugh king, and all knew it had happened while he lay fighting for his very life. He didn't realize that most thought of him as a tragic, suffering hero. To himself, he was just a man trying to get back in his life.

The three best chairs in the house were reserved for Stell and Lart, or Grandfather as Lart preferred all to call him, and Samesh, the youngest son of Lart and father of Sekale. It had been he who first saw Kaul-Leb after his crossing over. Sar found his lap and lay claim.

If the assembled women had had their way, Stell would not have had need of eating again for at least a year. They all thought him painfully thin and in need of fattening up.

Stell was, by nature, a shy, retiring type of man, preferring to be on the periphery of activity, not the center. This endeared him even more to the ladies present, especially the mothers of unbetrothed daughters each hoping their girl might catch his eye.

That he remained as handsome as ever, with his icy blue eyes, dark, wavy hair accented by his braids of citizenship, broad shoulders, and attractive face covered by just the right amount of facial hair more than offset the limp he displayed afoot. Sometimes when the weather was cold or wet, his side would ache where the sword sliced him open.

He spoke kindly to all introduced to him, but remembered few names. He remained cordial even though he was growing weary. Lart noticed Stell's fatigue and redirected as many as he could. He also noted that Stell's attention seemed to be drawn more toward Tinka than any other female in the house. She would be good for him. And she would need help with her children—they needed a father.

A father like Stell who knew what it was to lose a beloved father at a very young age. That he had known their father was a plus. That their father was Stell's Spirit Warrior made it even better. Lart felt that Sekale had brought Stell to Tinka. He had chosen the young man for his family.

And Lart knew what Stell would not tell him. Kaul-Leb, his father, had come to him and told him to be ready. Like Lod, his brother, had done, Lart would soon be crossing over and he wanted Tinka's future secured before that happened.

Stell slept later than usual the next morning. When he woke, little Sar was standing on the floor by his bed, looking at him. He was thankful he had decided to wear the long sleeping tunic his mother had insisted on packing. Otherwise, he would have been held hostage by the child as he usually slept with nothing but bed linens.

When she noticed his eyes were open, Sar ran from the room, calling out.

"Mother, Aunt Sica, Stell is awake!"

Stell laughed to himself as he heard Tinka's voice admonishing the child to be quiet and what was she doing in Stell's room?

A short rap sounded at his door.

"Stell, are you awake?"

"Soos, it is safe, come in."

Tinka looked around the door, holding to it.

"Forgive me, Stell, I had no idea she would come in to bother you."

"She did not bother me, she was very quiet until she saw I was awake."

"But still..." she said, her face reddening.

"Perhaps it would be better if I rose and dressed," he said.

"Soos," she said and firmly pulled the door shut. Stell slipped out of the bed and pulled on his drawers and britches then unbuttoned the sleep tunic and slipped it off his arms and back. Folding it carefully, he put it away and took a day tunic from his bag and put it on. He stayed close to the bed to lean on it when he felt off balanced. Then he sat back down and pulled on his low cut boots.

Rising, he took his cane from its place leaning against the wall and made his way to the privy at the end of the hallway to tend to his bodily functions. Completed, he slipped back into his borrowed room and splashed water on his face and hands and then took a handful of hair at each of his temples and braided it before pulling it all back and fastening it at the back of his neck. He finger combed his beard and mustache into a civilized shape and was ready to meet the day—and curious little girls.

He limped to the front of the house.

"Forgive me for staying in bed so late—yesterday tired me out more than I expected."

"Stell, I am truly sorry Sar disturbed you—I had no idea she had gone into your room."

Tinka sat at the table, holding her curious daughter in her lap.

"She didn't disturb me, she was just there, being quiet, watching me, waiting for me to waken. I didn't realize I could be that interesting," he said and laughed.

Sica put down a mug of steaming tea.

"Here, Stell, drink this. Would you like something to eat?"

He sat and took a hearty sip and swallowed.

"This is plenty, I am still so full from last night. I didn't know I could eat that much! That is probably why I slept so late—I was stuffed to my eyes."

"I'm afraid we overtired you," Tinka said.

"Everyone wanted to meet you."

"I don't see why, I am just me."

Tinka just smiled at him. He really didn't understand. Suddenly, she found herself wanting him as much as she ever had Sekale. It wasn't just with her mind or her heart. She had a craving from deep within her body crying out to be satisfied and it startled her.

"Is something wrong?" he asked.

"Esoos, I just…just thought of something I should tend to at home. Come, Sar, we need to go home."

She stood, having put Sar down and made for the door.

Sar didn't want to leave.

"I want to stay wif Aunt Sica and look at Stell."

"What do you mean to look at Stell?"

"He's pretty," the little one said and her mother turned red again.

"Sar, home!"

The tone in Tinka's voice warned Sar not to disobey and the child followed her mother out the door, with a parting glance at Stell.

Stell concentrated on his tea, it was really good, but Sica understood. She had never seen Tinka blush before, and now, she had turned red twice in one morning.

Sturl came in with two buckets of water from the well.

"Where did Tinka go? I thought she was staying to visit for a while."

"Oh, she'll be back, she thought of something she needed to get done at home," Sica replied.
He sat the buckets down and accepted a mug from his wife. He sat across the table from Stell.

"Did you sleep well, Stell?"

"Very well indeed. I only just got up."

"Being on display to one and all is exhausting, isn't it?" Sturl asked and laughed.

"Soos, it is." Stell laughed, too. "I am beginning to think battle is easier."

"Sometimes, it is."

Tinka did come back in a little while, without any children. Sica sent hers over to be with their cousins and the four adults sat and talked and eventually had a little to eat.

As the sun began to go down, they realized that they had visited the day away.

Tinka rose to leave.

"Let me walk you home," Stell said, surprising himself.

Sturl and Sica looked at one another knowingly as Tinka and Stell left.

"I've sat too long," Stell apologized as he walked slower than usual.

"Then this walk will do you good," Tinka said and immediately wondered why she had said that. She felt foolish.

They walked along, talking of nothing in particular and finally came to a stone walkway by a house. Water had been brought in for the night from the well by someone who had splashed some out of their buckets and it pooled on some of the stones. Stell's cane slipped in one little puddle and he started to fall forward.

He reached out automatically toward Tinka, and she reached for him.

They held to one another, closely. Tinka found herself leaning toward him and kissing him lightly on the lips. Then she loosened her grip on his arm and put both hands behind his head, pulling his face to hers and kissed him anything but lightly. Her body followed and pressed against his.

For a moment, he was lost in confusion, but found his arms enclosing her torso and holding her tightly. His cane dropped forgotten to the stones.

"We see where my daughter gets her forward manners," Tinka confessed after a while. She had reddened again. She bent and retrieved his cane, then handed it to him.

"Tinka, I..." he could say no more, he had no words to explain himself.

They walked on to shadows between two outbuildings. Tinka felt she could speak to him now that he couldn't see her turning red.

"Stell, I know I am your age. Older than most girls who..." she couldn't continue the sentence.

"But I want to... to be with you. To take care of you, to make you happy."

She turned to face him.

"I AM forward. But if I don't speak, I am afraid you will not, for you are so shy."

"Tinka..."

"Esoos, let me finish. I want you to...I want you to ... marry me."

She took his left hand in both of hers, leaving the right holding his cane.

"Why would you want me?" he asked. "I can't even walk very well or quickly. I can't walk far without my cane—I will never run again. I am little more than a cripple."

"You thick headed Dragon," she said. "If I want a race run, I'll get a horse. I love you, you big, sweet man. Don't you realize, I love you? I fell in love with you when you walked in the door yesterday. Something about you just, just took my breath away. The more I see of you, the more I want you—all of you, not just your leg. I hurt I want you much. I want you in my life—I want you in my bed! Marry me, please!"

She dropped his hand and turned away. He wouldn't want her at all now. Why had she gone on so? They had only met just yesterday, and now she was asking, no demanding he marry her. To her own ears she sounded like a mare ready to take any stallion that happened by. Tears welled in her eyes and spilled down her cheeks. She wanted him so badly she was sick to her stomach.

"Tinka," he said softly. "Come here. I can't chase you down."

He held out both arms to her, his cane propped against his right leg.

"I thought it was only me. I had no idea you wanted me as much as I wanted you. I didn't think it made sense, we had only just met. But soos, I want to marry you, if you will have me, bad leg and all. I want you with all my heart."

She melted into his open arms, her body clinging to his as if they were two halves of the same soul too long separated. They held to one another, their hearts beating close to one another, just holding.

"There isn't really time to prepare for in the morning, is there? Shall we be married morning next?" he asked.

"Soos," she whispered, breathing in the closeness of his body, the feel of his arms, the manly smell she had missed so acutely. "Morning next, we will come together Always and Forever."

"Soos, shall we go and tell everyone?"

"Just a few moments more, all alone, just us two. Let me have you all to myself."

In a little while, they entered the door of Lart's home, Tinka holding Stell's left hand in her right.

They made their way to the kitchen and found Lart with Steela, and Sturl with Sica.

"We came the long way around," Sica volunteered. "But we didn't stop to kiss one another."

Tinka and Stell both flushed lightly, but did not drop their hands.

"Do we have an announcement?" Lart asked.

"Soos, Grandfather," Tinka said, looking at Stell, and then dropped her eyes, deferring to Stell.

"We have decided to marry, if possible, by morning next," Stell said, and let go Tinka's hand to put his arm around her shoulders. "We...we do not wish to wait."

"Good," Steela said. "We have a day to prepare for it and for guests to arrive." She went to them and kissed them both on the cheeks, Sica right behind her.

Sturl was next, embracing and kissing them both.

"So which am I to do? Bring the bride or present the citizen?"

Lart answered him.

"You shall present the citizen, I reserve the right to give my granddaughter."

He kissed and embraced them both, as well.

"What guests?" Stell asked.

Lart laughed.

"You don't think I would allow you to marry without your mother and grandmother here, do you? I sent the coach that belonged to my mother for them this midday."

"At midday? But how did you know?"

"One advantage to being an old man is you learn to see the signs even before young people know that they are falling in love." He laughed again and gave Tinka another kiss.

The children, Tinka's and Sturl's, had heard the excitement and came in from the great room. The cousins all rushed in excitedly, all except Tinka's older son, Sekeel. He hung back, a look of concern on his young face.

"Sekeel? What is wrong, Son?" Tinka asked after she noticed he had stayed in the doorway to the room.

"Come to me."

He slowly walked to his mother's outstretched arms and held to her, tears coming to his eyes.

"What is wrong, Son? Tell me."

Stell, his leg beginning to ache, pulled out a chair and sat down, watching his beloved and her child.

"Where will we live? Sael, Sar, and me? Where will we live?"

"With us," Tinka answered. "Where did you think?"

"I thought you would leave us here and go with Stell—when Serone's mother married again after his father was killed in the war, her husband didn't want him with them and he had to stay somewhere else. He told me he hardly gets to see his mother since the new baby came and I didn't want to lose you."

Sekeel buried his face against his mother.

He felt a hand on his shoulder, pulling him away. Stell had hold of him and pulled him in between his knees.

The boy wiped at his tears as he looked down at the floor.

"Sekeel, look at me."

He looked up into Stell's face, afraid he had made the man angry at him. But Stell was not angry. There were tears in his eyes.

"Sekeel, I would never separate you from your mother, you must know that. When we marry, I will consider you my son, just as Sael and Sar will also be my children. You are a part of your mother, and I love her deeply, so of course, I love you, too. I want you to come to love me, as well."

"So Sekale will not be my father anymore?"

"Sekale will always be your father. I want you to never forget him. He was a great man and I loved and respected him."

"So, I can still get the Red Dragon with two heads when I become a citizen—or will I get a Black Dragon?"

"You may choose whichever one you want, you will have that right. In fact, if I were you, I would choose the Dragon of Sekale. It is what you were born to and you are a true descendant of Kaul-Leb. It will not change my love for you to honor your father."

Sekeel stepped closer in between Stell's legs and wrapped his arms around the man's neck. Stell pulled the boy up into his lap, settling his weight on the good, left leg. He enclosed the boy in his arms and kissed his forehead. Sar was immediately clamoring up on his right leg.

"Kiss me, kiss me!"

Stell kissed her and pulled her up high on his right thigh, away from his tender calf muscles.

"Sael?"
Sael joined his siblings, standing between his stepfather-to-be's legs and receiving a kiss.

"Don't forget me!"

Tinka stooped over, her arms around all four.

The morning of their wedding dawned warm and clear, the sun rising over the mountain to the east in excellent brilliance. In the same village center square where so long ago Grandfather Kaul-Leb was seen by the first Grandmother Steela and became her Second Husband, he a slave until freed by the Conclave, another full bloodied Song-hee and full bloodied Dragon pair united in marriage.

Sturl stood by his friend and lifted the marriage cape made by Lart's mother ages ago in preparation for her first son's marriage. On Stell's upper right shoulder was his Black Dragon Tribal tattoo of citizenship, demonstrating to one and all his eligibility to take Tinka as his wife by the Law of the Dragon.

The assembled witnesses also saw the deep scar on his right side that told of the wound that had nearly ended his life in the war. Then the hem of the cape was dropped back down.

Sturl helped Stell turn back around to face Tinka as Lart escorted her to the base of the steps leading to the platform. Sturl advanced to the steps and took Tinka from Grandfather Lart and led her to Stell.

Behind her came her children, Sekeel carrying Sar on his hip and Sael walking beside him.

Sturl held the cane as Stell took the right hem of the cape in his fingers and lifted the cape over Tinka and around her shoulders, touching it to his left shoulder, holding her close against his bare chest, and thus his heart. He demonstrated that he would hold her and keep her safe and secure for the rest of their lives. Then he loosened his hold just enough for the children to squeeze in between them and thus also be covered by his pledge of love. Stell's mother watched with tears in her eyes for she had feared that after losing Slia, her boy would never love again.

That night, two sons were conceived. Both to women who loved Stell. One was conceived in the bed of the humble Man of the Dragon, one in the bed of a king.

Chapter Seven
Slia and the King

Slia saw the Conclave Complex while still some distance away from it. Riding on the front of her new husband's saddle between his arms, she was awestruck with the enormity of the buildings.

I never knew it was so big, she thought. She looked it over, devouring every detail she could, knowing that this would be the one and only time she would see this great structure of her People.

The outer wall was fairly new, being erected after the attack upon the Conclave at the time of the wounding and near death of the Chief Elder Salar over a generation ago. Set back from the outer wall, Slia could see the ancient circular building erected some said a thousand years ago. It was enormous.

She could see evenly spaced windows marching up its walls—two stories high above ground, it was rumored to be even larger below, under the soil.

One huge domed roof rose above the rest of the Complex. That would be the Great Hall. The room held most sacred in all of the Dragon Tribal lands. In this room were held the most important ceremonies of the People of the Dragon.

Knowing that Stell lay somewhere within the vast array of buildings before her eyes caused a wound within her heart comparable to the one in his side.

She allowed herself one good long look at the magnificent complex of the ancient structure and wept internally at what she would never have.

I must increase the size of my palace, the king thought. These backward Dragons cannot have a palace greater than the Torbraugh. He wanted to impress the girl he had taken. The king of the Torbraugh knew that he had been incredibly selfish in forcing the marriage to this simple but beautiful Daughter of the Dragon. From deep inside himself, he knew that he would have to have her as soon as their eyes met. He knew she loved someone else.

He knew she was not delighted to be marrying a king. He knew that she would be unhappy, at least for a while. He resolved that he would live the rest of his life to make his beautiful young bride content in their marriage.

That night, after he had met within the walls of the Conclave and the ceremony for the signing tomorrow was set, he entered his enormous travelling tent and went in to his young wife.

She did not resist him, but neither did she come to him with the passion she had expected would happen if he had been Stell. Slia trembled slightly as the king slowly, gently removed her clothing. He kissed her softly as he revealed her body to himself in the light of the candles set around his luxurious bed. He had come to her with his tunic already removed in the outer rooms. Once she was standing before him with nothing but the Dragon Eye Stone hanging from her neck, he unfastened and pushed down his britches.

The man was very well built for a man of his age— for a man of any age. His broad shoulders were well muscled as were his legs. He believed in looking the part of royalty and had kept himself fit. His waist was fairly narrow and his belly only slightly rounded, but not fat. Besides his facial hair and the hair of his head, all the hair of his body had silvered. Despite his age, the skin of his buttocks was not wrinkled or saggy, but tight over the muscles he worked to maintain.

He was well aware how fragile was the trust of a young maiden, he had taken many in his lifetime. He no longer rushed as he had in his youth, but savored the beauty and innocence before him. His hands explored the child he had taken as a wife, hoping to spark in her some desire, but knowing that it might only come with time. Fully aroused, he lifted her slight, supple body onto the bed. He tenderly and carefully consummated his third marriage. She did not cry out with passion, but neither did she cry with pain.

The king's hands travelling over her body, Slia imagined belonging to Stell. Deep within, she could not forget that it was the touch of a stranger, now her husband, but trying to believe it was Stell made the ordeal tolerable to her. She knew with Stell it would have been sweeter somehow, because she loved him and both of them would have been virgin. They would have learned together.

The next morning, the king was up and dressing when Slia awoke. Naked under the bed linens, she did not stir out from under them, as the king was not adorning himself, but had various attendants hovering about.

He noticed her watching him and came to her, kneeling on the bed and speaking gently, bending down to kiss her tenderly. He turned to his attendants and barked an order. As one, they all turned their backs as he pulled a wad of something soft and fine from the side of the bed.

His large, strong hands eased her into a sitting position and helped her on with the beautiful garment, slipping her arms into the sleeves and pulling it closed across her breasts. Knowing he was on the search for a new queen, the king had caused various bits of women's clothing to be packed in with his travelling wardrobe. During the night, the soft, silken dressing gown had been retrieved to be readied for the young queen this morning. He showed her other things that had been unpacked for her and left them draped across the bed for her to dress herself with later.

He was pleased that Slia felt of the fine cloth of his offerings with appreciation. She smiled shyly and thanked him. He could not understand her words any more than she could his, but the look in her eye and tone of her voice told him that she was warmly accepting of his gifts.

Slia could have cried and shown distain to her new husband, but Daughters of the Dragon are taught from an early age that marriage is serious business, not to be dismissed lightly. She certainly would have preferred that the man in her bed be Stell, true. But it was not to be. What had happened to her must have somehow been ordained and approved by the Dragon Himself.

Had her lack of obedience to her parents caused this huge ripple in her life? She did not know and knew it fruitless to dwell upon. The fact she must face was that she had married this man, a king she did not want or seek out, and now she must live up to her responsibilities as best she could. She must do her best to honor him and their marriage, no matter what else she would have preferred. At least the clothing was pretty.

After the king had finished preening and was satisfied with his appearance, he and his entourage left her, but not before a platter of delicious smelling food was brought in and placed upon a nearby table. The king had pointed it out to her. She was to eat. She had smiled and thanked him again but waited to rise until she was alone. Slia didn't think it appropriate for the king's servants to observe her bare feet and legs emerging from the bed.

Believing that she would not be disturbed—who among the king's servants, all male, would dare intrude upon his young bride, Slia slipped from the bed and pulled on the clothing that had been left for her after washing herself in fresh water left in a large basin. Her discarded items from last night were draped across a bench not far from the bed. These she folded to keep as souvenirs of her old life. She also folded the dressing gown and placed it atop her old clothing.

The platter of food was more than she could ever eat, but Slia decided that probably a king's wife was not obliged to clean her plate of all she had been given as a daughter of frugal parents was.

Her parents—Slia hoped that she would be allowed to bid her father a farewell and send apologies for her disobedience to her mother. And her love to all her family. She would not mention Stell, that would be disloyal to her husband.

Slia found what she believed to be extraordinarily beautiful hairpins by her platter of food. And a comb made of brass. She carefully pulled it through her hair, taking out the tangles that had grown there during the night. She didn't specifically remember the king having taken out her hairpins, but he must have, for they were not in her hair or in the bed. Her belly full and her body and hair dressed, Slia looked about for footwear. All she spied were her own boots from her old life. At least they were fairly new and not badly scuffed. She put them on.

Slia noted that there was no pile of the king's clothing from yesterday. The attendants must have seen to it.

She went around the tent looking at and touching the fabrics and fittings. The cloth of the tent could not be seen through, but high up near the ceiling, at the top along the edge were some square openings permitting light to enter the area. The candles from last night were gone.

Slia did not attempt to lift the flap and look out into the outer room. She had learned her lesson about having to see everything. She did not wish to garner any undue attention from anyone. However, she felt free to pilfer through her immediate environment.

Doing so, she found the bag packed for her by the village women. Emptying it on the bed, she expressed glee at finding her current embroidery stuffed into the bottom. At least she would have something to do while waiting for the king's pleasure.

Slia packed her things from yesterday in the bag and replaced everything in it except her needlework. She moved a chair around to best catch the light and busied herself, her back partially to the tent flap to the other room.

Stitching had never been her favorite activity, but Slia found it calming to have something familiar and constructive to occupy her time.

The king did not know what he expected to see when he returned from the Conclave and entered the chamber where he had left his new bride. He even entertained the idea that she could have run away, slipping out somehow and gone. Or he thought he might find her weeping in their bed, bemoaning the man she could no longer have. She had to know he was somewhere in that enormous complex.

He nearly cried out at the scene he encountered.

Dressed in the finery he had provided, her hair beautifully adorned in the jeweled hairpins, there she sat the perfect picture of domesticity, stitching.

The bed had been straightened and the pile of things the servants had picked up from the floor where he tossed them last night had been put away.

There were minor changes here and there as she had rearranged to suit herself.

The king silently entered and lowered the tent flap behind him. As quietly as a cat, he crossed over to her, gaining her attention only as his shadow fell across her needlework.

Slia had been so lost in thought she jumped as the shadow startled her. She thought for a moment she had an intruder, but upon seeing the king, she smiled at him nervously and lay her stitching in the chair as she stood. She wasn't sure what she was supposed to do but thought showing respect would never be out of place. He was her husband, but also her elder—and a king.

He reached and grasped her hands in his, spreading their arms wide and admiring the beautiful sight before him.

"You are lovely," he said to her, admiration apparent in his voice. "What a beautiful creature you are, my dear girl."

She slipped her right hand from his left and touched it to her own chest.

"Slia," she said, patting at the neckline of her dress, then gestured toward him, a questioning look across her face.

"Maikel," he said, patting himself with his free hand.

"My name is Maikel."

"Maikel," she echoed, rolling the strange name around in her mouth. At least now she had a name for her husband. In her thoughts, he would no longer be known only as the king.

The treaty had been signed that morning in the Great Hall. Maikel, King of the Torbraugh had signed his name along with Salar, the Chief Elder of the Conclave of the People and the four Chieftains of the Dragon tribes. He felt a definite chill in the exchange of greetings from the Chieftain of the Black Dragon Tribe, Slia's father. Perhaps if the man were to see his daughter, the king thought, and observe she were not mistreated, the air between he and his father-in-law would be warmer. Maikel invited the man to his tent to speak with his daughter.

Maikel knew he was taking a chance on the girl being in presentable state. That was the reason he had come into their bed chamber alone. He would escort her out to the room of the tent where her father waited.

The king took his queen's hand and placed it on his arm, telling her in words she could not understand that he wanted her to accompany him.

"We have our first official visitor, my dear," he said and led her into the next room of the tent, escorting her under the flap between.

"Father!" she said excitedly and dropped Maikel's arm to go to her father once they were near him.

"Slia," he said, holding his child in his arms. "Are you alright? Are you happy? Has he been good to you?"

Her father, Shalim, spoke to her in low tones.

Maikel and the man he used to translate for him had retreated several paces to give the father and daughter privacy.

"Maikel is trying to make me happy, Father. He has been very kind and...very gentle."

Shalim looked into his daughter's eyes. He had always been able to discern if she were completely truthful to him. He saw no deceit.

"I think he truly wants me to be happy. He's just not—you know who I mean. Tell HIM I am so sorry, but, but I am married now. Tell Mother I am well. I, tell her I am sorry I did not obey her completely. But nothing can be done now. Give her and the boys my love. I love you, Father."

She rushed her words as she could tell her husband was ready to go back to the Conclave to finish the festivities and this might be the only time she could see her father. Shalim held his daughter to himself tightly, then let her go. Soos, she was married, and her life now rested with her husband.

"You look very pretty, Slia."

"Thank you, Father. Maikel gave it all to me." She turned slowly to show her new apparel to her father, and to demonstrate to her husband how much she appreciated his generosity.

Being a king, she knew he did not have to be kind, or gentle, or even generous with her.

It was time for them to go.

Shalim kissed his daughter on the forehead and hugged her once more. He willed himself not to shed tears, not in front of the Torbraugh king, even if he were his son-in-law. There would be time enough for that tonight alone in his bed. He wished he could be home to be in misery together with his wife. But he could not go home until tomorrow.

The king did not invite his new bride to the festivities, thinking she might find her way to the man she loved. If she soiled herself with him, Maikel knew he would have to kill them both and that would not be a good start to the new peace.

Slia would not have gone to the Conclave unless physically forced. She feared she might see Stell's sister or his sister's husband. She remained secluded away, she belonged to the Torbraugh king, and she would be as good a wife as she could. Slia would not even look toward the Conclave buildings on the day all the king's goods were packed up and the Torbraugh headed home. This land was no longer her home. Her home lay to the west, in a place she had never been and had never wanted to go.

Bit by bit, word by word, Slia began to pick a few words here and there of the Torbraugh language.

It's a good thing I come from Kaul-Leb's line, she thought. He learned Dragon quickly, now I am learning Torbraugh.

Day by day, riding with Maikel, she became at ease with him. To pass the time, she learned color names, numbers, and other simple words. By the time they reached the palace that would be her home the rest of her life, Slia could carry on simple conversations.

Maikel seemed pleased with her for her efforts in learning his language. He thought to himself, that having a mother with the intelligence Slia displayed, he would surely have remarkable children with her.

The countryside reminded Slia of home and a pang of homesickness ravaged her heart. The grass was the same green, there were the same kind of trees, and certainly, the sun shone the same.

The manner of dress on the people they passed was different, but then, so was what she wore now. The cloak she wore over her dress was of a soft red something but bore no embroidery or fancy work. Slia wondered if Maikel would mind if she embellished it some when they arrived at their destination. She heard the speech of the people as they shouted warm greetings at their king and at her, their new queen. A few words she understood now, but not all. Slia tried to smile warmly at them and would sometimes wave when Maikel did, though with smaller gestures.

Gradually, the roadway became wider and busier. There were more and more buildings. Slia realized that she was now in a city. There was nothing green except a tree or a small flower planting here and there. Then, at a distance, she saw what she took to be the palace. She found she was holding her breath looking at the large, white granite edifice that was her new home.

"It's beautiful!" she exclaimed in Dragon, then looked at Maikel and tried to say it again in Torbraugh.

She allowed she had at least gotten close to what she meant when he chuckled and gave her a quick hug.

After meeting the various members of the royal family, Slia believed she would be happier keeping mainly to her own assigned rooms. She felt too much an outsider to enjoy the continuous company of those born to rank. She developed a new obsession with her embroidery and attracted to herself servants and a few aristocratic women who were of the more retiring personality.

When she learned enough words, Slia asked her king to make a decree that when she died, whenever it was, sooner or later, that she would be sent to the Dragon in a funeral pyre so her soul could find rest. The other was could she, when and if the day came, name their first son Saan?

"Saan? Is that his name—the man? The man you still love?" he asked hotly, his countenance darkened.

"Esoos! No, my husband, I would never attempt to dishonor you by naming your child for the man I was betrothed to marry before you chose me. I have pushed him from my heart."

Slia knelt in front of his chair before the fire in their bedroom. She took her husband's hands in her own and looked up at him, her eyes eloquent with her heart's desire.

"Saan was the name of my great-grandfather, a man who has never had a child named for him. I have always wanted to name a son for him. Ever since I was a small child, I have wanted to use his name for my firstborn should that child be a boy."

The king studied her face. He could find no deceit nesting there. She had always been truthful with him as far as he knew. He searched his memory. What WAS the name he had found out belonged to the man who first held her heart?

Yes, he remembered now. Stell, that was the man's name. A boy still, by their reckoning, still a year too young to marry when the king stole away his beloved. He had been told the boy had not ever been truly awake since his wounding. Good. The king hoped that that Stell had died.

No, not dead, the king thought as he stroked the long, loose beautiful dark hair of his queen. He smiled at her. Let him be a hopeless cripple, forever wounded by a loyal White Eagle warrior. If his Slia were to ever have knowledge of his present situation, let the man be a hopeless cripple, a pitiful invalid, unworthy of such a woman.

Maikel wished now he could parade the shell of a man before Slia so she would know how much better off she was, that her sorry bit of wounded Dragon was nothing compared to the fine example of manhood who took her to his bed.

His bed. Did she ever think of that young man while in his royal bed? Did she dream of him while sleeping beside her king? Surely not. The girl knew nothing of deceit.

Sitting at the king's feet, Slia had lain her head upon his knees while he stroked her hair. She closed her eyes and imagined it were Stell touching her instead and sighed.

The king smiled, yes, he was positive his young wife, his queen, was content with him.

The king took her up in his arms and held her to him. She was used to him now and relaxed against him, her head on his shoulder.

"You have my permission to name all the children we have together any name you choose—except his, the man you almost married. Any name you wish."

She put her arms around his neck and sighed again.

Slia grew fond of her king, but in her heart, her love would always be Stell. Sometimes when the king came to her and she gave of herself to him, her thoughts were on Stell, wondering how well he had recovered, how had he felt about her when he found she had married the king, and most importantly, had he found someone else to love. She wished him happy, but it saddened her to think he could love someone other than herself. Her thoughts were of Stell the night she conceived her son.

The king had seen Slia smile, but the first time he heard her laugh she was playing with her child. She was speaking to Saan in Dragon, the king had given her permission to teach him her native language, it might be of use one day. The baby was only a month or so old and she was saying a simple rhyme to him when he burped loudly and smiled. For this, she laughed. The sound of her laughter sent a thrill through his soul. He found he had come to love her deeply.

When little Saan was three years old, Slia was brought to bed again with another child.
The pregnancy had gone well, but delivery was not.

The child was not advancing toward birth and seemed "caught" up within her.

Finally, after three grueling days, a child, a beautiful little girl was born. Her body was blue and she never took breath.

Slia wept weakly and asked to hold her baby, holding her arms out. Her face pale and covered in cold sweat, she held the baby tightly to her chest. She sobbed and Maikel came to her, sitting beside her on the bed. He gently leaned down, his hands on either side of her body and kissed her softly on the forehead. He, too, had tears in his eyes. He loved being a father and was almost as devastated as Slia at losing this baby.

It broke his heart watching Slia mourn her little girl.

The baby had fine, delicate features and for one so young, thick black, curly hair. Maikel sat and stroked Slia's hair, silently mourning with her. He gave her no ineffective platitudes about having other children someday. For today, this child was dead. No other would ever take her place, no matter how many more might grace their lives.

At last, Slia's sobs subsided, and she kissed her too still baby and handed her to the nurse. Maikel tenderly wiped the tears from her face with a very soft cloth.

"Please," she begged, her voice terribly weak from the effort of birthing the dead child. "Send her to the Dragon for me."

"I will, my love. It is late in the day. Will tomorrow be soon enough?"

"Soos," she whispered, so exhausted she could hardly speak.

Maikel was used to her one-word Dragon replies, and found it endearing when she occasionally reverted to her native tongue.

"Sleep now, you need your rest, you have had a hard three days."

"Three days?"

"Soos," he said back to her. Using the few words of Dragon he knew usually made her smile and he was not disappointed.

He pulled the warm blankets up around her and kissed her again. She was asleep before he rose from her bed. He turned to walk from the room, taking the dead baby from the nurse. He would watch over the little body tonight and direct the funeral pyre for tomorrow to be placed so that the grieving mother could watch from her room.

But for Slia, tomorrow never came. She was not asleep. She had slipped into unconsciousness, having hemorrhaged. Her insides had been too badly ravaged by the three days of hard laboring birthing the stillborn daughter.

By morning when her death was discovered, she was already cold.

Hearing the nurse's wailing cries, Maikel went to Slia's side. His tears dropped down upon her cold cheek as he bent to kiss her good-bye. Carefully, he slipped the Dragon Eye pendant from around her neck. Thinking it a family heirloom, he had never asked her its origin.

The widower king left his beloved wife's side and went down the hall, entering the nursery of their son, little Saan. Wordlessly, he slipped the pendant cord over Saan's neck, letting the stone fall to the boy's chest.

He picked the boy up from the floor where he was playing with a wooden toy horse and sat down on a chair and played with his son.

"Leave us for a while," he said to the boy's nurse, his voice barely audible.

The nurse bowed to the king and did as she was told. Later, he would see to the increasing of the size of the pyre. But for now, he just wanted to comfort himself with what little was left of his love.

Slia walked down the corridor of darkness. After several steps, she realized she was not alone, but held the hand of a little girl, her girl.

The child was not a baby, but the size of Saan at least. They did not speak, but just looked at one another, knowing. In the distance was the light, and Slia could perceive that they were nearing someone.

"Mother!" Slia called as she recognized her. She and the little girl ran to the open arms and hugged. No one spoke any other words. Words were not needed for they were all crossed over.

Slia knew that she and the girl and her own mother were among the dead. She had knowledge that she had never been destined to marry Stell, and that no matter her circumstances, she was to die having her second child.

And she knew Saan's destiny.

Chapter Eight
Slia Comes Home

There was a stir in the village the day a detail of the special guard to the Torbraugh king appeared in the Black Dragon Central Village. Their banner of the mighty White Eagle flew upside down, a sign of distress. So it would fly for a year to indicate mourning for the death of their young queen.

The chief officer of the detail dismounted outside the door leading to the dwelling where his king had found his Queen Slia just a few years ago and went to the doorway. Beside him was a man not in uniform, but in finery of the court. They had both been with the king the day he found and married his queen.

Alerted by a villager before the Torbraugh soldiers arrived, Shalim stood in his open doorway, his three boys behind him.

All three remained at home, not yet at the age of manhood, but showing signs of maturity. Salmar's face was going to be smooth with only a mustache, showing his Song-hee heritage, his two younger brothers were beginning to display facial hair, as well.

The two Torbraugh approached the door. The officer saluted and the court official bowed.

The official spoke.

"Sir," he said, his voice heavily accented with Torbraugh, but understandable. "Are you Shalim, father of Her Imperial Majesty Slia of the White Eagle, Daughter of the Dragon?"

"Soos, I am her father, and these are her brothers."

"Sir," the man said and bowed again. "It is with regret that His Imperial Majesty King Maikel of the White Eagle has sent word that our Queen Slia has perished in childbirth. The child perished with the mother, a girl."

Shalim stared at the man, his insides feeling both frozen and entirely liquid at the same time.

"My Slia? She is gone?" Shalim managed to ask at last. He felt the like he could no longer breathe. He took Salmar's arm to steady himself.

"Soos," the man said in Dragon. "But by her own request made shortly after her marriage to King Maikel, she was sent to the Dragon following her death, she and the stillborn princess together."

The man gestured to the officer and he held out to Shalim a jewel encrusted golden box.

"Inside this unworthy receptable is a portion of the ashes taken from their funeral pyre. His majesty believed you would wish to honor her ashes according to your ways of the Dragon."

Shalim gingerly took the box from the officer's hand. The grieving father held it in both hands, close to his body.

"The child," he said, having trouble talking about his own child being gone. "The child that died with her, was she the only one?"

"Esoos, Sir, there is a three-year-old young prince, a fine boy, who looks much like his mother."
Shalim started to speak, but the man raised his hand to forgo the request.

"His Majesty anticipated your desire for the prince, but Sir, His Majesty asked that I inform you that out of his great love for his dear queen, and his delight in the prince, His Majesty cannot let the boy leave him. I can assure you that from my own observation, His Majesty dotes on his son. He loves him dearly. As he loved your daughter, the Queen."

"I see. But if ever, for whatever reason, please tell His Majesty I would welcome my grandson—perhaps even for just a visit someday, or if he should wish to come to us, he is always welcome."

Shalim did not see. He wanted the boy with every bit of his being, but he knew that in the same circumstances, he would be unable to relinquish the child himself.

"Would you and your men overnight with us?" Shalim was not avid in his asking, but decided that it would be rude not to offer.

"We thank you, Sir, but it being early in the day, we wish to begin our journey home. We would not wish to intrude upon your time of mourning."

With that, the man bowed again, the officer saluted, and they retreated to their mounts, and the detail left the way they had come.

Shalim remained in his doorway for some time, clasping the remains of his daughter and her child against himself. Salmar was able to convince him to come into their home at last and the door was pushed shut by one of the younger brothers. Shalim realized later in the day that he had forgotten to even ask the name of his daughter's son.

Several villagers had dared to stand close enough to hear the exchange and soon the sad information was spread throughout the populace.

Tinka had heard the news from several before time for Stell to come in from the fields. Leaving Sar to watch her younger brother and sister, Tinka walked briskly out to see her husband, wanting to be the one to tell him.

Even though Tinka knew her husband loved her, she also had heard about the great love that had existed between Stell and Slia. She wanted to be the one to see his face when his heart had its first knowledge of the death of the one he had first loved before herself. She knew that she might be putting her own heart at risk for pain if her beloved husband was overly devastated, but she had to know how much he still loved the girl who had been lost to him.

Her oldest son saw her first.

"Father, it's Mother." All of her children had settled into calling Stell 'Father' since their wedding shortly over four years ago.

Her heart ached with love as he stood tall from stooping over a stubborn sapling he was hacking down in the middle of his cropland. His muscular torso glistened in the sun, browning under its light.

The Dragon marks on his shoulder blades undulated with the movements of his arms. The Black Dragon on his right shoulder appeared to be beckoning to the Red Dragon with the lion head on his left. She noticed that her sons emulated him and had their tunics off, as well. Sekeel proudly displayed the two headed Red Dragon newly placed on his right shoulder.

Stell smiled at first sight of her, then frowned as she neared as he saw her face.

"Tinka? What is wrong?"

She met him as he came up to her and he kissed her cheek.

"Sad news has come," she said.

Stell waited for her to speak. The last time she came to him in the fields, it was with the news that Lart had crossed over and they had made a hasty trip to honor him at his sending to the Dragon. It had been deep summer then and the days long, giving them time to make it to the Red Dragon Village just before the fire was lit.

She took his hands in hers before she spoke.

"Word came to Shalim today from the Torbraugh king that Slia crossed over, she and the little girl she was trying to birth."

Tinka looked into her husband's eyes and saw a sadness, but not the look of a man who had lost a sweetheart. She didn't know that Sekale had come to Stell and told him of Slia's loss the night she died. He had also told Stell to tell the news to no one.

"Poor Shalim, and the boys—hard for them to hear, I know."

"They also said that she had a son—about the age of Soth."

"Did they bring him to Shalim?"

"Esoos, they said that the king loved him so much, he would keep him. Also that he had greatly loved Slia."

"At least there is that. At least he loved her. I am glad to hear that."

He pulled Tinka into his arms.

"Thanks for coming out here to tell me. But look at me, I've gotten you all wet with my sweat."

"I don't mind at all," she said and pulled him close, kissing him softly.

Her sons looked at each other and smiled.

Chapter Nine
Saan Comes Home

King Maikel did indeed love his little son, the child of his third queen. The little boy's wavy black hair and green eyes reminded him daily of the beautiful young girl he had taken from the People of the Dragon for his own.

Maikel often held court with Saan at his feet playing with his little toys or sitting in the royal lap napping. The older princes became accustomed to their youngest brother monopolizing their father's time and took advantage of not being very closely monitored by their controlling father and king. They gave appearance of caring for him until Maikel's attention was elsewhere, then either ignored him or vented their distain for him in subtle, or not so subtle slights or cruelties.

Rondol once walked by as Saan was eating one of his favorite desserts and snagged a large piece of it, popping it in his mouth.

The child said nothing, for his oldest brother, the crown prince, had been known to pinch him hard if he did. As Saan reached for the last piece of his food, Rondol flipped it off the child's plate onto the floor where Rondol's dog scooped it up and swallowed it.

The older prince smiled hatefully, defying his baby brother to complain. Saan, no fool, said nothing.

A puppy given him by his father was found dead. When asked if he would like another, Saan had declined.

"No, Poppa," he said. "Everything dies, like Mother."

Tears swam in Maikel's eyes as he pulled the little one into his arms and hugged him closely.

Rondol got rid of the little vial of poison, since the child refused another pet. He hated the child of the third queen mainly because his father loved him.

Rondol never remembered being so coddled, nor had his own mother been so pampered as that Dragon witch. He felt his father had been bewitched by that scheming creature, that she had tricked his father into wanting her and making her a queen. He considered Saan a witchling and had no desire to show him any affection. To him, Saan was not royalty, he was no more than a mongrel in a kennel of purebreds.

For over a year, Saan was the target of Maikel's extreme love and Rondol's hatred. Then came to Maikel as comes to all men. His decline was rapid, a growth within his insides first took his appetite, then his vigor, then his life.

The king was succeeded by his first born, Rondol. Rondol's mother had died after seven years of marriage.

The day of King Maikel's burial was cool and overcast causing the old people to say the skies were in mourning. Seating for those not of the royal family was at a premium in the mausoleum courtyard where he was to join his ancestors and his first two queens. Ashes of his third and their stillborn daughter had been carefully gathered and collected into an ornate golden box, a larger version than the one taken to the queen's kindred in the Land of the Dragon. The golden box would lie in his tomb with him by his own decree made shortly after their deaths.

The royal family filed in led by the new king, His Imperial Majesty Rondol Maikel. Beside him, on his arm, walked his queen. Behind them, their children.

Then came each royal sibling with spouse and children by order of birth rank. At the very tail of the procession, behind the others, little Saan walked, his right hand in that of his nursemaid. He had wanted to bring his favorite toy, a little wooden horse given him by his father recently, but Rondol had said no.

The tiny prince was pitied by many who saw him. It was well known that no love was wasted on him by the one now sitting the throne. It was dangerous to even show concern for the child. Several had, in quiet secret, voiced fear that the boy may well come to harm and be the next to be interred.

Crown Prince Rondol had been making plans to rid himself of the child once their father expired. Once Maikel's illness had manifested to the point that all were sure he was about to join his wives in death, Rondol had entertained himself with visions of how the child would die. His favorite method would be to build the little Dragon his funeral pyre and throw him in it, crying out with pain as he burned alive.

He knew, though, that anything so overt would weaken the loyalty of his followers.

He had decided that the little brat would be sent to one of the distant palaces to be raised and educated, or so it would be told. Once there, the child could be slowly poisoned. He would be seen to be growing sickly. His eventual demise would be of no surprise to anyone.

The night after Maikel's death, the first dream came.

Rondol dreamed of a huge white beast. It flew from the Eastern sky, flapping its powerful wings slowly in the coming dawn, coming toward him. In his dream, he thought it to be the White Eagle of the Torbraugh coming to give him its blessing as the new king.

As the beast neared, fear captured his heart and he thrashed about in his bed. It was not an eagle, but a dragon, its icy blue eyes staring at him intently. Just as the creature neared him and he became afraid it would attack, he woke.

Rondol's body was covered in cold, clammy sweat. His mouth had a bad taste and his breath came in great gasps as if he had been under water and suddenly surfaced.

Still under the dream's influence, he stared around his royal chamber. There was no one with him. He slept alone. When he wanted her, he visited the queen then left her, the same with the others he bedded. He had never liked sleeping in the same bed with anyone.

The fire across the room still emitted some light, as did the three candles placed about the room. Nothing he saw had the shape of a dragon.

Gradually, his breathing became normal and the sickly sweat on his rotund frame dried. He did not go back to sleep that night, nor the next.

The second night's dream brought the dragon, the white dragon, back to him. It did as before, but hovered in front of him, its breath sickly sweet and rancid both. Rondol sensed that the beast had a message to give him, but that it was not yet time to tell it.

The third night, the creature did as before, but finally spoke.

"Do no harm," it said.

"No harm?" Rondol heard himself asking. "No harm to who, or what?"

He woke before the beast answered. But he thought within himself who it must mean.

The fourth night, he discovered he was correct in his assumptions.

"Harm not my child. The Son of the Daughter of the Dragon. My child Saan is not to be harmed."

"What am I to do with him?" Rondol asked and woke, frustrated.

Am I supposed to keep him with me? He wondered. Rondol avoided the child during the day, easy to do as he was kept in his nursery far away from the rest of the royals.

The fifth night, the white beast came as before, his icy blue eyes penetrating to the center of Rondol's being.

"What am I to do with Saan?" the new king asked.

"Send him unharmed back to my land, to my people. Send him back to the People of the Dragon. Back to the home of his mother, to her father, who wants him. See that no harm is done him, or my wrath will fall upon all who lay harsh hand on my child."

Rondol did not dream of the Dragon again, much to his great relief.

Seven days after King Maikel died, he was buried.

The next morning, shortly after eating his morning meal, Saan saw ten soldiers and one of his father's court officials come into his nursery. The Captain of his father's guard, now his brother's guard ordered his nurse to pack some of his clothing for a short stay in two small bags.

"Where is he going, Captain?" the nurse asked. "I've not been told of any visit, I have nothing of my own packed."

"He goes alone." The Captain answered. "Get his things packed or he goes without them. We leave immediately."

The nurse pulled several items from a drawer, making sure to include his little night shirt. She noticed a parchment in the bottom of one of the bags, but was afraid if she brought it to the Captain's attention, he would grab the boy and go without the child's things.

"Just a moment, his boots are in the dressing room," she said and went to get them. Returning, men, bags, and boy were gone. The nurse ran after them, down the hallway and down the steps.

Through a window, she saw the detail trotting away, her little prince riding on the saddle in front of the court official.

"They didn't even let me kiss him good-bye," she said to no one.

"Good-bye, my sweet baby."

She blew her little charge a kiss and returned to the empty nursery to cry and put his things away.

"They didn't even take any of his toys."

Two weeks later, the child hungry, exhausted, dirty, and frightened, they arrived in the Black Dragon central village in front of the house of Shalim, his grandfather.

It was the time of Conclave, and the grandfather was gone. The brothers were not home, for they were out in the fields, tending to crops or cattle. A neighbor boy was sent by his mother to inform the brothers of the Torbraugh visitors. That he was informed of a small dark-haired child with light green eyes being with them did not thrill Salmar at all. What he dreaded most was happening.

Salmar did not want the king's whelp.

By the time the brothers neared their home, most of the village residents had already gathered around the detail still mounted on their horses. The animals pranced about, wanting to be headed back toward their own stables far away, or at least relieved of the men that had been on their backs for so many days.

As Salmar and his brothers were seen by the villagers to be coming toward their home, they informed the official who could speak Dragon. He was the same who had spoken over a year ago when they brought the Queen's ashes.

"Are you the brothers of Queen Slia?" the man asked.

"We are," Salmar answered. "I am Salmar, the oldest. Our father is away at Conclave and will be gone several more days. Is that the king's?"

He had gestured with his chin toward Saan, still in front of the man talking for the detail.

"Soos," the man answered. "This is the child of King Maikel and Queen Slia. His father the king has died and King Rondol has sent the child to be with his grandfather, father of Queen Slia."

"We don't want him," Salmar spat out. "I—we want nothing of the Torbraugh king here."

"We were ordered by our king to bring the child and to deliver him to the home of his grandfather. That the man is not here does not matter. Our mission is complete. Here is the child."

The man eased Saan down, holding to his little arm as he leaned over and positioned him slightly away from his horse. The child dropped the last several inches. He landed on his hands and knees, a dirty little bundle with wide, scared eyes. Carefully side-stepping his horse around him, the court official reined his animal around and it trotted off the way it had come. The rest of the detail followed, dust swirling in the air, a good deal of it settling on the boy.

One of Slia's younger brothers started forward to collect the child.

"Leave him, I will not allow him in the house," Salmar ordered. "Nothing, nothing from that king is welcome."

Strella, Stell's mother, standing in the crowd, could not believe the words she heard.

"This is your only sister's only child, all that is left of her in this world, and you don't WANT him? What is wrong with you? Have you no heart?"

The child's eldest uncle stared at her.

"His father forced Slia into a marriage she did not want and took her away from us to die. Why should I," he spit out and gestured at his younger brothers.

"Why should I or my brothers want him?"

Salmar stomped away, his brothers looked at Strella and the child, then turned as one to follow their eldest brother. They had each felt his wrath too often growing up and feared his hot temper. They knew he could be tender and kind, but he could turn completely hateful when crossed, an attribute he acquired after the loss of their sister to the king he hated.

Strella looked down at the little one in the middle of all the arguing. He might not understand the words, but the high emotions and heated speech had him upset.

His lower lip and chin quivered as he fought the battle against tears and lost. He did not cry out loud, but streams of hot tears tracked down his dirty little cheeks and fell on his filthy clothing.

She could stand it no longer and stooped over, wrapped her arms around the little pile of unwanted flesh and lifted him up against her, marching resolutely toward her home.

"Mother," Stell called and caught up with her, his limping exaggerated by his rushing. "What are you doing? This is none of your concern." He no longer needed his cane, in normal walking his limp was barely noticeable.

Strella stopped and turned toward her son, the little boy's head resting on her shoulder, his arms around her neck.

"None of my concern? Do I really hear your mouth saying those words? This is the child of a girl we both loved. It is not his fault who his father is! How could I rest at night knowing I left this poor, abandoned baby wandering the streets unloved and unwanted and uncared for?"

With that said, she started home.

"At least let me help you with him," he had said as they walked along, offering to carry the little load. Stell noted to himself that the little boy looked the same age as the son he had fathered with Tinka, Soth.

"He's frightened," she said. "I'm not going to try to peel him off me in front of the whole village." In little time, she was at her door, child in her arms, her son on her heels.

Stell opened the door to his mother's dwelling and escorted them in. She stood the child on the table in the kitchen. He was a pitiful sight. Tear tracks had washed down through the grime on his face. His shoulder length dark hair was tangled and matted.

His clothes were well cut but would probably never wash clean again. He was missing one shoe and his bare stocking sole, once white, was black. A hand sized bruise adorned his left cheek. But his light green eyes were clear and alert and moist with unshed tears.

"Get the tub out of the closet for me and get two buckets of water from the well, please."

"Soos, Mother."

Stell pulled out the tub and got the two buckets beside it and went back out the door. He was gone only a few moments and had his buckets full.

Strella poured a pot of simmering water she took from a hook by the fire into the tub and poured one bucket of fresh cool in the pot to heat. Strella always had water heating. The other bucket of water she motioned Stell to pour in the tub. She wasn't trying to cook the child.

"Go get one more, that may still be too hot for him."

"Why didn't you just put the other one in it?"

His mother gave him her stern, don't ask me questions look.

Stell, a grown man, but still his mother's son, did as he was told.

"Pour half in the tub," she said to him and continued what she had started doing, undressing the little dirty child standing patiently on her table.

"Oh, my" she said almost in a whisper as she pulled his little shirt away.

Stell turned to look.

Around the boy's neck was a leather cord with a red stone attached.

Stell stepped over to examine the pendant. He reached out to touch it and the child grabbed it, enclosing it in his little fist.

"No!" he said in his own language, which they did not understand. Then he added, in Dragon. "Mother!"

He started to back away until Stell caught him, just before he stepped backwards off the table.

"It's alright, little one, I'm not going to take it from you, I promise."

He patted the child's back, smiling at him. He finished undressing him by unbuttoning his once fancy little britches now dirty with travel and sleeping outdoors. Seeing that his own Mother was standing by the tub ready, he picked the boy up, and carried him to the washing tub, the little behind perched on his right arm. The child held his mother's pendant in his hand, guarding it.

Walking slowly across the floor, his limp was barely apparent. Stell gently sat the child down in the water, testing the temperature with his left hand in it first. He decided not to worry the child over the stone, but would get a closer look when he could.

Strella scrubbed the boy softly until she was satisfied that no hint of grime remained on his little body.

"You can lift him out now, Stell."

The man carefully grasped the child under his armpits, with his fingers spread widely to make sure the slippery little body didn't fall and lifted him up and over the edge of the tub.

The boy's legs bent like a little frog's as he was pulled from the water. He straightened them out as Stell lowered him to the thick rug next to the tub.

He held to the stone again. Strella started at his head with a warmed cloth drying him off. With the boy's face momentarily obscured, and his hands down, Stell closely studied the pendant around the little neck. It was definitely the same one.

He took another cloth and warmed it as his mother finished drying the boy. Stell knew his mother's boy-washing routine well. The fresh cloth went around the little body before he could chill.

"Do we have anything to put on him?"

"Perhaps there is something in one of these packs," a voice said from the door. It was the village executioner. He was a boyhood friend of Stell's.

He dropped two small bags on the table.

"They were still in the square after everyone left. I thought they might hold something for the child."

Stell emptied them out on the table. There were a few small britches, stockings, shirts, and finally, what appeared to be a night dress of some sort. A scroll of parchment rolled out of the bottom of the bag, almost flattened by the weight of the other objects.

The three adults looked at the scroll, written in lettering they could not understand.

"No shoes or boots, though," Strella said, picking through the scant offerings. "He lost a shoe on his journey."

Taking what they considered to be appropriate night clothes, the child was soon dressed for the evening.

"I'll check around to see if anyone has a pair of outgrown footwear that will do for a while," the executioner, Stol, said.

"Don't bother, Stol, but thanks. I'm sure Tinka will have something put back that will fit him," Stell said to his friend.

While the boy's hair was still damp, Strella combed through it lightly. Done, she patted his flat little belly.

"Time to feed this baby. I can only imagine that has been neglected like everything else."

Stell, will you get him seated? Stol, would you take a mug of cider?"

"Always," Stol answered. He had spent much of his youth running in and out of this house with Stell. It had been his second home. He sat down beside the boy.

"What's his name?"

Strella and Stell looked at one another.

"I don't think they said," Strella answered. "It's nearly two weeks before his grandfather will be back, we can't just call him Boy."

Stell became thoughtful for a moment.

"Slia always talked about wanting to name her first born son after her great-grandfather, maybe she did."

He turned to the child.

"Saan?"

The boy looked up and answered in the language of his former home.

"Yes, Sir?"

No one understood him, but by consensus, he would be called Saan until they found a better name for him.

Strella set a mug down in front of him and in front of Stol.

"You're giving him hard cider, Mother?"

"I think Stol can handle it," she laughed. "Saan's is diluted with water and has honey added. The cider is to help him relax."

She also gave the child an ample slice of hearty bread generously spread with soft cheese mixed with more honey.

Saan looked at her with inquiring eyes as if he wondered if he might eat.

"Soos, Saan, eat," she said and picked up the bread and put it in his now clean little hand.

He attacked it and the mug of watered-down cider with the vigor of the hungry boy he was.

"I wonder if that's how he got that bruise," she said. "Eating something they didn't intend for him."

Strella brought two more mugs to the table and she and Stell sat and sipped with Stol as the child ate.

He finished his bread and Strella gave him another.

She wondered if those men had fed the child at all on their journey. He ate this one in less haste.

Saan was almost finished with his second piece of bread when Tinka appeared in the doorway, followed by Soth. She carried various pieces of boy clothing folded over her arm. Soth carried a pair of low-cut boots, passed down from his brothers, intended to be his soon. He had been allowed to choose which ones to bring and had proudly picked out the best pair he could find.

"Where's the rest of the brood?" Stell asked, rising from his seat and taking the clothing from Tinka. He kissed her lightly on the cheek then guided her to his chair. Strella brought her a mug of hot cider.

Tinka sat down slowly, her body awkward so close to bearing a third child to Stell.

"Sira is still napping with Sar watching her, the older boys are studying, and I thought our little fellow would be overwhelmed with more than one descending on him," she said and rubbed her rounded belly as she sipped the cider.

"So good," she said and took another sip.

Soth stood by his mother, minutely observing the child he did not know.

"Come here, son," Stell said, holding his hand out. He had sat next to Saan, Stol still on the other side.

"Come meet Saan. He doesn't know anyone here and will need a friend. Do you think you could be his friend?"

"Soos, Father," Soth said and went to Stell. He turned to Saan.

"I brought you a pair of boots. Mother saw you needed some."

Saan looked at Soth but said nothing.

"Saan doesn't understand our words yet, son."

"How can he not understand, Father? Doesn't he talk?"

"Soos, he can talk, but mostly only Torbraugh words. You will have to help him learn how to talk in Dragon."

"Mother said his mother was a Dragon, didn't she teach him Dragon words?"

"I would think that she would, but you see, his mother died and he had no one to talk to him in Dragon, then his father died and he was sent here to live with his grandfather. But his grandfather is at Conclave, so he has come home with Grandmother for a while."

Soth looked solemnly first at Stell, then Tinka, then back to Stell. Tears came to his eyes.

"He must be sad."

"Soos, that is why he will need a friend."

Soth, one boot at a time, slipped them on Saan's bare feet and smiled at him. Saan just stared back, not knowing what to do.

"Boots," Soth said and smiled again, tapping the toe of one boot.

"Boots," Saan repeated and tapped the boot himself. Both boys laughed.

"Has Saan been to the privy yet? He's been here a while. He better go before he has an accident and gets embarrassed," the ever-practical Tinka asked.

"I'll show him where it is," Soth volunteered and took Saan's hand, directing him to come with him.

Saan slid off the chair and went with Soth.

Two little boys, both with the black hair of the People, one with the green eyes of his ancestor Kaul-Leb and his mother, the late queen of the Torbraugh, the other with the icy blue eyes of his Dragon father, both conceived the same night and born the same day, walked hand in hand together.

The mothers of both had been thinking of the same man both when the child was conceived and the day he was born.

"Will you let Soth stay the night to keep Saan company?" Strella asked of Tinka.

"Soos, his night clothes are on him under the other. I thought your little one might need someone his own age to make him comfortable."

Stell reached out and took his wife's hand in his and lifted it to his lips, giving it a long kiss.

When the boys came back, still holding hands, Stell told Soth that he would spending the night with Grandmother and Saan.

His smile lit up the room as he hastily unbuttoned his short tunic and britches to reveal his sleeping tunic below. He kicked off his boots. Seeing this, Saan kicked off his, as well. They both laughed in the universal language of children.

Soth took Saan's hand and led him into Grandmother's main room to play with some of his toys he kept there in a basket to the side of the fire. His basket had once been his great-grandmother's sewing basket, given to him for toys after she crossed over when he was two.

He had three wooden horses and two made of cloth in addition to a small wooden wagon.

The boys busied themselves moving the toy horses about sometimes with the wagon, sometimes not. That night, Saan relearned the Dragon words for boots, privy, horse and wagon. And he learned the names Soth and Grandmother.

After Stell and Tinka went back home and Stol said his good-byes, Grandmother Strella let the boys play for a while before calling them for a bowl of stew.

The three of them sat and ate together. The boys played some more for a bit while she cleaned up and then she directed them to the privy again and then bed.

Except for the occasional grandchild, Strella's big bed had been unshared since the death of her young husband when Stell was nine. Tonight, she had two wiggly little boys, who each chattered in their own language for a while then fell into sleep almost at the same time.

Strella slept nearest the door, Saan in the middle, close to Soth.

In the morning, she was almost finished making their morning meal before she heard giggles coming from her bedroom.

"Boys, go to the privy then come eat," she called.

They came in to her, both fully dressed, Soth wearing the clothes he had had on over his night clothes, and Saan in some of the ones brought by Tinka. Both were barefoot, their naked feet slapping the flat stones as they ran together, hand in hand, giggling.

Both boys ate well then went back to playing with the toy horses. Strella relished the sounds of happy children playing. She dreaded Saan's grandfather's return when she would have to give up Slia's child to him. She already loved the little son of the dead Torbraugh king and the girl her son had loved.

Saan and Soth were like twins separated at birth, now reunited, both her grandsons. Strella wondered if she might be allowed to keep him.

Saan had been told he was being taken to his grandfather, his mother's father. He had not seen anyone he would consider a grandfather. The man who came with the woman who had taken him home was not old enough to be his grandfather, nor the other man who came and left.

He had seen the other men and the woman argue, over him, he rightly judged, but they were too young to be his grandfather, he was certain. He thought a grandfather would be older than his own father. He knew that his father had not been a young man, but a grandfather for him must be older still.

His mother had taught him long ago, long ago to him, words like the ones these people used and he was beginning to remember some of them.

The man who had first come into the house had been very interested in his mother's red stone, but had not tried to take it from him. He was glad he had hidden it from the soldiers when they brought him. They had not been good to him, and he thought that they would have taken it from him, if they had known of it. Father would have punished them if they had treated him so before he died. But he knew that his brother, Rondol, did not care.

The woman the men argued with, Soth called her Grandmother, but the younger man called her Mother. Saan knew what "Mother" meant, that was a word he knew still. So he surmised that "Grandmother" meant she was Soth's grandmother and the younger man's mother and Soth was that man's son. The woman with the baby in her belly must be Soth's mother, for they had come in together and she had left with the man who called Grandmother "Mother." Who the other man might be was still a mystery to him, but he had come in with the clothing of Saan's that the soldiers had. Perhaps he was just a friend to Soth's father. Saan wondered if his grandfather had died, too, like Mother and Father.

And just who were those men Grandmother had argued with? The one had seemed to be angry with him, why, he could not understand. It had scared him the way he spoke with such anger in his voice.

And Saan had been so very tired and hungry and dirty and alone. Then Grandmother had grabbed him up and Soth's father had come with her and things started to get better. He had been cleaned and fed and talked to nicely, even if in words he could not understand. Then Soth had come in with the woman with the baby belly and he had a friend. And they had brought clothing for him like Soth wore. And boots. He felt love for Grandmother and Soth. Maybe if his grandfather never came, he could stay always with Grandmother and Soth.

He liked sleeping in the big bed with Grandmother and Soth, it reminded him of the special times he got to sleep in the big bed with Mother before she died with the baby that died.

At first, after she died, Father had let him sleep with him in his big bed. But after a while, Father had other people sleeping in his bed, women people.

Then Father had died and Rondol didn't like him and didn't have to act like he did anymore and had sent him away with the mean soldiers.

Now he was here and Grandmother and Soth and Soth's mother and father were nice to him and he got to play with Soth's horses. Soth's brothers and sisters came by some, but only Soth stayed. And no one tried to take the red stone that had been his mother's.

After three days he and Grandmother and Soth went for a walk and went in a nearby house and saw Soth's mother holding a little squirming baby and she didn't have a baby belly anymore. Saan was glad Soth's mother did not die with the baby the way his mother did.

Grandmother held the baby some and talked silly to it then gave it back and they went back to Grandmother's house and ate and played and then went to bed in the big bed.

Several days later while he and Soth were playing in a mud puddle with some rocks, an old man came running to them and picked Saan up and hugged him and didn't mind that he got mud on his nice clothes.

This must be the grandfather he was sent to be with, he thought, and he was right.

"His name is Saan, Sir," Soth said to Shalim.

"Saan, I am your grandfather," Shalim said and hugged the boy to himself and kissed him several times.

"He only knows a few words, Sir," Soth told him.

Shalim sat on a nearby bench, holding Saan in his lap. Soth came to them and pointed to Shalim.

"Grandfather," he said to Saan. "Say it."

"Grandfather," Saan said and hugged the old man.

The old man's face, especially his eyes, reminded him of his mother.

"Soos, I am your grandfather."

The old man's eyes filled with tears as he held the boy close.

Grandmother came out of the door and looked at the three of them.

"Shalim, your Conclave clothes, they are covered in mud!"

"Soos, they are, but I don't care. I finally get to see her boy. And Soth tells me his name is Saan, after my grandfather."

"Soos, Stell said Slia always wanted to name her first son after him so he tried it and the boy answered to it. The men who brought him to us didn't say what he was called."

"I hear he arrived filthy and half-starved, too. You can't know how much I appreciate your taking care of him for me. I am ashamed of my sons for refusing to take him."

"They still hate the king for taking Slia—or at least Salmar does, and he influences his brothers."

"Still, he is their sister's child. But now he is with us! Isn't he a fine-looking boy?"

"Soos, he is, and very sweet. He and Soth are already fast friends."

"Sir?"

"Soos, Soth?"

"Are you going to take Saan away from me?"

"I will take him to my home, but you will still be his friend, won't you? You may still play together and see each other every day, but he will live with me."

"Can he still come here and stay some with me and Grandmother? Sometimes?"

"Shalim, Saan is always welcome here, and when you are gone to Conclave, couldn't he stay with me?" Strella asked. "With me and Soth?"

Shalim looked at Saan and then back to Soth and Strella.

"I think we would both like that very much, thank you Strella."

"Shalim, would you like Soth to be with you and Saan your first night together, to be, well, a familiar face for him in your home?"

"He has had to face a lot of changes lately, hasn't he?" Shalim said and ran his hand over the boy's head, as though trying to see for himself what the child had been through.

"Do you think Tinka and Stell would mind if I kept him with us for a day or two, just to make the adjustment a little easier for Saan?"

Shalim glanced at Strella but had difficulty looking at anyone but Saan. Here on his lap was the child he had so long wanted to see. The only bit of his Slia still in the world.

He suddenly felt very overwhelmed. How was he supposed to raise a child alone? He wasn't so sure he had done well even with the help of his dear wife, now gone for years.

Once, following well meant advice, he had talked about the possibility of marriage with Strella. She had laughed. Not mean, not derisive, but matter-of-factly.

"Don't be silly," she had said. "We would both of us be terribly unhappy within a month. We are not suited for one another—and I have been alone too long to easily get use to another man!"

Shalim turned to her again.

"Will you help me raise this boy, Strella? I'm not exactly sure how to go about it all by myself with one so small."

Strella sat down beside him on the bench.

"Let the boys go back to their mud puddle for a bit, they are so like brothers, they love one another. But there is something you do need to realize."

Shalim's brows gathered together in the middle of his forehead.

"Soth, take Saan and play for a little while longer, then it will be time to clean up."

"Soos, Grandmother."

Shalim eased Saan back to the ground and allowed Soth to take him by the hand and return to churning the mud around.

"Now, what is this great mystery I must realize?" he asked.

"Even though Slia married the king both under a marriage cape and again in the king's own way, he was not of the People of the Dragon. He had no tribal markings, no citizen braids. Saan has no inheritance of the Dragon. No tribe. He will not be a citizen, not by his birth. Only if he is adopted. By law, it must be one of your sons as you are beyond age. And no one else may because he has them."

The old man sat, thinking within himself. He rubbed his chin and pulled thoughtfully on his long, black beard, beginning to have more gray than black.

"You are right, Strella, the thought had not yet come to me, I was so excited about having him here with me. He will have to be adopted, or risk attempting to rise to manhood with the Dragon's forgiveness."

"Shalim! The child is not even five years old yet, do you think you can be assured that you will live another twenty years?"

"If the Dragon wishes to grant His forgiveness, I will."

"It would be safer for him to be adopted by one of your sons."

"If one of them would."

"Do they still hate the king so much?"

Strella raised her eyes up to look at the sky.

"Of course, they do—I could not get any of them to see reason to take Saan the day the soldiers brought him. But if you have him marked, you know what will happen if he doesn't get forgiveness."

"Soos, I know."

Strella let it drop. She stood.

"I'll take the boys in and scrape the mud off. Why don't you stay, the both of you, and eat, then we can take them to your house. We can stop and ask Tinka to make certain she doesn't mind Soth staying with you, though I don't think she will, she's got the new baby to contend with. Another boy."

"Good," Shalim said, and stood, brushing drying mud off his clothing. "I would like a chance to see the new one."

While the two youngsters splashed themselves clean in Strella's tub under Shalim's watchful eye, she prepared their meal. Later, the four of them walked over to see the baby and ask permission for Soth to stay with his new friend at Shalim's."

Strella tucked the boys into bed in what had once been Slia's room and kissed them both. Shalim decided that he would let them stay together there without him. It would become Saan's room.

After the death of Slia's mother, Shalim had changed his bed for a narrow one, not wanting to sleep in their marriage bed alone, so there was no room for two wiggly boys in it.

"Be good tonight, Soth, and be helpful in the morning. And don't giggle all night, either," she said and kissed them both again."

"I will see your Grandmother out and be right back in," Shalim told them, showering more kisses on both boys. "Tonight I will be in my room, right across from you with both doors open, if you need me."

Soth, on the other side of Saan, told him what to say.

"Saan, say 'Goodnight, Grandmother, and goodnight, Grandfather.'"

Saan echoed his friend and they both giggled.

Grandfather Shalim took the candle from the bedside table and moved it to one out in the hallway. He escorted Strella to the door.

"Thank you so much for taking care of my boy, Strella, and for loaning me Soth. You are right, the boys seem like brothers."

Strella patted him on the arm and walked briskly home in the deepening twilight. She didn't want anyone to see the tears beginning to fall down her cheeks.

She missed the boys already. She wished desperately she could have Saan with her, she loved him so much. She would always have Soth close, but worried over what would be in Saan's future.

To the People of the Dragon, the day of a person's birth was a sacred detail. After Saan came to live with him, Shalim searched the delicate parchment that had been sent with Saan's pitiful few clothes, hoping it would tell him. The Torbraugh words told him nothing. He determined to take it to the Conclave, perhaps there, the Elders would have someone to tell him what it said—hopefully, it would tell when he had been born.

It was indeed a certificate of the boy's birth, proclaiming him a royal prince of the Torbraugh Nation, descended from kings of old and giving his full name and date of birth.

He was named The Most Honorable Prince Saan Maikel of the White Eagle, son of His Empirical Majesty Maikel Railen of the White Eagle and Her Empirical Majesty Slia of the White Eagle, Daughter of the Dragon. The date of birth listed, when the Elder scholars at the Conclave matched the calendars used by the People and the Torbraugh, was the exact same as the date of Soth's birth.

By the time Shalim took the document to the Conclave Elders and they poured over it and examined it thoroughly, Saan had learned enough of the Dragon language to understand when Grandfather told him what it said.

The two boys were thrilled to learn that they had been born the same day and declared themselves to be actual twins. Others, both in the village and at Conclave wondered at the coincidence, for they knew of both mothers and their love of the man Stell. They began to recall to themselves old Kaul-Leb's prophesies.

The boys were frequently at Strella's house, running in and out, always welcome. Whenever Shalim was away on Tribal duties or at Conclave, Saan stayed, usually with Soth right beside him. Until they were about ten, they slept in Strella's bed, moving to another room for their visits after they considered themselves too big to sleep with Grandmother.

Chapter Ten
The Detail

The fire brought relief to the cool night. There was a large one in the middle of camp as well as three smaller ones to warm the sentries. No need to be on high alert, they were back in their own country again, far away from any possible threat from the backward Dragon people.

They had eaten food requisitioned from a nearby farmer and all were bedded down, save the sentries. The horses were tethered and resting, bellies full of fodder from the farmer's barn.

The court official did not sleep in a bedroll on the ground like the soldiers, but in short legged bed under a tent.

It was he who had slapped the young prince when the child, chilled sleeping on the ground near him, had sought to climb into the bed to get warm the night before their arrival in the Black Dragon village.

The official had been relieved that the boy was so ill received in his mother's village—no one would care, and certainly not send word of complaint back to the king. Not that the king would mind, he was glad to be rid of the little mongrel.

Towards morning, the moon still ruling the night before being overpowered by the sun, a serpent slithered into the camp. Normally, it would be in its burrow waiting for the warmth of day, but it was under a direction it would not understand, if it had had reason to contemplate.

It passed by the sentry, whose watchful eyes looked for larger enemies. It momentarily warmed by what was left of the feeble fire, its tongue dashing in and out, tasting the air. Under other circumstances, it might have neared one of the men on the ground, to share in his mammalian heat, but it was driven to seek one particular man, a man the snake's cousin the Dragon wanted him to find. A man who had somehow wronged the Dragon.

He tasted the air again and caught the flavor he sought. Turning from the heat of the fire and the men directly around it, he followed the trail in the air and slid under the flap of the tent.

The flavor was much stronger here, he relished its taste. The man on the low thing, yes, that was his target.

And the man was very warm. Much warmer than those around the cooling fire. There were many layers of warm soft things over him. Layers he had selfishly kept to himself, not sharing with the Dragon's child and had struck the favored one. Struck him when he only wanted to warm himself. Struck him that the Dragon had warned should not be harmed.

The creature lifted his head and burrowed beneath the soft things, the warm things, and rewarded himself with the heat trapped beneath them. The man lay on his stomach, his legs slightly apart. Into the warm crevice between the two limbs the snake made his way. The man was deep in sleep and did not notice.

The pulsing of the blood in his leg, yes, there it was, the artery the Dragon wanted him to find. The snake waited for the Dragon's last command. The man must know before the strike, must know why he was to die.

The man's sleep became disturbed as he began to dream his last dream. A mighty white beast with icy blue eyes frightened him into the space between awake and asleep.

"You struck my child," it hissed at him. "So now shall you be struck, as well."

The snake buried his fangs in the artery of the man's leg, high up on the flaccid thigh and pumped his venom into the one who had harmed the child.

The man came fully awake, screaming and thrashing about, kicking away the coverings keeping him warm. Moonlight weakly illuminated his tent as one of the soldiers threw back the flap. On his bare white upper leg, the snake rode, his hold releasing from the writhing man in time to avoid being struck by the other man. He quietly slipped through a small opening and entered the refuge of the dark.

His mission complete, he sought the safety and quiet of his nearby burrow.

The man lay dead, his eyes open wide both from the terror of his dream and the pain of the venom.

"Snake got him," a soldier observed. "Must have been cold and crawled up in with him to get warm."

"Get him covered with some of his bed things and bind him up. I don't want to see that face staring at me on the way home," the detail captain ordered.

"We may as well break camp, there'll be no more sleeping after that, and the sun should be up soon. We'll be home all the sooner."

He looked at the dead man.

"Some of us will, anyway."

Chapter Eleven
The Boys Grow

Salmar hated his young nephew. Even so, being underaged himself, within the confines of his hated, he remained obedient to his father. He could have left home, some did if life became intolerable, but he did not wish to abandon the rest of his life or his heritage.

Besides, of late, his eyes had fallen kindly on a daughter of the village, and hers upon him. Like many descended from their old ancestor Kaul-Leb, he had inherited a tendency to be lean with well defined musculature.

His wavy black hair had one streak of lighter hair that bleached in the summer to a pale red. He knew that the young women of his village found this streak becoming and he took care that it was readily displayed when he braided the hair from his temples.

Before the loss of his sister, Salmar had been of a generous, kindly nature, at peace with everyone. The pain of Slia's being taken away and then later her death, added to it the death of his mother, had sown a bitterness within his soul he could not dampen.

Even though Slia had not died birthing Saan, it was with a child of the same man, and that, Salmar could not forgive. The pain in his heart convinced his mind that somehow, it was the boy's fault.

The day Shalim returned from Conclave, Salmar had observed his father hastily making his way to the home of Strella after being told by some busybody of the child's being there. He knew that when his father returned, he would not be alone.

Salmar watched from the door of their home until he saw the group coming from the house of Stell and Tinka, then closed it and retired to the quarters he shared with his brothers.

"Salmar, it's rude to stay in here with guests in the house," Solot said as Salmar blocked the exit of their room.

"They are not guests," he hissed under his breath. "Strella and the son of Stell are NOT guests, not mine, anyway. They have brought that brat of that king into our home. I will not welcome them, and neither will you."

"Father wants him here, doesn't that mean anything to you? He IS Slia's child."

"Slia was forced to bear him. Forced to...give herself to that tyrant when she should have married Stell. She should have stayed here with us, with people she knew, where she was loved. Instead..."

His voice caught in his throat, he blinked away the hot tears welling in his eyes as he thought of his beloved sister taken away, far away, where she was to die, never to be seen again by them, never to hear her speak, or laugh, or even—anything.

"Instead, she was taken away, ravaged by a so-called husband without a Dragon mark, without braids, to die in a foreign land."

Salmar spoke quietly, not wanting to be heard by their father, but with such hatred and force that tiny droplets of spittle came with his words and settled in his beard.

From experience, his brothers knew there was no reasoning with him. He would have to seethe for a time before he could calm down enough to be civil.

In this state, isolation in their room was far better than confrontation. They lay back on their beds, staring at the ceiling, walls, or dimming light at the window, waiting for the muffled sounds of conversation to end so they could be released from their confines.

Their room was fairly large, but the three narrow beds took much of the available space. Salmar finally calmed enough to sit on his with his back to his brothers, watching the door.

Stant hoped Father would not summon them out. He did not wish to witness another scene with Stell's mother and Salmar over the child. He would have liked to have gone to the boy and held him in his arms and seen what there was of Slia in him, but Salmar WAS the oldest, and the closest to being a man. And he could be very spiteful.

It had been quiet for some time when Solot spoke.

"Salmar, may we at least go to the privy? You rushed us in here so quickly, and it has been quiet for some time."

"Go," he said, his voice flat.

At least he had calmed down.

They both left the room, the only light the candle in the hallway and the banked fires. When they returned, Shalim stood in their doorway, waiting. He motioned them to enter and followed them in, quietly slipping the door nearly shut.

Salmar rose from his seat on his bed and faced his father. Solot and Stant stood next to him. Shalim stood looking at them for several moments before he spoke.

"The three of you have shamed this house and your sister's memory—and the memory of your mother."

The two younger brothers stared at their own feet.

Salmar stared back at his father defiantly for several moments, his jaw muscles clinching and bunching with raw emotion. Then he spoke.

"Strella lost no time informing you we did not want that child, did she?"

"I knew long before I reached Strella's house, Salmar. Your ill-mannered performance was on display for all to see."

Salmar lowered his gaze slightly away from his father's eyes, his jaws demonstrating his agitation.

"Your sister is gone, all that is left of her is within that little boy. A child not at fault with who his father might be."

Salmar again looked directly at his father and spoke.

"He is the son of that king, the man—the man who took Slia away and killed her having his brats. She should have stayed here and married Stell and lived."

"We don't know that the same thing could not have happened if she had married Stell."

"Esoos, Father, she would have been happy here and she would have lived!"

Hot tears sprang to Salmar's eyes. He blinked rapidly, trying to will them away, but they came and spilled down his cheeks.

"She would have lived, Father, don't you see? She would have lived."

He covered his face with his hands and felt his father's arms surround him, holding him like he had when Salmar was a child with childish problems.

"She would have lived," he said once more, little more than a whisper.

Shalim held his son until the tears were gone and his composure returned. He stepped back and holding to Salmar's shoulders talked quietly, but firmly.

"Salmar, no one can change the past. Slia was taken away by the king and she died. But she left us with a child. A little boy who has no one else. His father loved him, but his brother, the new king, does not. I want him now as much as I wanted him when we were told Slia had crossed over. And I will keep him. He is my grandson, your nephew. I cannot force you to love him, or even respect my love for him. But he will live in this house. Do you understand?"

"Soos, Father."

Continuing to hold Salmar by the shoulders, Shalim looked from his older son to the other two.

"Never forget, I love the three of you more than my own life, but I shall also love your sister's son, no matter who his father was. You are almost men, before many years, you will no doubt marry and have your own families. Perhaps then, you will understand how I feel about Saan."

Shalim stared blankly for a moment, thinking.

"For now, he has your sister's room. With him is Stell's son, Soth. They have become close friends and Soth will be staying with us for a few days helping Saan adjust. I expect the three of you to at least treat Saan as well as you would a stranger, and for Stell's sake, be hospitable to Soth. Will you at least promise me that?"

Almost in unison, they answered, "Soos, Father."

He released his hold on Salmar.

"Now, have you eaten?"

"Soos, Father, we ate when we came from the field," Stant answered him.

"Good, the little ones are already asleep. It has been a long day and little boys tend to rise early when they are well rested. I suggest everyone get to bed soon."

Even though Shalim had long since stopped kissing his sons good night on a regular basis, he did tonight, taking each one in a gentle hug and kissing him lightly on the cheek. He opened the door and went toward his own room.

All three stripped to their drawers, the younger two slipping into bed while Salmar walked quietly to the privy. When he returned, he lay down on his bed, but did not sleep.

After a while, he rose and went to the doorway of what had been his sister's room, barely touched since her leaving. By the weak candlelight in the hallway, he studied the two boys sleeping peacefully in the bed that had last held Slia. He still felt nothing but hatred for the half-Torbraugh, but for his father's sake, he would tolerate him, for now.

He went back to his bed, sleeping a deep, but not very restful sleep. In the morning, he was awakened by childish laughter and his anger rekindled with a slow simmer. He kept his feelings to himself, saying nothing to anyone. He completely ignored Saan to his face, almost never speaking to him, then never with any affection.

The day after Salmar turned twenty-five and was thus a full man, he married and moved out of his childhood home into the home of his bride's parents. She had one sibling, a much younger brother on whom he showered his affection. He continued to work his father's fields, for one day, most of them would be his.

The next year saw Solot marry and move into the countryside.

Almost a year and a half after that, Stant became of age and married, as well. His new wife was an only child and he moved into a home where he would someday be its lord and master.

When Saan and Soth were twelve, like the other boys of the village, they began to learn weaponry.

Much of their early training mirrored what had been taught for generations among the Song-hee, except no one was expected to kill a man in practice merely to live himself. They trained under the guidance of men who had been to war. There were few still living who remembered when the most dreaded enemy were the Song-hee. But all were wary of the Torbraugh.

Saan came to grips with the knowledge that the biggest threat to peace among the People of the Dragon was the menace to the west, their king, Saan's half-brother Rondol.

Their grandfather, Railen, had wanted all the Song-hee lands and had begun eliminating the Lion Brood.

After what was left of the Lion Brood, the Song-hee, joined with the People of the Dragon under the Chief Elder Salar, it became their father's war when he became king. Now, they feared that Rondol was planning to continue the quest for all of what had once been Song-hee territory to add to his possessions.

The day after Saan and Soth turned fourteen, Saan sat alone on a big rock waiting for Stol the executioner to come down the path to the village from the home of a child with a broken arm. He had seen Stol go this way earlier and wanted to speak with him.

Soth was not with him, a rare occurrence. For Soth was speaking with someone, Sailk, his uncle by marriage about life in the Conclave as an Apprentice.

It made Saan feel hollow inside, thinking that in another year, Soth could be gone from him, learning the Law. But he had seen the light in Soth's eyes discussing it and would do nothing to sour his friend's dream. Saan only wished he had something to hold to that thrilled him. Instead, he had a confused dread. He scratched at the loose dirt of the path with the toe of his boot.

Soon there were sounds of a horse coming purposefully down the path. Saan stood and looked toward the sound. He saw Stol on his horse round a large tree and prepared himself to ask questions that were bothering him.

Stol's attention went to the movement he saw from the corner of his eye. Realizing it was Saan before him, he smiled. Then his looked turned to concern.

"Is there illness at your house, Saan?"

"Esoos, Sir, I, well, I just wanted to ask you something without anyone hearing."

"Sounds serious, Saan, sit down," Stol said and dismounted, holding to the reins.

The rock was large and flat, they both sat, one on either side of it.

"Now, what is it that you wish to ask me?" Stol asked.

"My birthday in a year, I will be fifteen, you know that, though."

"Soos, I know."

"Grandfather wants me to take the mark, did you know that?"

"Soos, he and I have spoken of it."

Saan stared down at his hands, clasped tightly in his lap.

"But my father was not a Dragon, so by Dragon Law, I'm not really eligible, am I?"

"Esoos, you are not, Saan. But there is one way around it that the Law has provided. Actually, two ways. You could be adopted, and since you have near kinsmen, your uncles, it would have to be one of them. No one else may. Or you could be sponsored, which is what your grandfather intends to do. But it is risky, very risky. Your grandfather will be your mentor, or so he has told me, sponsoring you until you are twenty-five, a full man. But if the Dragon does not forgive your boldness of taking the Dragon mark without having a real right, the consequences will literally be quite painful for you."

Saan dropped his head down, looking now at the dirt between his feet.

"It will have to be cut off my back if Grandfather crosses over before I am twenty-five, true?"

"Soos, it will have to be cut off. The skin peeled away. And then you will be claimed."

"If I remained unmarked, I will be claimed when I turn fifteen, soos?"

"Soos."

"And if I allow Grandfather to have me marked and he crosses before I am twenty-five, I will be claimed then. Plus my back will be cut. So I will most likely be enslaved, either way, am I right?"

Saan's throat felt like it was closing, choking him.

His emotions threatened to envelope him in misery.

"Soos, Saan."

Saan stood and turned his back to Stol. He didn't want the man to see him cry. But no tears fell. His chin quivered and that was all.

"Grandfather really wants me to take the mark. I guess he is trying his best to keep me free. It doesn't seem fair, does it? I was freeborn in a palace, the son of a king and his queen, but no one who CAN help me will. My brother throws me away, and my uncles don't care enough about me to...save me."

Stol rose and put his hand on Saan's shoulder, gripping it tenderly. He noticed that the boy was getting tall for his age, but then, his Torbraugh father had been quite tall.

"Esoos, Saan, much of life is not fair. You are having to face very difficult problems at a very young age. But you are strong, and there are those who love you, never forget."

Stol dropped his hand from Saan's shoulder and turned back to his horse and mounted.

"Come, ride beside me."

Saan untethered his horse from a nearby bush and got on it, doing as Stol asked.

They rode in silence for a while.

"Have you made a decision about the marking?"

"Grandfather wants it, I will accept it. Perhaps I will be forgiven. If not, at least I know the Executioner," Saan smiled coldly.

"True," Stol answered, reaching over and patting Saan's arm. "And you are one of his favorites."

Saan's smile warmed. He knew whatever happened, Stol would treat him decently.

Chapter Twelve
The Leaving

Saan lay back, looking up into the sky, watching the clouds chase across the sky. His hands were under his head, fingers laced together, cradling his hair just above where the braids joined the rest behind his neck. A long, stiff blade of dried grass rolled around in his mouth, chased by his tongue.

Soth was in much the same position, but his grass blade was still green.

Their souls communed on the gentle hillside, best friends, not needing to always talk. They had turned fifteen only days ago, their shoulder blades still rough to the touch where the black ink had marked them with their tribal Dragons.

Soth's Dragon was magnificent, true, but Saan's, as he was descended from the Poet Prophet Kaul-Leb, was two-headed, one head a Dragon, one a Lion.

But today, as they lay in the grass, contemplating the enormity of life, their braids were all that denoted their citizenship. They were fully dressed in tunics, britches, and boots.

Saan turned on his side to look at Soth.

"Have you ever thought that if my father hadn't taken my mother away and she had married your father instead, that we would have been just one person, not two?"

Soth gnawed his grass blade for a moment and turned his head to answer.

"Esoos, I haven't. Where do you get these ideas?"

"I don't know, it's just some of the things that come in my head when Grandfather and I are alone in the evenings, and he goes to sleep in his chair in front of the fire. Even before then, even when my uncles were home before they married, they didn't say much to me—Solot and Stant were afraid of Salmar and then when he left, we were just accustomed to being quiet. I guess they were afraid to talk to me much, afraid he would find out."

He lay back again. "I'm going to miss you, Soth."

"I know, it's a little scary thinking about leaving, but I will be back in three months."

"Conclave furlough isn't the same as every day."

"Esoos, it's not. I wish you were going, too."

"Studying all day every day is NOT the life for me. I like weapon practice more."

"You could be a Conclave Custodian."

The boys looked at one another and laughed.

"We better get on to Grandmother's, she won't like it if her meal gets cold waiting on us."

"True," Saan said, and they stood. "I'm glad Grandfather had to go see the Green Chieftain."

"Soos," Soth answered, and they walked to Grandmother's side by side.

They both knew that next time Grandfather would be gone to Conclave, Soth would be there, too, no longer staying at Grandmother's to keep Saan company. Never again.
Saan normally liked seeing Soth's Aunt Sisten and her family when they came on Conclave furlough, but not this time.

When the Conclave Custodians came to collect the Elder Sailk and his family for the trip back at end of furlough, Soth would go, too. And so would Grandfather. The time of year for all tribal chieftains to attend to the bulk of their Conclave duties would be upon them and Grandfather could be gone for nearly three weeks.

At least Grandfather had allowed that even though he was a citizen now, this one last time Saan could overnight at Grandmother Strella's during the Conclave. He would not be totally alone. They could miss Soth together.

The month of furlough with all the business of visiting and so many people, for Stell's sister had a brood of eight now, plus the houseful of Stell and Tinka's own children numbering ten in total, made Saan feel often alone in the crowd. The last week of furlough this time, Tinka's brother Sturl came with all his family to see Soth off.

The evening before the leaving back to Conclave brought a big celebration, for it was considered an honor to be apprenticed to the study of Law. To add to the chaos, Sailk's extended family was in attendance. Saan was glad that he and Grandfather had been invited to be there, but really wished he could see Soth alone without so many around.

It was common in most of Dragon society for young Dragon males to be drawn into the laps of adult males. It emphasized that they were still considered children and were treated as such. Many of the People of the Dragon were extremely affectionate with their children and had no qualms or hidden agendas in demonstrating it. It had not happened often with Saan. Once in a while, Grandfather had wanted him in his lap, and sometimes Stell had sat him on his knee, but not often and not lately. It had never been with Saan's uncles.

He was surprised, but had forethought not to struggle, when Soth's Uncle Sturl caught his hand as Saan walked by him and pulled him onto his knees.

"I hear you prefer war practice over studying, soos?" Sturl asked, smiling broadly.

"Soos, Sir," Saan answered. "I was glad when my school time was done. I would rather be out active in the sun."

"I quite understand, but no archery, though?"

"Esoos, Sir, I just don't have the eye for it. I am much better with a sword or spear."

The Song-hee Dragon rubbed the boy's back affectionately.

"It is good you recognize your gifts and limitations; you don't waste time that way. We will be here a few more days, perhaps you and I can spar a few times before we leave, would you like to?"

Sparring with Sturl? Saan had lived to hear Stell's stories of his brother-in-law's battle prowess.

"Could we, Sir?" Saan asked, amazed that Sturl would invite him to practice against him. Sturl saw no reason to mention that his sister Tinka had given him the idea, knowing how lost Saan would be with Soth gone.

At least now he would have something to look forward to in the coming days.

The next morning, though, Saan felt no happiness, Soth was leaving. Their life as constant companions was over.

Just after sunrise, in front of Strella's home, the group gathered to leave and say their good-byes. Saan had already hugged and kissed Grandfather, and Grandfather had mounted his horse, ready. Soth was only halfway down his family, but making progress. Stell and Tinka, and Grandmother Strella had tears in their eyes and Soth's brothers and sisters and some of his cousins held to him.

At last, he came to Saan. They embraced as only brothers of the heart can do, wordlessly, for a good while. Saan did not weep but knew he would later.

Everyone was mounted on horseback or in the Conclave transport wagon, waiting. The Conclave Custodians did not act impatient, they had been foretold this would be a hard farewell.

They released their holds on one another and stepped apart. They both knew that at this moment, their real childhoods were over. Soth's home would be the Complex of the Conclave, Saan's future was uncertain.

"Always and Forever," they both said at the same time, then laughed. Always twins, forever friends.

Soth mounted his horse and the whole party of travelers left. No one looked back, that being an insult to faith in the Dragon. Stell and Tinka went to their home, Sturl and Sica and all the children with them. They did not offer for Saan to come with them, they knew that he would need to be alone. And he did.

He went to his room to get his things to stay with Strella, but first spent his time in mourning over his loss. It would be late in the morning before he felt the signs of his crying had abated enough to be seen in public.

Strella noticed Saan's eyes were still slightly swollen when he brought his things to her house, but said nothing, allowing him to think no one could tell.

Chapter Thirteen
Another Loss

Saan opened the door and walked into the kitchen.

Something was wrong. All of his cousins were gathered there with their mothers. His uncle's wife, Serra sat with one of the baby cousins in her lap.

Normally, he would have politely nodded and continued on to his room to change out of his sweaty practice clothing. No one here ever attempted to engage him in conversation. He knew he was unwanted, but he was worried.

"Grandfather?" he asked to the room, hoping someone would be civil enough to answer him.

As she was closest to him, Serra answered.

"It looks to be a stroke, Executioner is in there with him and your uncles now."

Now Saan politely nodded and headed for his grandfather's bedroom.

The door was open. He saw his grandfather propped up and laboriously breathing, the four men around the bed. Salmar noticed him and turned toward him.

"Go to your room," his uncle said to him harshly and turned his attention back towards the bed.

Saan said nothing, but obeyed his uncle. He wanted desperately to go to his grandfather but did as he was told.

Once in his room, he pulled off all but his drawers and poured fresh water into his basin. He picked up and dampened the cloth lying beside the basin and washed himself. After drying, he pulled on fresh clothing, sat on the edge of his bed, and waited.

After what seemed like forever, a light knock sounded at his door.

Saan crossed the small room and opened the door to Stol, the Executioner.

"Your grandfather is asking for you."

"Am I allowed to go to him?"

"Your uncle has agreed to allow you."

Saan wondered what kind of argument Stol had used as he followed him across the hall back to Grandfather's room.

Salmar stood with his arms crossed, on the other side of the room, looking out the small open window, his back to the bed. Clearly, he did not approve of Saan's being there, but had allowed it. Shalim still lay propped up, but his eyes were open and looking at the boy. His hand reached out.

"Come here, Saan," he whispered hoarsely. Saan went to his grandfather and held the outreached hand.

"Sit," the old man managed to say.

Still holding his grandfather's hand in both of his, Saan sat beside him, fighting back hot tears.

"I am so proud of you, my boy. I love you more than you can know."

"Save your strength, Grandfather, please."

"There is not enough left to save," he gasped. "I have failed you, child."

"Never," Saan whispered back.

"I am leaving you too soon. I was not able to take you to manhood as I wanted to do...as I intended to do."

The old man stopped to gather more air. His eyes fluttered shut and he crossed over.

Saan held his grandfather's hand to his cheek and wept silently, his tears bathing the cooling skin.

After a few moments, he heard Salmar's voice again say, "Go to your room."

Then, "I'll deal with you later."

It was Stol who gently took Shalim's hand out of Saan's grasp and tenderly pulled him to his feet. With his arm around the boy's shoulders, he guided him back to his own room and shut the door.

"This is a hard day for you, Saan. There will be no easy ones for you for a while."

He led the boy over to the bed and sat him down on it, sitting himself by the boy's side, his arm still around him.

"Tonight, I am your friend. Tomorrow, I must be the Executioner."

The boy turned to look at him, his cheeks wet.

"The village elders will send me to collect you at dawn to pronounce sentence on you. I know this to be so for they spoke to me earlier while you were in here."

"Knowing the signs, they satisfied themselves that Shalim would not survive."

Stol took a deep breath and continued.

"Tonight, after dark, your grandfather will be sent to the Dragon. No one, not even your uncle may prevent your coming to the ceremony."

"Tomorrow, though, it will be different. Tomorrow, I will not be your friend. I must take you to the village square as if you were no one to me."

He sighed deeply.

"It is within their rights to demand your mark in the morning, you must be prepared. Don't eat tonight. Or in the morning before I come. But if you wish to mourn your grandfather, you may ask for a month's stay to do so. I suggest you do it. Give yourself a month to mourn in confinement. The Ordeal you face is too harsh to have loss of Shalim weighing on your heart so freshly."

He told Saan the words to say to get his month's stay and made him say them several times.
Stol pulled the boy against him and allowed him to place his head on his shoulder. He hugged the child fiercely then released him and stood.

"I will be here shortly before dawn."

With that, the Executioner opened the door to the boy's room and left to tell Salmar when to expect him in the morning.

Saan reached to the back of his head and removed the cord holding his hair in place at the nape of his neck.

One side at a time, he finger combed the temple braids of citizenship away. After retying the cord, he reached into the top of his tunic and grasped the leather cord holding his mother's pendant. He pulled it over his head and placed the only remembrance of his mother he had on the chair beside his bed.

He could own nothing, not even that. Not his horse, not even his clothing. When he left for good, maybe not tomorrow, but when he left for good, nothing would go with him. Nothing.

There he sat as the day wore on. The sunlight was nearly gone before the door to his room opened. No knock, no "May I come in," it was just opened, and his uncle Salmar entered.

The boy stood.

"Stol has informed me that you must be allowed to go. We leave soon. I expect you to stand with the servants, is that understood?"

"Soos, Uncle."

"Go now, and stand by the door with the servants, and wait."

"Soos, Uncle. Sir?"

Salmar had started to leave, but turned back to Saan.

"What?"

"Will I return to this room, or...or stay somewhere else?"

Salmar looked around the small room. There was little in it. Saan was not a collector and had spent much of his time out and about, only coming to this room for sleep, washing off, and dressing.

"Return here. Stol told me he suggested you ask for a month's stay tomorrow. If granted, you will stay in here for your confinement. Your meals will be brought to you. You may leave it as you wish for the privy, as long as you limit yourself."

Salmar turned again and left. Saan followed after to go wait outside. He glanced in his grandfather's room as he passed by. It was empty. The bedding was gone from the bed, he could see that much.

The servants outside the door waiting for the family parted as Saan walked out among them.

"Sir," he heard from various ones.

"Please," he answered. "Please, no longer address me as Sir. I am no longer a citizen since Grandfather's crossing over. I am...I am nothing."

Tears welled in his light green eyes. He made his way to the rear of the waiting servants, behind those who were enslaved of the household. He had no status, he knew. They knew.

They also knew how he was regarded by his uncle Salmar. And Salmar was now the head of the family.

No one would dare differ with him.

The mass of servants began to move, Salmar and his own had passed by from their dwelling next door.

Tomorrow, he would move into his father's home, further laying claim to family head. His hot temperament had not been improved by learning Stol had advised Saan to ask the elders for a month's stay. He wanted the boy gone.

As Salmar took the burning brand and lay it to the kindling of his father's pyre, all he saw in the growing flames was the empty stare of his dear sister as she left their village that day after her wedding with that foreign king. Now he must endure the presence for another month of that animal's whelp.

His ire was abated momentarily as the Chief Elder came to him, speaking to him for a bit about Shalim and how he would be missed.

To hear Salar praise his father caused him to smile in gratitude, revealing the handsome face he usually kept hidden in a scowl. Behind Salar came the other High Elders of the High Council of the Conclave and the other tribal chieftains.

Salar spoke to the younger brothers, then seeing that Salmar was fully engaged with the other dignitaries, he sought out Stell and spoke with him.

"My dear boy, I see you no longer need your canes, Tay will be pleased. I wanted to tell you how well your son, Soth, is doing. I enjoy hearing his reasoning. The Law comes easily to him, and he debates like a seasoned veteran."

"Thank you, Sir," Stell managed to say, overwhelmed at being singled out by the Chief Elder.

"And this must be your lovely wife, the mother of my favorite Apprentice," Salar said, his smile directed at Tinka, standing at Stell's side. Tinka beamed at hearing her child so praised.

"Now, I need your help, the two of you, in a little conspiracy," Salar said looking sideways where the sons of Shalim stood, still deep in talk with the Conclave visitors.

"Point out to me the child, the grandson of Shalim, Saan," he said almost in a whisper and smiled. "My favorite Apprentice has charged me with delivering an important message."

"Soth?" Stell asked, perplexed that his son had asked a favor of the Chief Elder.

Tinka leaned over and whispered into Salar's ear.

"See the tall youngster over there, in back of the crowd of servants?" she asked as she gestured only with her eyes, to be more secretive.

"The boy off to himself?" he whispered back.

"Soos, that is Saan, Soth's best friend."

"Thank you, my dear," he said and patted her hand, then kissed her cheek.

"Being an old man, I can kiss all the pretty girls without their husbands getting jealous," he said laughing. With that, he turned and walked to Saan, aware that being who he was, it would not be a secret he talked to the boy. But he knew no one would try to stop him, either.

Several paces from the boy, Salar stopped and called his name.

"Saan?"

Saan, watching the fire burn, had not noticed the Chief Elder's approach. He startled slightly at hearing his name called.

"Sir?"

"Come here, child, let me look at you."

Saan walked up to the Chief Elder and bowed slightly, showing his respect.

Salar noted the wet tracks down the boy's cheeks as the burning fire glimmered across his face.

"You and I are distant cousins, Saan," Salar said. "Kaul-Leb was my grandfather, and your...I believe...great-great-grandfather, soos?"

"Soos, Sir," Saan answered quietly. He glanced toward the knot of people around Salmar.

"They will keep your uncle busy for a bit yet," Salar said and placed his hands on either side of Saan's head, where the temple braids had originated until earlier in the day. Salar still stood tall, but he was not as tall as the young one in front of him. He gently pulled the boy's forehead down and kissed it.

Then his hands coursed down his cheeks, his neck, his shoulders, then his arms, coming to rest grasping the boys' hands.

Saan had felt a crisp something in Salar's right hand as it made its way down his left side. As Salar held Saan's left hand, a piece of parchment was transferred to it.

Both of the Chief Elder's hands closed on Saan's left, enfolding the boy's fingers around the thing. Salar winked at him and smiled, then left him, going back to the crowd from the Conclave.

Saan understood. He would not look at it until alone. Was the Chief Elder just enjoying being a little mysterious? What could it be? The old man had winked at him, a friendly gesture, surely.

Whatever it was, the Chief Elder had sought him out and pointed out their shared bloodline. Was it a veiled note of encouragement? Kaul-Leb had come to the People of the Dragon a slave, a non-citizen, and had risen above it all.

Perhaps, I will, too, he thought and took a deep, calming breath.

Slowly, the mass of people dissipated. Chief Elder Salar, his Conclave Custodians, the other High Elders, and their Custodians retired to the little village inn, filling it to capacity. Even Saan's uncles and their families left. None of them asked after him to join them.

Saan stood alone in the dark until the last embers had lost their color, clasping the folded parchment scrap in his hand. There was no one left but him. Except one he did not see. Stol watched him, barely able to make out the lonely form in the weak moonlight.

Would the boy slip away in the night? Go away where he was not known and profess to be a homeless orphan to hire himself out? Or would he stay and face the sentence of having the Dragon removed from his back by knife and lifelong servitude? Stol questioned himself what he would have done facing such a future at that age. He was not pleased with the answer.

Finally, the boy moved. He was not walking away from the village, but toward his home of the last thirteen years. The home that was no longer a haven, but at best, a jail.

Stol watched until he could see him no more then turned to his own home and what he feared would be a sleepless night.

Rather than disturb his wife, he decided to attend to his blades to make certain the keen edges were as sharp as possible. Should they be called upon tomorrow, he wanted the Ordeal to be as quick and painless as possible.

Saan returned to his room, quietly. He knew there would be no one else in the family quarters but welcomed the night's emptiness. If the village elders allowed his stay, he knew when he returned tomorrow, the house would be full and he an unwelcome guest.

An aroma beckoned him from the chair that held his mother's pendant. A mug of broth, grown cold, had been placed there for him. He realized he had not even sipped water since coming home what seemed years ago to find his grandfather dying. Thirst and hunger attacked him, and he lifted the mug to his lips and drank down its contents. The broth would be out of his belly by morning should he have to face the Ordeal then.

In the light of the candle that had been left lit for him, perhaps by one of Grandfather's servants, he sat on his bed and unfolded the precious bit of parchment secretly given to him by the Chief Elder.

In the bold handwriting he immediately recognized it to be from Soth. Three words: Always and Forever.

Always his twin, and Forever his friend.

Despite everything he faced, Saan laughed.

Soth using the Chief Elder, the most powerful and respected man in the whole land, as his delivery agent.

From across the village, Stol and Saan kept vigil together, each in his own thoughts.

Saan spent the night alone in the home he had shared with his grandfather for most of his young life.
Several of the servants watched over him from a distance. Just before the first threads of light stitched the day together, they saw the form of the Executioner in his official uniform of total black tunic and britches with no adornment enter the dwelling. With him were his two apprentices, similarly clad. One carried a length of thin, black rope coiled in his hand. Should there be resistance, the boy would have to be bound.

Their pathway through the house was lit by a small fire laid and started by one of the men serving the property. They cared for the boy and respected Stol.

A few moments later, with Stol in the lead, the small company of four left the house. Saan had offered no resistance and was unbound. He followed Stol with the other two behind him. Wordlessly, they made their way to the public square and mounted the platform as the day began to take on light.

Standing facing the eastern sky, Stol stood beside Saan with the two apprentices directly behind them.

Between them and the east on the platform was a row of five chairs, placed just as Stol was entering Saan's room.

In front of the platform sat the members of the Conclave, including the Chief Elder and the Chieftains of the tribes. Everyone knew how dear the Law of the Dragon was to the Chief Elder. No one, least of all Salmar, would try to push to rob Saan of his rights, not with the controlling force of the Conclave assembled and watching.

Saan wondered, had he just seen the Chief Elder wink at him again? Having Salar there and friendly towards him gave Saan even more courage to face what would come.

One by one, village elders mounted the platform in a solemn row. They sat, staring back at the standing group. The large metal cylinder behind the wall of the platform was struck five times to call to assembly any residents not already in attendance. Its echoes had hardly ceased when the ranking elder, who had been Shalim's second in command, rose from his seat.

Salmar and his two younger brothers were close to the platform to witness and verify the proceedings.

"Saan, grandson of Shalim," the man said, reading from a scroll of tanned animal skin he held in his hands. The scroll was lit by the rising sun.

"You are charged with the taking of the Mark of the Dragon without due rights."

"Is it true, Saan, that your father is not of the Dragon?"

"Soos, Sir."

"Is it true that you were aware of this fact when you accepted the Mark?"

"Soos, Sir."

"Is it true that you have not yet attained the age of manhood and been forgiven by the Dragon for your arrogance?"

"Soos, Sir."

"Is it true that your protector, Shalim, has crossed over and can no longer protect you from the Wrath of the Dragon?"

"Soos, Sir." For the only time, Saan's voice quivered slightly as he thought of his grandfather being dead.

"By your own admission of guilt, Saan, child of a stranger, you are hereby sentenced to forcible removal of the Mark of the Dragon. Before time of sentence is set, have you any remarks or requests?"

The elders knew that Stol had advised him to ask a stay to mourn and they were ready to grant it, but he had to ask.

During the long hours of the night, Saan had considered asking and not asking. He had thought that getting the Ordeal over with and done would be good. But would it be respectful to his grandfather's memory? He knew that living with Salmar under the same roof would not be pleasant, but it was the roof he had shared with his grandfather most of his life.

He would like more time to say his farewells to his old life before the new and vastly different one, whatever it may be, began.

"I pray the elders will grant a month of mourning for my grandfather."

There, he said it. Just as Stol had practiced him yesterday.

"Granted. Twenty-eight days from today, you will be returned to this assembly for completion of your sentence and to be claimed. Until that time, you are under confinement in the home from whence you came today. Executioner, you may return Saan to his home."

For today, it was over. Stol and company would march him back home and officially remind him of when and where the sentence would be carried out.

He would also be reminded that he was under order of confinement and might not leave the confines of his home. He would be allowed no outside visitors, other than the Executioner. No friends to ease his heartache. No well-wishers. Only those living there.

By evening, that would include Salmar and his family. He began to regret asking for the extra time.

"Stay in your room," had been Salmar's reply when Saan asked his uncle if he could help in bringing their possessions into the interior of the house.

Saan retreated and only heard the bustling of others through the walls.

When he entered his room, a tray with some of his favorite foods sat on the chair. His mother's pendant had been moved to safety on his bed. He sat down beside it and looked at the tray. At first, he wasn't interested, but his adolescent system overwhelmed his emotions and he started nibbling, then enjoying until it was all eaten. He felt better with his belly full.

Mid-morning, the sounds of activities lessened, and he took a chance that he might avoid his uncle taking the empty tray and dishes back to the kitchen on his way for a privy visit. He was relieved that he only saw his aunt and two of the smaller children on his foray.

He wasn't certain how his uncle would respond if he found Saan had gotten chatty, so he only nodded to his aunt respectfully and silently completed his errands.

As he returned to his room, his aunt wordlessly motioned to him to come to her. The children were no longer running about her. She pulled a cloth covered something from somewhere under her apron and quickly put it in his hand and kissed his cheek. She smiled at him as she nudged him to get to his room.

He found a mug of hot cider sitting on his chair, the aroma filling his room. Inside the cloth was a fresh baked pastry, still warm. He savored both. He had a friend.

Stol came to see him in late afternoon. He asked about what the boy had had to eat and quietly gave him messages from various friends, including Stell and Strella, to let him know he had not been forgotten.

Before Stol left, he asked Saan to remove his tunic to allow him to examine his back. He planned to check it daily, not to watch the condition of the skin, as he said, but to make certain the uncle's ire did not sink into physical abuse.

On the third day of his confinement, Saan was making his now regular trip to take his tray and see to bodily functions when he noticed his uncle was still in the house, using the same room Grandfather had as his personal room of reflection among the rare and beautiful volumes.

He did not peer into the room or speak. His aunt was in the main room of the house as he passed through, but they did not say anything to each other, not with Salmar in the house.

On his way back to his room, as he passed his uncle's private room, he heard his uncle speak.

"Saan, come in here, please."

His heart sank. What had he done?

He entered the room. His uncle stood with his back to the door, gazing out the unshuttered window.

"Sir?"

"Come over here by me."

Saan walked to his uncle's side. He was startled to see Salmar had tears on his cheeks.

"The day my sister was taken from us, all I could remember was the deadness in her eyes. I hated your father for that deadness, I hated him for taking her away, and I hated you because you were his."

Salmar turned to Saan.

"Last night, she came to me in a dream. For the first time since the day she was taken away, I saw her face. I had forgotten her face. You have her face, her same green eyes, even your voice is much the same as hers. Though deeper."

The corner of his mouth turned up slightly.

"And she had no whiskers over her lip."

He touched his nephew's upper lip where the few hairs grew.

"You're like me, got the Song-hee lack of beard like old Kaul-Leb. Only I didn't get the green eyes. None of us are blonde except my youngest girl looks like she might be."

He mused for a few moments, looking at nothing in particular. Then he turned his gaze to Saan.

"You really look nothing like your father, except you are tall. I wonder why I never noticed before. My judgement has been clouded by hate."

He took Saan's hands in his and looked at them as if counting to see if he had all his fingers.

"She only said one thing to me. She said, 'Love my boy.'"

He lowered his head and looked at the floor.

"I failed her."

He looked back at Saan and pulled him into his arms, holding him close against him, his tears falling down on the boy's back.

"I should have taken you into my heart the day you came, but I let my hate turn me against you."

He caressed him, rubbing his hands across the boy's back.

"You wouldn't be facing this except for me, I could have made you mine, or Solot. He wanted to, and I persuaded him not to...and now...now it's too late. I'm so sorry, Saan. So sorry."

Salmar's quiet tears became hard sobs.

"I'm so sorry."

Saan lay his head on his uncle's shoulder and just let the emotion wash through him.

Soos, it was too late.

Saan was eighteen years old. To be made the adopted child of anyone, he had to be under the age of fifteen. It would have to have happened at least three years ago. Not now. Now was too late.

Now he would have to face the Ordeal. He would have to face being claimed by someone and taken into their home. He would have no choice but to comply with the life they chose for him to live.

But now. Now, at this moment, his uncle, his mother's brother, loved him. At last, he had family again. Even if only for a few days. He could carry the memory of being loved with him, wherever, whatever. He had love again. His arms snaked around his uncle's waist and he held to him.

In the kitchen, activity ceased as Salmar's wife held the corner of her apron to her eyes. She was glad she had fed the children early and sent them out to play.

When Stol came later in the day, he said nothing about the two other uncles in the house. In his mind, the boy had lived in confinement most of his life and was entitled.

But he noticed one thing odd. To him, the Mark of the Dragon on the boy's back seemed smaller. That could not be. He measured it against his hand.

Hadn't his hand covered less of it a few days before?

He mentioned his puzzlement to no one.

Day by day, the boy's happiness in the face of what was to come encouraged Stol. But his confusion over the boy's mark increased. Toward the end of the month of confinement, he laid his hand on it and completely covered it. He knew his hand had not grown.

The afternoon of the last day of Saan's confinement arrived, and with it, Stol's last visit as friend.

"As before, I will come for you just before dawn," he said as he took his hand away from the boy's back. He frowned—the mark had to be almost half the size it was four weeks ago.

Saan turned to look at him as Stol spoke.

"Eat nothing tonight after dark. It might come up in the morning and cause you to choke. By law, you will have a gag in your mouth, you will be able to scream, but not talk."

He continued the recitation of the speech that must be given, word for word.

"I will wrap you in a cloth that will later be burned as sacrifice to the Dragon, for it will be soaked in your blood. Nothing else will adorn your body during your Ordeal other than the bonds that hold you. I and my helpers will take you from your home as dawn approaches, no one else may accompany you. So will your sentence be carried out."

Then in his own words, Stol continued.

"Afterwards, you will be claimed, as should have happened when you were fifteen, except for your being marked. I will continue to come to you to make certain your wound is properly cared for. You will be in your second confinement, but this time it is to accustom you to your new home—and to the one who claims you."

"What if I am not claimed as a Second Husband?" the boy asked. "What if I am only a servant in someone's service, will I still have confinement?"

"Esoos, you will begin service after you have healed enough. But I am certain you will be a Second Husband, there have been several inquiries concerning you." Stol smiled. Speculation about the boy had been a frequent topic in the village. Several eligible widows had asked Stol questions about him.

Those of lowest rank had little chance to get him.

To be eligible, a widow must be beyond the years of childbearing. After that, rank of widowhood depended on how long a woman had been a widow.

To claim, she only had to declare for him, there was no selling of children being taken from their families. Any male child at or over the age of fifteen unmarked was taken to be claimed as Second Husband or into servitude. Only with a demand for Seeds Rights could their genetic line continue, for their Blood Children were not considered their own.

"Who?"

"Esoos, I cannot say."

"Stol!"

"I cannot say, Saan. It would break confidence. But don't worry, that is all I can say."

Stol pressed his lips together. He had to tell Saan another thing.

"Tomorrow, when I come. It would be best to only have on your drawers. Or not, I will not be offended if you are nude. But I can place the wrap around you and then slip your drawers off. The Wrap of the Sacrifice is all you may wear—that and the binding belt. You will have to be bound, I have no choice."

"I understand, Stol."

If the weather were very cold, Stol had the option of allowing the subject to wear boots and a cloak until they ascended the platform. But with pleasant weather, such as now, nothing but the wrap—a white loincloth wound just below the waist, providing a bit of modesty and a way to catch some of the blood.

Stol left him and moments later, Solot knocked gently on the open door.

Saan was putting his tunic back on and turned.

"Uncle?"

Solot came in and quietly pushed the door closed.

He had the green eyes of their Song-hee ancestor, but with black hair and full, black facial hair.

"Saan, Salmar told me that he told you I had wanted to adopt you as my own several years ago."

"Soos."

"I regret that I was not more forceful in my desire to do so now, but …"

He picked at a miniscule flaw in the board of the wall.

"But, would you mind, or think it bad of me...if...after you are...claimed, if I file intent to, to demand Seeds Rights?"

He quit the wall and looked at Saan.

"We want a child, but none has come. I would rather raise your child, if possible, than someone else's. I know the Ritual is difficult, would be difficult for you."

"I would not mind, Uncle."

Solot crossed the space between them and cupped the back of Saan's head in his hand, pulling him closer and kissing him gently on the forehead.

"Now, Salmar, Stant, and I want to give you a proper night before—we feel certain you will be claimed as Second Husband. Come."

Solot took his hand and led him down the hallway, through the great room, and into the washing area. Saan's other two uncles were there with the bathing tub half full of water.

Tradition among the People was that men were physically cleansed by their closest male friends the night before their weddings. Saan would not undergo a traditional wedding, but his uncles wanted to show their affection for him. This private, intimate interaction would suffice.

Together, they undressed him, helped him into the water and washed him as if he were a small child.

To them, he was still a child, and would be for several years yet.

Salmar lay his hand on the boy's back.

"I always thought your mark was larger," he said.

The other two looked and indicated their agreement.

"Has Stol said anything about it being so ... small?"

"He has started placing his hand on my back every visit, in that same place you did, Uncle. Is it fading?"

"Not fading, but...smaller."

"How can that be?" Saan asked.

His uncles had no answer. But each thought, *Perhaps the Dragon...*

Perhaps the Dragon, in His Wisdom, knowing the boy had not sought to be unlawfully marked, had intervened to reduce his coming suffering.

As he rose from the water, they dried him and redressed him. His two younger uncles led him back to his room as Salmar poured a mug of hot hard cider with special herbs to help him sleep.

They would all three keep vigil with him over the night, leaving him only as time for Stol came. Salmar's family spent the night with Solot's wife in their home. The men pulled three other chairs into his room, leaving the one he had for Slia's pendant as it was.

The brothers watched as their nephew slept, dozing off and on themselves. Shortly before dawn, they stirred and roused the boy, each embracing him briefly, then allowed him to visit the privy. While he was there, they left.

He returned to his room alone and slipped off his long britches, leaving his drawers. Moments later, Stol and his apprentices entered without knocking.

He stood in the center of his room, waiting.

No one spoke, and would not unless necessary.

Stol unbuttoned the boy's drawers, but left them hanging around his body.

Stol's apprentice carrying a long, white cloth moved to Saan's left side. He unfolded the cloth and reached around the boy, an end of it in each hand. Stol, on Saan's right, took the ends from the apprentice and pulled until the middle of it fit snuggly against Saan's left hip. He crossed the ends over the right hip and handed them back. The apprentice took the ends and tied them on the hip in a tight knot.

The legs of the drawers hung slightly longer than the wrap. Stol gently grabbed the drawers and pulled them down. They puddled at Saan's feet. He had not been told to step out, so he did not.

The other apprentice held a leather belt, treated to be also white. He handed it to Stol, and it was tied with the knot in front of Saan. White leather straps protruded from its back. First his right wrist, then his left, were fastened in those straps. Stol made certain that they were tied well enough to hold him securely, but not too tight. Satisfied, Stol turned and walked to the door, not before noticing that the red stone pendant of the boy's mother was no longer on the chair where it had always been during his visits.

The apprentices each held to one of Saan's elbows and guided him to follow Stol. They were not only to keep him moving, but to ensure he did not lose his balance and fall.

Saan finally stepped out of his drawers and left them where they fell on his room's flooring. He would never sleep in this room, nor could he expect to ever step foot in it, again.

Before exiting the home, Stol stopped and turned.

"Saan, hold your back straight and your head up, you have done no wrong. Your family failed you. You have not failed them. Never forget, either, that you are the legitimate offspring of a king. He just wasn't a Dragon."

With that, Stol stepped out the door followed by the others. He walked at a moderate pace, slowing as they walked through rocky ground in consideration for Saan's bare feet.

They neared the square. The crowd hushed as they drew near. Saan avoided looking at anyone, keeping his gaze on Stol's back. He was afraid if he looked anyone in the face, he would tear up. He wanted to make Stol and his uncles proud of his behavior. Even his uncles. Even if they had failed him. For the last several weeks they had tried to make up to him for their previous shortcomings. Stol had said he thought he would be claimed to a good place, he had to hold to that.

Stol climbed the steps to the platform, his apprentices and Saan in tow. They walked to the wall at the back of the platform as the big, metal bell was struck the last time, its echo seeming to shake the boards beneath their feet.

The village elders were again in their seats on the eastern side of the platform. Saan's sentence was again read aloud. No response from the boy was expected this time. It was time to carry it out.

The apprentices guided Saan close against the wall, pushing on his waist where the belt was strapped to get him as flush as possible. The belt was anchored tightly against hooks in the wall. Straps were passed around his ankles, calves, the back of his knees, and thighs, immobilizing his legs. A strap was passed from his left shoulder crossing his back under the right, leaving uncovered the area to be removed.

Several straps travelled over his arms. One went around the back of his neck, not too tight, but restricting. Before Stol fastened the strap holding the top of Saan's head, he placed a moist wooden gag in the boy's mouth, tying it taut at the back of his neck with the other. Then the strap around the top of his head was tightened down. All the movement Saan would be capable of would be a twitch. Even if the pain of the removal made him lose consciousness, he would remain upright and basically still.

While Stol had been strapping Saan down, the apprentices brought up a narrow table with a cloth packet on it's top. Below the packet was a cloth bag that would hold the skin with the Mark of the Dragon they were taking from the boy. It, and later the very cloth around the boy with his blood soaked into it, would be burned, going to the Dragon.

Stol turned to the table and untied the cloth strap around the packet, revealing a collection of various keen-bladed knives. He selected one with a very narrow, sharp tip.

One of the apprentices stepped forward and rubbed a dampened cloth across the detailed tattoo of the two-headed black dragon, one head a dragon, one a lion. The solution on the cloth was meant to cut the risk of infection afterwards. He could tell by the tingle in his hand that his mentor had added something to the usual mixture for this boy. His hand was almost numb before he finished. The boy's even breathing told him that the gag moistened with much the same had put him to sleep. Part of his training had been to recognize when they must do the unspeakable to the virtually innocent and ease their suffering as much as possible.
Stol began by circumcising around the outer line of the mark. Then, lifting the edge of the skin at the top, he sheared the tissue away from the boy's back with the blade's long edge.

Blood began to seep down toward the wrap around Saan's hips. In a few moments, the flap of skin was disconnected and placed in the open bag held by the second apprentice. As the two left to go burn the bag and its contents, Stol gently spread a mixture of honey and herbs over the hole he had created in the skin of the boy's back. The mixture would impede infection and promote healing.

The bleeding had nearly stopped by the time he carefully patted a clean cloth with the same on it over the wound. Stol was amazed that the cloth around the boy had caught all the blood—none had run down his legs and down through the planks of the floor as usually happened. There just hadn't been that much.

"Sentence has been carried out," Stol announced to the elders and then added. "The boy is unconscious." Thus, signaling that Saan could not be made to stand facing the crowd as he was claimed.

Directly in front of the platform, seated in a row by rank, were the widows of the area eligible to claim a Second Husband.

For over thirty years, Strella had been a widow, Stell's father killed in the waters of the river. Only the last ten had she sat with the eligible widows. Until then, she had been capable of having a child, but no longer.

Due to her long widowhood, she had been ranking widow for those ten years. Each time a male had been offered, she had stood and declined, passing the opportunity to the next in line.

She was content. She loved her husband and his memory. She had Stell and his sister Sisten. They had given her a heartful of grandchildren.

Time after time, she stood and declined. The newly enslaved boys and young men offered had not interested her. She had wanted none of the young males offered for a Second Husband as companion and lover. She appeared to watch impassively as Saan was stripped of his mark. The child had frequented her home since his coming as that small ragged lost baby.

Stol had told her his secrets. She knew Saan would not feel the knife as it cut through his skin, she knew he would be asleep during the claiming.

Her name was called. She stood as she had every time, knowing what she would say and that Saan would not hear it. This time her words would be different.

"I claim Saan as Second Husband."

He was hers. She had wanted him in her home to stay since that first day. Over the years, her love for him had changed from motherly to desire.

If she could have convinced his grandfather not to have him marked, she could have had him three years ago. He could have been spared the pain he would eventually feel. None of that mattered now.

What mattered was that now he was hers. Legally. Hers.

Stell and Stol both had known of her intent to take him. They had told no one.

Her boy was being unstrapped. Stol's knives waited for his apprentices to return and take them. For now, his concern was the boy and treatment of his wound.

Stell stood ready to help Stol take him off the platform and to her home. The boy's uncles also climbed the steps and asked could they help move him. Strella was touched. They had come to love him late. That they could have spared him did not matter now, for if they had, she could have never had him.

She watched as Salmar pulled something from inside his tunic and placed it on her boy. Slia's necklace Stell gave her. He was allowing the boy to have the one thing he had ever had of his mother's.

Suddenly, she loved him for it.

Saan didn't know how much longer he could remain calm feeling the straps tightened against his body.

He trusted Stol, but he was still going to have skin taken off his back with a knife. He was afraid he would begin to tremble uncontrollably; afraid he would become so agitated that he might even soil himself like an infant. He feared that more than the pain he imagined would come.

It was then that the gag was placed in his mouth. It tasted odd like...like...

He became aware of softness surrounding him. He was on his left side with something against his back, some pressure he couldn't identify. There was the same in front of him, holding him gently still, his right arm draped over it.

Slowly, he realized the room was not quite dark, but dim. It was still day, but not bright where he was.

He remembered the Ordeal. Or remembered being strapped to the wall. Not much else. It must be over. He slowly flexed his shoulder, waiting for pain. There wasn't much, not as much as he had expected.

He worked to force his eyes open. They fought him. Gradually, he had slits to peer through.

He was in a bed. A big bed. A big bed with plump, generous bed linens, soft linens that caressed his body. He was so comfortable. He was so comfortable except he needed to get up and empty his bladder. The more he tried not to think of it, the more it nagged at him.

He gingerly pushed the rounded-up linens in front of him away and carefully fought his way up to sit. His mother's pendant moved against his chest. He held it against himself, thinking of her.

His eyes finally focused and he remembered this room. He had slept here often when he was little.

He knew where he was. He smiled. He knew who he belonged to. He was where he had wished to live many times.

His feet touched the thick rug on the floor as he began his slow attempt to stand. At first, he was wobbly, his head swimming. The more he stood, the steadier he became. His shoulder gnawed at him, but wasn't bad. He had on drawers, but not any he had ever worn before.

He padded through the open door, took care of himself in the privy, then went down a hallway, and through a big room that opened into a warm kitchen. He had detected delicious smelling whiffs back in the bedroom. The closer he got, the more his nostrils affirmed his familiarity with the smell.

Strella was at her fire, stirring a pot emanating enticing aromas. Saan saw a platter of his favorite pastries cooling on the table.

"I don't call you Grandmother anymore, do I?" he asked softly.

Strella turned, her dripping spoon held above the pot. She smiled at her boy. Her boy. He was at last her boy. Soon he would be her man.

She tapped the spoon twice on the edge of the pot and lay it aside. Strella held her hand out and Saan took it in his own, then pressed closely against her as she drew him into her caress. They stood together several moments, enjoying the embrace of gentle affection. Saan, inheriting his father's height, was already a full head taller than Strella.

He enclosed her in his arms and sighed with contentment. Strella snuggled him, taking care to avoid touching anywhere near his right shoulder.

"You claimed me." Not a question, a simple statement.
"Soos, I have always loved you," she said, talking to him with her cheek against his collar bone. He was still warm from the bed.

The light scent of the aromatic lather his uncles had washed him with mingled with that of the sweet salve Stol had spread on his back and his own natural post pubescent smell. Stella found herself aroused in a way she had not felt since she last held her husband that morning before he died.

She spoke to him again, still nestled against him.

"You are nearly grown now, not the little child I first loved. The thought of anyone else having you—I could not stand it. I had to claim you for my own."

Saan relaxed his embrace enough to lean down. His hands gently caressed her face as he brought his lips close to hers and kissed her. For the first time, it was not the kiss of a boy considering her as his grandmother, or the grandmother of his best friend, but of an adolescent discovering physical desire.

By the Law of the Dragon, they were in marriage, and he found he dearly wanted to fulfill his marital duties.

Strella returned his kiss, relishing the reawakening of want. Her hands roamed over him, heightening his arousal and her own. She led him back down the hallway to her bed. There she taught him more about being a man.

"Are you hungry, my love?" she asked him as they lay, sated together.

"A little, but I don't want to leave this, not just yet."

He basked in the feeling of romantic love fulfilled, enjoying her idle twirling of his chest hair in her fingers, feeling her face against his shoulder, and his own hands stroking her long, unpinned hair falling across him.

Strella had always loved him, he knew that she was his mainstay. She had taken him when he had no one and loved him. Now, when he most needed love again, Strella was there for him, her arms open to him, loving him as no one else could.

Saan was slightly amazed that his shoulder annoyed him so little. He surmised that whatever Stol had done to relieve residual pain was working well.

One thought bothered him.

"How do you think Soth will take it, my being your Second Husband? I don't want him upset, but—it is what it is."

"I have been thinking of taking you since you neared the age of fifteen. The day after both of you were marked with your Dragons, he came to me worried that if your grandfather did not live until you were twenty-five what would happen to you. He began suggesting then that I take you if that happened. I reminded him what that would mean. He just laughed and said he would call you 'Grandfather.'"

Strella loved the deep bass of his laugh, and he was particularly amused by Soth's answer.

"Oh, I miss him, well, I miss him most of the time, maybe not as much today," he said and nuzzled his face in her hair.

"Conclave furlough will be in five weeks, he and Sisten and her family will be home then."

"How will Sisten react, my being here?"

"I have kept no secrets from her, she knew of my intent. She's never spoken against it."

Strella pushed up on her elbow and looked seriously at Saan.

"One thing, though," she said and could not keep from smiling, despite how hard she tried. "I will NOT want Soth sleeping on the other side of you like he used to!"

Saan's deep laughter echoed through their bedchamber as he rolled her down on her back and smothered her in kisses. Her hands explored his adolescent frame, urging on his desire for her. He did not disappoint.

"Strella," he said later, looking in the cabinet across the room. "These are all my clothes, plus more."

"Soos, I made you some over the last month, but then your uncles brought all your things this morning while you slept."

His hand went to his mother's pendant hanging on his chest.

"Soos, that, too. Salmar put that on you before you were even brought here. Shall I tell you about it?"

He looked at her, puzzled.

"It was my mother's, soos?"

"Soos, but before that, Stell's father gave it to me on our wedding day. Stell gave it to your mother the day he left for war."

He picked it up from his chest and kissed it.

"Now it means even more to me, much more, for it has returned on OUR wedding day."

"Soos," she said and went to him, holding him close. "And I love the way it looks on you, however..." She lightly swatted his bare behind.

"You do need to wear more than that, my love. Unless you intend to stay in bed all the time."

"I am getting hungry."

He pulled britches from the cabinet and slid them on after his drawers.

"Saan?"

"Soos?"

"Your back, the patch Stol put on your wound, it's gone, and your back, it's—it's healed!"

"Are you sure?"

She lay her hand on the place that only that morning been an open wound. Saan felt no pain, only her light touch.

"It's only a scar!"

He raised his arm up and bent it down at the elbow, feeling his shoulder blade. There was no wound, only the dimpled skin of the scar.

He searched their bed and found the patch Stol had applied only hours before. It had dried blood, but not much, and the residue of the ointment.

"How did...?" he asked.

"I've never heard of it happening," she said. "We'll have to ask Stol, he will be by before night, he said this morning."

His stomach growled.

She giggled.

"I'm always needing to feed you!"

She took his hand.

"Mysteries later, food now."

This time she led him back into the kitchen and they both ate heartily. It was late afternoon when they finished.

Stol arrived soon after.

He knocked at the door and entered, carrying a bag with his healer tools.

"How are you feeling, my boy?"

"Better than I expected, Stol."

"Oh? Let me..." he said and stood gawking at Saan's bare back. "See."

"What happened?" he asked.

"We thought you would tell us," Strella answered.

"I feel like an insect being examined by a group of nosey children," Saan said after having Stol and Strella looking at his back and touching all around it.

"I've never heard of this before," Stol said and sat at the table. "I've taken off several marks, all but you have been condemned men that were executed right after, but a wound is a wound. I've never seen any skin heal this quickly."

He sat and stared for a few moments, lost in thought. Then he started up in his chair.

"Oh, I almost forgot! Your Uncle Salmar brought you something earlier, a surprise."

Strella looked around then back at Stol. She arched her eyebrows in question.

"Wrong room. Go open the door to the stables."

Strella's house had an attached stable where her own old mare was housed.

Saan rose from the table and went to the door in the hallway that led to the stable.

His tall stallion nickered to him in greeting. The big boy was tethered in the stall next to Strella's mare.

Barefooted, Saan padded out to his horse and threw his arms around the animal's neck, hugging him closely.

To the side of the stall, Saan noticed something else, all his weapons, both for practice and for real battle were carefully lain to avoid dulling the blades.

The thick shield Grandfather had given him for his fifteenth birthday was propped against the wall, his saddle and bridle next to it.

He came back into the house, tears in his eyes. He carried his shield.

"Salmar has given me back everything! Everything I had is mine again!"

They all knew, that by the Law of the Dragon, Salmar was under no obligation to give Saan a single thing.

He held the shield up to show to Strella.

"May I keep it in the house somewhere?"

"This is your home, Saan, of course you may," Strella answered. "There is in the main room, to the side of the fire where it won't get too hot, a hook in the wall where the shield Stell carried into battle hung. I think it would be the perfect place, then we can always admire it. And there are hooks for a sword, as well. I've never had them removed."

Saan lay the shield against the wall and went back into the stable for his sword, the one his grandfather had carried into war.

"Those were your husband's, weren't they, Strella, the ones Stell carried?" Stol asked softly.

"Soos, the shield was lost when they nearly killed Stell, but he still has the sword. It will be good to see the room decorated again."

Saan came back from the stable with his sword, quite a large one, but he was physically big like his father and had no trouble handling it even though he wasn't fully grown. He picked up the shield and carried them both into the room with the hooks and hung them up. They glimmered in light coming through the open windows.

Strella and Stol followed him into the room and watched him place his prized possessions.

Strella noticed the rippling of his muscles as he lifted his armament to the hooks. Stol noticed more the shape of the scar on his back.

Saan stood back to admire his display, a wide smile on his face. His things—on the wall—of his home.

"Saan, come stand with your back to the window, please," Stol said.

Saan moved over and turned, letting the afternoon light bath his back in light.

"Now, raise your right arm."

He did.

Strella saw what Stol had seen.

"How?" Strella asked.

"What is it?"

"Your scar, Saan, when you raise your arm, it looks like an eagle in flight," Stol answered him.

"Why did you cut it that way?"

"I didn't, I cut a circle, the way the mark was. I have no way to explain. Except, except, the Dragon is reminding all of us that your father was an eagle. We may have had no right to mark you...or no right to take it away... or it may mean nothing, I don't know."

"He has healed and is not in pain, for me, that is enough," Strella said.

"Saan, are there any other things that need to come in out of the stable? We can put up hooks to hang a spear or bow if you have them."

"I am no good as an archer and my spear is nothing special, but I might like to bring in my knives."

"Go get them, they can rest on a table for now." Saan went to get his knives.

"You've already made him happy."

"I hope so, he deserves to be happy—forever."

Saan came back in carrying several knives, small scabbards, and a whetstone. He carefully laid them out on a side table.

"I'll have to put them somewhere else when Sisten's children visit," he said. "Those blades are too sharp to be safe around little ones."

"Only the last two, the others are your age or older."

"I guess I'm just being a grandfather," he said and laughed.

"You look awfully good for such an old man," Strella said, placing her hand on his arm. They looked into one another's eyes.

"I think it's time I went home," Stol said and left, gratified that the boy was doing well, but mystified over how his back had healed—so quickly.

Two weeks after taking Saan as her Second Husband, Strella had the Maker come to her home. It was the earliest she could declare her intent complete and have their marriage finalized.

He carried in his bag of inks and needles and healing salve and set it on the table.

"Well, child, here I am again, this one you get to keep, no matter what."

"Soos, Sir," Saan answered, smiling shyly. He knew that the Maker knew what he and Strella did, but still being only a youngster, he embarrassed easily.

The Maker gestured toward the chair at the side of the table and Saan pulled it out and turned it around, and sat down in it backwards, leaning on the crossbar of the seatback.

Strella brought a mug of hot cider for the Maker and set it down near his tools. Then she sat down herself and watched the Maker put the marriage Dragon of her tribe on her boy's left shoulder.

Before he started marking Saan, the Maker had given a good look to the scar on the boy's right shoulder. He looked at Strella, questions in his eyes, but said nothing. She only smiled back, she had no answers.

By Law, the only other visitor during Saan's confinement of marriage after claiming could be Strella's son, Stell. He always tried to come when he imagined it would not be an inopportune time. He came in now as the Dragon Maker was finishing.

"Beautiful job," he said as he entered and saw Saan's freshly marked back. He set down a basket that had delicious aromas wafting out of it.

"What have you brought this time?" Strella asked.

"Tinka is convinced the two of you will starve to death, it's a bit of roasted rabbit the boys got out hunting. Well, it wasn't roasted when their arrows hit, Tinka did that."

Strella took the platter out of the basket and put a loaf of fresh bread back in it.

"Now I know you won't starve, either!"

The Maker had packed up his things as they talked. Strella took several coins off the other end of the table and handed them to him.

"Thank you, Milady, quite generous. Thank you."
He bowed and left.

Chapter Fourteen
Ritual

"I don't know how the Dragon Fire will affect him," Strella said to Stell. "He's never had it. Be careful with him, don't let him get sick, please."

"Mother, he has to have enough for the ritual, you know I'll take care of him. Everyone who will be there loves him. He will be just at Solot's home, we'll bring him home the next day. Then you can pamper him all you want."

Stell started to leave his mother's kitchen, then turned and flashed a wicked grin.

"What do you mean he's never had any Dragon Fire? Never needed it, hmm?"

He ducked as his mother's wooden spoon sailed toward his head. He looked back at her and winked.

She laughed at him and went to get her spoon.

Saan came into the kitchen carrying his bag and set it down on the table.

"I wish I didn't have to be gone so long, are you sure you will be alright?"

Strella took his face in her hands and kissed him deeply.

"I have been alone before—but I won't really be alone, Stell's little ones will keep me busy."

"That's not the same," he said and held her close against his chest.

"Esoos, but you will only be gone tonight and tomorrow night, and the next, and then, the night after the Ritual, then I will get you back."

They had decided that even though Saan would likely be sick and in pain, they would bring him home the day after the Ritual.

Saan nuzzled her ear and kissed her again and then let go of her, got his bag and went out the door to Stell's wagon waiting for him. He would have preferred to ride his horse, but being carefully brought in a wagon was part of it. Coming home, he did not expect to be in shape to want to ride.

Solot's house was close enough that they were there before long. Ordinarily, very few other than the men conducting the Ritual would see the subject in the middle of it.

Since everyone involved was well known to Saan, it was not considered necessary. His aunt, Solot's wife, did remain in seclusion, preparing herself for what she hoped would be a successful Ritual. Today, he had to leave home to primarily make sure that there was no coming together with Strella this close in time to the Ritual.

By midafternoon, Saan was restless. He was not at ease being so idle, specially thinking ahead to the Ritual. He was not allowed to leave the house and yearned to be outdoors and active.

"Come sit with me, Saan," Salmar said and held his hand out to his nephew.

For the first time in his life, Saan was pulled into his uncle's lap.

Salmar said nothing, but held Saan against him with his arms around the child he regretted so misjudging. He placed his hands over Saan's and laced his fingers through them, enclosing him tightly in a warm hug. Saan, feeling a peace he had rarely known, leaned back and relaxed against Salmar. He knew his uncle's love had come late, but what mattered to him was that it had manifested at last.

At one time or another, each of the uncles, and Stell, as well, embraced him. They knew he had consented and was not being forced by the Law into giving himself to the Ritual.

That night, they ate well, going to bed with full bellies, for tomorrow Saan would be allowed almost nothing to make sure that the next morning he would quickly drink down the full cup of sweet cider mixed with the Dragon Fire, bringing on the Ritual and the giving of his seed.

To appease Saan's restless spirit, Stell told of his war experiences, including the day he almost died.

It seemed the right time to tell them of Sekale's coming to him as he lay in his long recovery and how he told that someday he would come to Slia's aid, even though he would never see her again.

"I felt I had failed her, the night of Shalim's sending, that I had done nothing. But Sekale came to me that night—I've never told Tinka any of this, but when I asked him what I was supposed to do to help Slia. That night, he told me," Stell paused for a moment reliving it within himself, stroking his beard, noting the first few strands of gray beginning to appear.

"That night he told me I had already fulfilled my mission, my task—my purpose, and the rest of my life was my own to live to its fullest.

He said I had given Saan the one gift only I could give, I had given him the other half of his heart—I had given him Soth."

Stell could speak no more. He put a knuckle against his mouth, composing himself.

Saan came to him and knelt before him, resting his cheek on Stell's knees.

"Sekale was right," the boy whispered. "I couldn't love Soth anymore than I do if he had been my twin brother. And you did more, you didn't disagree with Strella when she decided to claim me. So much of my happiness in life is because of you."

Stell leaned down and kissed his mother's Second Husband on the temple where he had once had his braid of citizenship.

"You have made Mother very happy, Saan, very happy."

For some time they sat, Saan resting his head on Stell's knees and Stell stroking the boy's hair, thoughtfully. The only sound in the room was an occasional sniff from one of the uncles.

As it grew dark outside, sounds could be heard from the kitchen as a meal was prepared for the older ones by the women attending to Solot's wife in her seclusion.

"I'll go prepare for bed," Saan said. "All of you go eat."

He rose and before they left him, each uncle hugged him.

"I'll bring your cup of sleep elixir shortly," Stell said and joined the others moving toward the kitchen.

"Soos," Saan answered and went to the hallway leading to the room he and Stell shared for this visit.

It wasn't long before Stell came in with the mug of cider spiked with calming herbs to help Saan relax and sleep through the night. He drank it straight down and belched lightly, then laughed. Stell laughed with him and tucked him into bed, kissing him on the forehead as he had done when the boys were little and overnighted together in his home.

"Stell?"

"Soos?"

"I miss him."

"I do, too."

"He had to go, though, didn't he? I mean, it was that important to him to study the Law, he had to go. He loves it, I can see it in his eyes when he's home talking about it. I don't understand it, but I can tell he does."

Saan yawned, the herbs were starting to work on him.

"Soos, he does," Stell answered quietly.

"I think I could have made him stay, if I had begged him. But he, he, he wanted...it so...much."

Saan's voice was fading as he finished talking, then Stell heard another yawn and just soft breathing.

"Sleep well, little prince," Stell said and pulled the linens up higher over the boy's shoulders. There were two candles burning in the room. Stell blew out the one on a stand between their two beds but left the one burning near the door. They were in a house they didn't know and if they had to get up during the night, would need to know how to get around.

In the morning, Saan was awake before Stell, but waited for him to get up before going to the privy.

He knew he wasn't supposed to be alone today, wondering about.

After taking care of bodily needs, they returned down the hallway, but to a different room, the room to be used for the Ritual.

Saan stopped just inside the door and looked at the bed he would be on. There were ropes, straps, and chains waiting to bind him down, as much for his own protection as to protect the others around him.

Solot was not there, he would be waiting in another room, waiting for the Receptable to introduce Saan's seed to the prospective mother.

There were Stell, of course, with Salmar, Stant, and Stol. Traditionally there must be four, so Stol had agreed to be the fourth. Saan was relieved to see Stol, another someone he felt he could trust.

Stol held the mug of drink Saan must consume to begin the process.

"Sit on the edge of the bed, Saan, then drink this," he said to Saan, handing him the drink after the boy sat.

Saan drank it down quickly, he was very thirsty and hungry, his stomach welcomed anything it could get. He handed the empty mug back to Stol.

"Now, we'll need your drawers off, you can pull them down under the covers, if you want."

Saan stood and slipped them off.

"I don't think I have any secrets with anyone here," he said, and stepped out of them.

As his eyes began to droop, the men guided him to the bed and settled him in the center. While he lost the battle with forced sleepiness, they began tightening the bindings around several points on his legs, torso, and arms.

They finished only moments before the restless twitching began, signaling the beginning of buildup to completion of their purpose.

Stol, besides being the Executioner, was the area's general healer and often conducted the Ritual. As such, he readied the Receptacle that would hold the precious seed to take to Solot.

As the time of gathering neared, some men would seethe with violence, some cried and moaned, while others produced a steady stream of profanity, or simply screamed. Not Saan. He breathed rapidly and hard, his back arched, and had release.

Stol carefully removed the Receptacle from Saan's body and carried it to the room where Sotol waited. There, it was carefully turned inside out and Sotol pulled it onto himself and prepared to go in to his wife. He went into the room where his wife waited and introduced the seed.

Stol returned to see if assistance was needed with Saan. He had already been relieved of his bindings and they had been removed from the bed where he lay, sleeping peacefully.

He was on his side, rounded up bed linens propping him up and holding him still should he vomit. He would not choke on it if he did. Thick cloths were placed to catch anything that might be brought up from his practically empty stomach.

"I thought he would move around more," Salmar said. "That's what I've always heard. He hardly needed to be bound down."

"I have never seen such an easy time of it," Stol answered. "Never."

"Could it be because he is half Torbraugh—are they not affected the same as other men?" Stell asked.

Stol shrugged.

"I have no idea—it's like with his mark shrinking, and his back healing in less than a day, that can't all be because of his bloodline. If Torbraugh bodies were so resilient, how could they die in battle? Or die, ever?"

"I KNOW that they can die, during the war, I saw many fall. And the badly injured died. Those who recovered healed like the Dragon and the Song-hee. Their bodies are no different," Stell said.

They all sat vigil with the boy. Since he was in a drugged sleep, they did not worry about waking him with their talking. He never retched, never moaned, just slept.

Solot appeared with a tray of celebratory drinks and joined them.

Towards evening, they brought their food into the room to eat. They were eating and talking when Saan stretched, then sat up. He rubbed his eyes and looked at them. His stomach growled.

"Would you like to eat?" Stol asked him. He had never seen anyone eat so soon after the Ritual, usually they had dry heaves by now.

"Soos, I'm hungry," he said, sleepily.
Salmar handed him a piece of fresh bread, heavily buttered.

"See if you can keep this down. If it stays with you, I'll get you some more to eat."

"Thank you, Uncle," Saan said and steadied himself, sitting cross-legged in the middle of the bed, linens covering his lap. He enjoyed the buttered bread and licked his fingers clean after he finished it.

"Let's wait just a bit before anything else, just to make sure that doesn't come up," Stol said.

"Could I make a trip to the privy while we wait?"

"Certainly," Stol answered and retrieved Saan's drawers from the bedside table. "Let me help you get these on."

Saan allowed Stol to move the pile of coverings out of his way then eased his feet and legs over the edge of the bed.

He looked and acted as if slightly tipsy, but did not appear to be in the great pain that usually accompanied the Ritual.

Stol pulled Saan's drawers over his feet and up his legs. Salmar helped him to stand and steadied him while Stol slipped the garment up to his waist and buttoned. The boy was groggy, but not ill.

Stol and Salmar held him between them and took him down the hallway. When they returned, Saan was propped up and given more to eat. To drink, Stell held on to the mug for fear the boy would not hold it steady.

With his belly somewhat satisfied, he snuggled down into the bed and went back to sleep. Stol gently pulled him on to his side should his meal decide to leave him after all.

"Have you ever seen anyone be able to eat so soon after?" Solot asked.

"He is the first," Stol answered. "The very first."

It was barely daylight when Saan woke the next morning. Again, he felt the need to visit the privy.

All the men were asleep in the chairs they had used to sit vigil with him. He decided not to wake anyone, but quietly got up.

The grogginess had left him and he padded carefully and quietly across the hallway to the room where his things were and slipped on a pair of britches. He wasn't sure if there would be any women about the place, but even though he was still considered underaged, he WAS married, and didn't think it appropriate to parade around half naked.

After taking care of himself in the privy, his hunger returned, and he went to the kitchen to see if he could find any more of that tasty bread. Anything would seem tasty right now, he was a completely ravenous adolescent.

There must have been at least one woman up and around at some time, no man he knew of could so quietly load a table with so much delicious smelling food. He chose one his favorites, a meat and vegetable pastry like Strella made, and placed it in a small wooden bowl and went into the great room to sit on a rug in front of the small fire to eat.

"How is it you are up and everyone else is still asleep?"

He jumped up still holding his bowl, a big bite in his mouth. He quickly swallowed and set his bowl on a chair.

"Strella!"

He went to her and enfolded her in his arms, nuzzling his face in her hair.

"Have they not had the Ritual?" she asked.

"Soos, but I haven't been sick at all, just very sleepy last night."

She kissed him, tasting her meat pie on his lips.

"Go sit and eat. I'll sit behind you and rub your shoulders."

He sat obediently and relished both her cooking and her touch.

"Mother! What are you doing here?"

"I'm feeding my boy and rubbing his shoulders, I think you can see that for yourself, son."

Stell looked at her, a crooked smile on his face.

"I can see that, I mean, why are you here? I thought Tinka was bringing food for this morning."

"She was going to, but the baby is teething and his little belly is upset. She didn't want to leave him feeling so miserable. I told her I would come. I wanted to check on my boy, anyway."

Licking his fingers, Saan leaned back against her knees and wiggled his back in between them. Strella kissed the top of his head, his hair unruly from the Ritual activities.

Stell looked down at Saan comfortably sitting on the floor, leaning back against Strella.

"Are you not sick, or sore, or anything?"

"Esoos, just still a little tired, but hungry."

"That's odd, I mean, that's good, but odd."

By the time the others had wakened and come into the main room, basically asking the same of him, Saan had eaten two more meat pies and was finally no longer hungry.

"May I go home now?" he asked of Stol.

"You are not in pain, I see no reason for you to stay."

Saan collected his things, loaded them in Strella's wagon, handed her up onto the seat, and climbed up himself, taking the reins. Shortly, they were home, amazing those who saw him, knowing where he had been, and why.

His only aftermath was a residual fatigue lasting less than a week.

He did not experience the expected pain. Other expectations did not occur, either. There had been no conception. Nor did one occur the next three attempts. Solot's wife wept.

The legal limit of four Rituals had been reached.

There could be no more.

"Well, there IS a way," Soth told Saan during his Conclave furlough after the fourth try. "I read it in the Law, but it is not an easy thing to get a special consent."

"Tell me," Saan said as they sprawled together on their favorite knoll, watching the clouds race above them. He felt bad for Solot and his wife, and personally empty—he had looked forward to knowing he had a Blood Child.

Soth raised up and propped himself on an elbow, facing Saan.

"First, you have to wait until you reach manhood—twenty-five before the attempt is made. Before that, everyone involved, you, Grandmother, Solot, and Sheroma must petition the Conclave in person. Your Chieftain must be there, too, and verify that there has been no issue, not even a miscarriage resulting from the other attempts."

"That shouldn't be a problem, getting the Chieftain, since they chose Salmar."

"True, but it could be embarrassing for Solot and Sheroma, but if they want it bad enough, they could try. There's no guarantee that it would be granted, though. It would be particularly hard on you because it calls for a full portion of Dragon Fire, no dilution with anything else. It's considered to be very debilitating, there have even been deaths from it. Grandmother might not want you to try."

"Does she have to know about that? I mean, couldn't she just be told I could get very sick?"

"Esoos, it is all told in Conclave, there can be no secrets kept from her. Plus, you couldn't lie to her, could you?"

"Esoos, I cannot."

"Absolutely not!" was the answer Saan got from Strella when he asked her. It was three years since the first time he had undergone the Ritual and he had had no ill effects other than a vague tiredness for several days each time.

Chapter Fifteen
After the Furlough

Saan and Soth were almost twenty-one. Soth was now a Senior Apprentice and already considering what question to work on toward rising to Senior Elder.

He had finished his Apprentice works and worked on refining his expertise in the Law and teaching lower Apprentices. He was pleasantly overwhelmed to occasionally be invited to dinners with the Chief Elder Salar and his family.

It was at one such dinner he was introduced to the youngest daughter of the High Elder Sed, Salar's oldest son and Tay's twin.

The two of them exchanged shy glances at one another, much to the amusement of Salar. He remembered fondly the days when that was all the contact he and his Sheelta had when her father was Chief Elder.

To Senior Apprentice Soth, Shela was the most beautiful and virtuous creature to ever grace the eye of mankind. She had the light golden hair and icy blue eyes of Salar's mother, the Blood Daughter of the Poet and Prophet Kaul-Leb. Her quiet voice and gentle demeanor thrilled his heart. That she seemed to be pleased when he came to dinner drove him to distraction, making it difficult to keep his mind on his studies and duties.

Consulting with his son over a coming case, Chief Elder Salar quipped to Sed.

"If you don't approve an understanding between Soth and Shela soon, the boy is going to be worthless, he grows more distracted day by day."

Sed smiled, he liked Soth, and trusted he would be a good man for his baby girl.

"When is he next coming to your table, Father?"

"I was planning on having him in two weeks, but for the good of the Conclave, I could invite him for tonight."

Both men laughed. Salar loved working so closely with his son. He knew many fathers did not enjoy the closeness they shared.

Three of Sed's sons had also joined the Conclave. Two were already Junior Elders, one was a junior Apprentice, just taking his initial vows last year. Two others worked with their Uncle Tay and were skilled in the healing arts.

One of his daughters had married within the Conclave, the other two who were married had fallen in love with good men they met while their family was on furlough. Now Shela was interested in Soth, another good man, almost.

It would be four more years before he reached full manhood and could advance to Junior Elder and be married. Four years! Salar hoped the Conclave could withstand it. He also hoped he could listen in while Sed talked to Soth about an understanding with Shela—that would be fun, knowing Sed had every intention of allowing it, but watching Soth stammer his way through would be heart-warming. He loved that boy.

Soth wondered why he had a sudden invitation to the Chief Elder's home for dinner. Had he done something wrong and the Chief Elder in his gentle manner, wanted to chide him out of hearing range of others, or had he decided on a duty he wanted Soth to take on, or had some other guest become ill and the Chief Elder and his dear wife simply needed another to round out the table?

When the Custodian who ran many of the Chief Elder's errands informed him he was to come, Soth immediately accepted with thanks. One did not say one could not come—not to the Chief Elder. He closed the book of opinions written long ago by the Chief Elder's father-in-law and hurried to make sure of his appearance and put on a fresh set of Apprentice robes.

Arriving at the appointed time, Soth was a little taken aback to find that the only other guest for the evening was the High Elder Sed.

As always, the Chief Elder's wife, Sheelta, served an excellent meal. Her hair was now not only gray but shone like fine silver. Shela mirrored her grandmother's good looks.

Soth wondered why the High Elder was here without any of his family. He was a little perplexed when Sed indicated he had something to discuss after Sheelta left the room. Knowing what the men intended, she had set herself up with her needlework close enough to hear, smiling.

Salar had decided to simply just stay where he was, not to miss any of the evening's entertainment.

Soth had stood, thinking that they would retire to the main room, as usual.

"Please be seated, Soth."

Soth noted that Sed had not addressed him as Apprentice. He became slightly alarmed. Salar smiled. He loved the way Sed had this going.

"It has come to my notice that of late your mind has not been entirely on your studies or on your duties."

"Sir?" Soth's heart began to beat a little harder—was he to lose his appointment to the Conclave, or merely to be reprimanded? His mouth became dry.

"Your dedication until lately has been extraordinary. I feel we must find a solution to your recent, shall we say, less than your usual standard."

"Sir?" Soth's eyes widened, what was going to happen to him?

"Your distraction is, I believe, mainly my fault."

"Sir?" Where was this heading?

"My fault for having such an enchanting daughter," the High Elder said and smiled. "What I have in mind may only make matters worse, but there is little else I feel we can do."

Both men laughed at Soth's dumbfounded expression.

From the other room came Sheelta's voice.

"Sed, quit teasing the boy and get to it."

"Soos, Mother."

Sed turned back to Soth.

"I have spoken to Shela, and she is in agreement, if you wish, Soth, I will allow the two of you to become betrothed."

Soth's mouth fell open, but he could not speak, he could barely breathe.

"I, I mean, she, we? We may plan on marriage?"

"Soos," Sed answered and patted Soth's hand. "As soon as you rise to Elder, when you reach full manhood."

Soth stood and grasped Sed's hand. He finally remembered to breath. Excited tears swam in his eyes. Salar beamed, how he loved this boy!

Sheelta was at Soth's side.

"Now that these old men have had their fun, let me kiss my new grandson-to-be." She said and pulled his face close to hers, kissing both cheeks.

"You will come to dinner again tomorrow night, Shela and her mother will be here, as well, and we'll make it completely official," Sheelta said and accepted a kiss on the cheek from the excited youngster.

"Though, I'm afraid your studies tomorrow will most likely suffer," she added and laughed.

"I suppose I better have Soth help me tomorrow in the archives doing some heavy lifting—he won't have to do any thinking," Salar said, then added,

"Come here, child, and sit with me. Tonight, you are not an Apprentice, but the lucky boy promised to my granddaughter. We will send a message by a Custodian in the morning informing your parents."

"Thank you, Sir," Soth said and went to his betrothed's grandfather, now his grandfather, as well.

Stell ran to his mother's home as best he could, only limping slightly. He was too excited to walk.

"Mother! Mother!" Stell called, running through the door of the kitchen.

"Right here, Stell, what is it?"

Strella rose from her chair in the main room where she had been sewing. Saan came in through the door to the stable, muck rake still in his hand, to see what was causing the excitement.

"It's a message from Chief Elder Salar! He had a Custodian bring it to us this morning—Soth is betrothed to the Chief Elder's granddaughter!"

Stell held the parchment out to his mother.

"Let me see," she said, putting her sewing in her chair. Saan came to read over her shoulder.

It was warm and sweet, telling how much the whole family loved Soth and looked forward to the marriage as soon as he reached his majority. He told them that they would receive more information as the time grew near, but that the wedding would take place in the Conclave itself, by tradition, the next morning after his taking his oath as an Elder.

"Why so quiet, Saan?" Stell asked, noting that he had said nothing.

"Will they allow me to attend either ceremony? I'm not a citizen."

"They will have to," Stell answered. "You are his best friend—and a kinsman."

"The Custodian is waiting for a reply, we have to give our permission since he is underaged. I will ask the Chief Elder. They will have to let you go, too. It wouldn't be right not to."

Stell walked purposefully back home to write his reply.

Salar's answer came the next day. He would be greatly disappointed if Saan were not there. There had been no royalty at the Conclave since King Maikel. Being born a prince in the Torbraugh kingdom would circumvent the requirement of Dragon citizenship.

At next furlough, Saan heard every detail of Soth's beloved and the fright he had had the night of their betrothal. Now, he could laugh about it. He wished he could bring her to meet Saan before, but only descriptions could be had until the day of their wedding.

Soth was worried at first. How would Saan react? Would he be happy for him or feel rejected? Soth nearly worried himself sick stewing over the thought that Saan might be hurt over losing his friend to a mate.

Soth got permission to ride separately from his sister's family and arrived earlier, having come on horseback with his Custodians.

Saan had not been expecting Soth until mid-afternoon, like usual. He was again in the stable mucking out stalls when the door from the house opened and Soth came through it, smiling.

Saan heard the door and turned, expecting Strella. Instead, he saw "their" grandson. Saan leaned on his rake and smiled.

"Well, if it isn't the young husband-to-be?"

He dropped the rake and went to his friend, his arms open. They embraced and then looked into one-another's eyes.

"My boy is growing up, getting himself betrothed and all—to the Chief Elder's granddaughter, no less!"

He put his arm around Soth's shoulders and they walked back to the door to the house.

"Let's find Strella and you can tell us all about it."

"She is at our house, she saw the Custodians bring me home and told me to come get you so I could tell everyone at once."

To an outsider, it might seem strange to see a Conclave Apprentice and an enslaved, braidless, non-citizen walking arm-in-arm together, but not in this village. The Custodians who accompanied Soth would wait for the ones with the wagon and all return in the morning together. They liked overnighting here and looked forward to it.

The four weeks home on furlough went quickly for Soth, but not quickly enough. He was anxious to return and see Shela again. He rode beside the wagon with his aunt Sisten and their growing menagerie of children, but wanted to kick his horse in the flank and rush to see his sweetheart.

Knowing the impatience of the young, Sed had invited him to dine with their family the first night back.

Shela had cooked most of the meal with her mother only running supervision. Soth was certain he had never eaten better. Her sweet smiles and gentle ways flavored the meal for him in a way that neither his mother nor grandmother could compete with. When it became time for him to return to his own quarters, they were allowed several moments to say their farewells alone. Her chaste kiss on his lips inflamed him. But he wanted her to remember nothing but gentleness from him, his sweet, delicate flower, so he kissed her lightly on the lips and again on the forehead. He looked into her beautiful blue eyes and took each of her hands in his and kissed them, as well.

Sed ushered him out firmly, but gently—he remembered being a youngster in the throes of love.

Soth didn't really remember walking to his quarters, but he arrived, and went to bed. He was surprised when he realized in the morning that he had actually slept.

The routines of the Conclave gradually made their way back into his life now that he knew Shela would someday be totally his.

Seadol was of the Green Dragon tribe and had returned to Conclave alone without his wife and children. He had been nearly twenty-seven before completing the requirements for rising to Junior Elder, and at thirty-five, was resentful of those younger than he who had risen to Senior Elder.

He had returned alone from furlough because his mother-in-law was ill and his wife stayed in their home village to care for her. At least that was the reason she gave. In truth, she was tired of her husband's pettiness and needed time away from him. The children had been glad to see the Custodians escort their father away, leaving them to play with their cousins far away from the slaps and ill-temperament of their father.

Day by day, his quarters in the Hall of Junior Elders became less tidy, as he had never learned to pick up after himself, leaving that to his wife and children. He ate in the food hall of the Apprentices. After a month of bachelor life, he became restless and wanted female companionship, or at least, gratification of his physical need.

Sed had reprimanded him earlier in the day for his incomplete research regarding a case upcoming in Conclave Court and instructed him to rectify it as quickly as possible.

Sed's wife and mother had gone to one of his older children's quarters to admire a new baby. Shela was in their family quarters alone working on her embroidery, embellishing linens that would one day grace her marriage bed. Her thoughts were of Soth and the home they had started planning.

As usual in the Corridor of the High Elders during the day, the door was unbolted. Custodians manned all entrances to the corridor, keeping the homes of their leaders safe and secure.

Seadol stated his business to the Custodian and was allowed access. He had been to High Elder Sed's quarters before and knew the way. He knocked on the door and heard Shela's cheery greeting to come in.

She had no idea who could be coming to her family quarters, but expected it might be a neighbor dropping by to pass the time.

"Beautiful stitching, Shela," she heard and was startled to hear a man's voice. Looking up, she saw it to be Seadol. He always made her feel wary and she did not think it appropriate for him to be here with her alone.

"Father isn't here," she said, and stood. She kept her stitching in her hands.

"I have a document he wanted, do you know when he will be back?"

"He should be home any moment, he is behind his usual time, as it is."

Shela's instincts were sending her warning flashes, but she didn't know how to make the man leave.

"Your mother, is she home?"

It was obvious she was not.

"She is next door and should be right back. You can leave your document and I will give it to Father."

"I hear congratulations are called for, you are to marry Soth in the future."

"Soos, we are betrothed."

"It will be several years, though, soos, he is still a boy. A young woman of your beauty should not have to wait."

"I don't mind, I love Soth."

Seadol began to edge closer.

"Please go," she said, backing away.

He edged closer, the sting of the earlier reprimand biting into him.

Shela turned to go and felt his arm around her waist. His hand covered her mouth. She dropped her stitching and began fighting against him, scratching deep welts across his face as he tried to kiss her.

"You'll let that half Song-hee touch you, but not a full Dragon? Let me teach you, girl."

His hand covered her mouth, muffling her scream as he carried her into the nearest room with a bed.

The Conclave was buzzing that there had been something happen in the Corridor of the High Elders.

Soth, like the other Apprentices, ran to the entrance to be stopped by the Custodians.

He could see several Custodians near the entrance to Sed's family quarters and heard cries coming from it.

"What has happened?" he asked. "Please, what has happened?"

At the moment, his greatest fear was that Salar or Sed had fallen greatly ill or crossed over.

Then he saw Salar emerge from Sed's quarters. He had never seen anyone look so sad. The old man saw Soth among the crowd being kept away.

"Soth, come here, child."

The Custodian let him pass.

"What has happened Chief Elder? Is it High Elder Sed, or his wife?"

"Esoos, child. It is Shela. She is...she was. Attacked. She is gone."

Soth felt as though his heart had stopped. He pushed by the Chief Elder and through the door.

Shela's parents were there, her mother weeping in Sed's arms. Custodians were massed in the room, but Soth was able to slip by everyone to the room with the most activity.

He saw her then. So still. Her throat bruised and at an uncomfortable angle. Her clothing was torn and disheveled. One boot was lost off her feet.

Seadol was not there. He had been discovered by Sed and nearly beaten to death before the Custodians, hearing the sound of a fight, intervened and took him away.

Tay was with her now, covering the beautiful body, tears streaming down his cheeks at the horrific loss of his niece.

Soth wanted to go to her and hold her and make her live again, but was afraid he would hurt her more.

He knew it made no sense, but he couldn't think, he forgot how to stand and fell to his knees, hands on his face, hiding the ugliness in the room from his eyes, but knowing he would see it forever.

He felt firm, gentle hands lift him up and help him to stumble away. He didn't know who or where they took him. All he could see was Shela lying dead and hurt. He became unaware of anything but that Shela was gone. Forever. Their future together. Gone. Forever.
He could think of nothing else. He could see nothing else.

He wasn't aware of being undressed or being forced to drink something that put him to sleep. When the blackness lifted, it was no better, and they put him to sleep again and again.

A Conclave Custodian knocked on the door to the home of Strella and Saan. It was fairly early morning and she had just finished one of her favorite tasks, combing Sann's hair and pulling it back to tied it at the back of his neck. He sat at the table in britches and drawers, his first meal of the day just making it into his belly.

"Who could that be so early?" she asked.

"I'll go to the door and see," he said and rose.

Unbolting and opening the door, he saw the Custodian.

"Are you Saan?" the Custodian asked.

"Soos, I am Saan."

"You are needed at the home of Stell. His son, Soth, needs you. By request of Chief Elder Salar, please come."

"What is wrong?" Strella asked from behind Saan. "I am Soth's grandmother, Stell's mother."

"Just over a week ago, Apprentice Soth's betrothed was raped and murdered, Milady. His mind, Apprentice Soth's mind, has gone. The Chief Elder and the Healer Tay are hoping his friend Saan may help him."

Barefoot, Saan ran to Stell's home. There were several Conclave Custodians around the home. The Chief Elder's coach stood in front of it, the door open. Had Saan looked, he would have seen that one whole seat was covered with bed linens.

A Custodian stopped Saan at the door to the home.

"Let him in," a voice called, "He is Saan."

Saan saw one of Soth's usual Custodians who accompanied his friend home on furlough. He was the one who allowed him in.

The man took him by the arm and led him to the room where Soth had slept as a child. Saan momentarily wondered where all the other children were, but only for a moment.

He saw Soth on the bed. Sitting up. His face blank. He saw Stell holding Tinka as she wept in his arms at the immobile creature that was her son.

An older man with indication that his beard and hair had once been red was with him. He was gently guiding Soth down into the bed linens. Soth's eyes were open, but Saan saw no light in them.

The man finished nestling Soth down and turned to see the Custodian holding Saan's arm.

"You must be Saan, Soth's dearest friend, soos? I am Tay, the Healer from the Conclave."

"Soos, Sir, I am Saan. What is wrong with him? The Custodian that came to get me said his mind was broken. And that Shela was, had been..."

"Soos, and Soth saw her just after it happened. He has been like this ever since. I had thought that, with time, he would come back, but he has not. I can only get him to drink a little and he will not eat, food just sits in his mouth until it is taken out. I know there is a special bond between the two of you. I need your help, Saan. I am afraid he will die, really die of a broken heart if we cannot bring his mind back."

Saan went to the bed and looked at Soth, lying there, his eyes open, breathing, but no real life in him.

"I'm going to lie beside him, like we did when we were little for a while," Saan said to no one in particular.

He lifted the coverings and slid in beside his friend, lifting Soth's head and putting his shoulder under it. His left arm under Soth, he put his right over him in a loose hug and rested his head on top of Soth's, cradling him in his arms. Before long, he found himself sobbing quietly, as if he were taking on Soth's pain.

Soth's eyes had closed, Saan surmised he was asleep. Saan drifted off, holding him.

He heard voices around him at a distance, fading away. He dreamed dreams, but he couldn't remember them.

He heard his name being called lightly and roused to it. He looked at Soth and saw his friend's blue eyes focused on him. He was aware of others around them, looking on.

"Saan?"

"Soos?"

"How did you? Where? Am I home?"

Saan held him tightly.

"Do you know about...?"

"Soos, I know."

Tears rolled from Soth's eyes, down the sides of his face. Then came the great, heaving sobs. Saan sat them both up and held him against himself, letting him cry it out. His tears ran down Saan's chest and were caught in the waist of his britches. Saan held Soth against his heart and rocked him gently like a small child.

He continued holding his dearest friend against his chest, just holding, allowing the sorrow to wash around them both. Saan was aware that various ones came by and watched them for a while, then moved on. Just checking to see how Soth was doing.

Tay seemed the most pleased, his patient was recovering, his prescription was working.

The tears ceased, but Soth stayed as he was, holding to Saan, soaking in the supporting love. He knew others loved him, but Saan was different, Saan was himself, the other half of himself, they had always been so. Always and Forever.

Soth's stomach growled.

Saan laughed softly and rubbed Soth's arm.

"Are you hungry? I've been smelling some good stuff the last little while."

"Soos, I am, very."

Tay came in, a mug in his hand. Steam rose from the contents.

"Let's try a little broth, first, to wake your stomach up. It's been empty for quite a while."

Saan accepted the mug from him and blew on it lightly. Satisfied it was a little cooler, he placed it against Soth's lips and tilted it gently, letting him sip slowly and swallow. When it was about half gone, Soth raised his hand to help hold it and drank down the rest. Saan handed the empty mug back to Tay and enclosed Soth in his arms again, letting him lounge against him.

"Saan?"

"Hmm?"

"I don't think I can ever love again, this has hurt too much."

"You don't have to, Soth."

"Saan, could you help me to the privy, I'm not sure I can make it by myself."

Saan stood and helped Soth rise from the bed, holding him firmly, but allowing him to try his limbs.

Youth won out, he had more strength left in him than he thought and rapidly became steadier as they walked together, Soth's hand up on Saan's shoulder and Saan's arm around him. When they returned, Soth held to Saan's arm, but walked on his own.

They saw Tay standing by the door to the bedroom.

"There is food on the table for you, if you would like to eat."

"Let me straighten this mess out first," Saan said and playfully touched Soth's matted hair.

He sat Soth in the chair by the bedside and gently took down Soth's braids, strands of hair sticking out in odd directions from being in bed and uncombed for so long.

Tinka came in and handed Saan a stout wooden comb. Stell brought a basin of warm water and two cloths, one for washing, one for drying. They kissed both youngsters and left Saan to work on Soth's appearance.

He dipped the comb in the water and brought the black, wavy hair into compliance with his wishes, braids and all. Tying it at the nape of Soth's neck,

Saan wetted the cloth in the still warm water and carefully washed his friend's face, neck, and torso, drying him off with the other cloth. Soth did not have a heavy beard yet, and being half Song-hee, might never, but Saan brought what there was under control with the damp cloth and pronounced Soth fit to be seen. He was rewarded with a slight smile.

Neither of them had on a tunic, and Soth only had drawers, but Saan considered that no one in the house would mind. He helped Soth to stand but allowed him to walk on his own into his mother's kitchen.

Saan realized that he, too, was hungry. It was getting toward evening and he had not eaten since early morning.

Only Tay and family were in the kitchen. Saan had the impression that there had been others, most likely Custodians, but the room had practically emptied before their entrance. He knew that no one would leave Tinka's kitchen without being fed.

Stell led his son to the table and sat him down while Tinka brought his plate. Stell then guided Saan to the seat beside Soth and Strella placed food in front of him, lingering to stand with her hand on his shoulder, gripping it softly.

A small boy wandered in, the youngest of Stell and Tinka's brood and climbed up in Saan's lap.

Tinka started to fuss at him, but Saan smiled and hugged him.

"Sakil is fine, he can sit and eat with me, I don't mind."

The little brown-haired boy looked at Soth and then looked up intensely into Saan's face.

"Unca Saan?"

All the younger children of the household had been taught to call Saan their uncle.

"Soos, Sakil?"

"You make Sof feel better?"

"Soos, he did," Soth answered for him.

Soth ate slowly, his system sensitive from not eating for several days. Tinka hovered over him, not pushing him to eat, but just wanting to drink in the sight of her child in recovery. She had been terrified she would lose him to his deep sorrow.

"Tay, I want a full detail of Custodians to accompany you to Soth's village. He is to never be left alone until we are absolutely sure he is no longer despondent."

"Why, Father?" Tay had asked.

"You have heard me talk of my best friend, Sareen?"

"I see," Tay said. "We are all torn apart by Shela's loss, but to a youngster...and his first and only love. Soos, I understand."

Saan had eased Soth out of his catatonic state, but Tay had to be positive Soth would not harm himself over his loss.

Salar granted Soth a six month leave from the Conclave. He wasn't certain his favorite Apprentice would want to return ever, there would be so many memories, but he also wanted Soth to heal, whether he returned or not.

The next morning Soth and Saan walked to their favorite knoll out in the fields, distantly trailed by two Custodians.

"They think I may want to kill myself," Soth told Saan. "I heard people talking when they thought my mind was gone. I could hear, I just didn't care, then."

"Do you?" Saan asked sitting down and plucking a grass blade to chew on.

Soth sat, facing him.

"Esoos, not now. I did at first, but not now. Those first few days, all I could do was weep inside, thinking of her...and how she... died. But then," he said and paused. "But then they brought me home."

He chose a piece of grass and put it between his teeth.

"When I realized I was home and that you were holding me, I knew then, I was not ready to die, too. I knew the pain of loss, and I didn't want anyone I loved to go through it."

For a while, they said nothing, but sprawled back and looked at the sky. There were no clouds today, only birds.

Soth sat up, his knees drawn up to his chin, and his arms around his legs.

"I had the oddest dream."

"What?"

"At least, I thought it was a dream, but now it seems so REAL."

"What was it?"

"I roused up once, knowing you were holding me, and it was you, but it wasn't you I saw."

Saan raised up on his elbow and squinted in the light, looking at Soth.

"Who was I?"

"Not a who—a what."

"Very well, WHAT was I?"

"A Dragon, a white Dragon."

Saan sat up.

"I was a white Dragon?"

"Soos, you were asleep, but your wings covered me. I lay on your left shoulder with your arm around me, but your left wing was under me, with your right wing covering me and your right arm laying across me. Your chin rested on my head, you had me all covered and protected."

Saan stared at him, he paled.

"Saan? What is it, what's wrong with you?"

"That is the dream I had as I held you and I slept, I recall it now."

They looked at one another, munching on their grass pieces.

"We've always known we were special together," Saan said. "Perhaps the Dragon is reminding us how rare our friendship is, or it could mean something else, I don't know."

"For now, that's good enough, Saan."

"Soth, I'm getting hungry, how about you?"

"Soos!"

They stood and started back, the Custodians joining them for the walk back to the village.

Three days later, Tay sat at Strella's table across from Soth and next to Saan.

"The two of you have been best friends without a single quarrel?"

"They have never fussed at one another as far as I know," Strella answered.

"We met the day my brother's soldiers brought me here and left me. Soth became my playmate, and in a way, my real brother."

"The parchment they left said we were born the same day, so we've said we were twins ever since Saan's grandfather discovered what it said."

"I've seen the document, Shalim gave it to the Conclave along with your mother's ashes in the jeweled box. They are displayed in the archives alongside the works of Kaul-Leb."

"Why with Kaul-Leb's works? He's the Poet, Mother was just a young girl, and I'm just me."

"Both of you are his descendants, to begin with. And because of your mother and King Maikel's wanting her for his queen, his armies were completely stood down. You see, we knew that they were still assembled just over the border even as he came to sign the contract for peace. We feared that it was just a ploy to trick the People of the Dragon into disarming, with another attack of the Eagle pending. But with Slia becoming his queen, Maikel completely honored the peace. Your birth sealed it."

"What about Rondol? Do you think he will ever attack?"

"There is always the chance, but your brother is not the king your father was. He is weak and lacks purpose, other than the feeding of his own pleasures. Your father strove to carry out the plan of your grandfather Railen—to unite the Eagle, Dragon, and the Song-hee Lion into one. And in a way, he accomplished your grandfather's mission."

"The Dragon and the Lion's Brood are one, now, but they are not united with the Eagle," Saan said.

"Soos, they are, you thick headed Torbraugh—you are all three," Soth said and threw a small piece of bread at Saan's head, laughing.

Saan caught it and threw it back. Soth caught it, and seeing the mock stern look Strella gave him, popped it in his mouth. All four laughed.

After the laughter died down, Tay took a long look at the two friends.

"I think Soth, you are well enough to continue your healing without me—you have your own healer, and others need me. The Custodians and I will return to the Conclave in the morning. Although, I love being in your village, this has been a most restful time for me, letting Saan do my work."

"You will be greatly missed, Tay," Strella said and placed her hand over his. "We have much to thank you for."

"Soos," Soth said. "Especially me, if not for you, I would have never been born."

"Exactly, we would have lost Stell during the war." After Tay and the Custodians left, Strella and Tinka made it their personal missions to feed Soth all his favorites to tempt him into gaining back the weight he lost after Shela's death.

"How do you think Soth is doing?" Strella asked her beloved boy one night as they snuggled together. "Is he fully recovered?"

"I don't think the hurt will ever all go away," he answered her. "But he can speak her name now without tears coming to his eyes. And I think he's missing the Conclave life and his studies. He tells me more and more about it. I think when Sisten comes home for furlough, he will return with her family when it's over."

"But Chief Elder gave him a six month leave."

"I don't think he wants to be away from Conclave that long. He loves that life."

"Won't it be hard on him, going back?

"Soos, whenever he goes back. I think he wants to face it and get the hard part over."

"You'll miss having him with you every day, though, won't you?"

"Soos, but... he loves that life. Why, I cannot understand. I like this one much more."

He held her against him and gently reminded her of his love for her.

Furlough came, and with it, Sisten's family. When it was over, just as Saan thought, Soth went with them back to Conclave.

Sakil became a daily visitor.

"You lonely now, Unca Saan? Now Sof gone?"

"Soos, I am a little lonely, but I have you and your grandmother, don't I?"

"Unca Saan, you play horses wif me?"

"Soos, I will play horses with you, Sakil."

They went into the main room where the old sewing basket with Soth's horses he had shared with Saan as children still sat. The old horses were worn, and had been mended many times, but were still enjoyable for small boys, and not so small boys.

"Saan?" Strella asked him in the dark that night.

"Soos?"

"You did enjoy playing with Sakil today, didn't you?"

"Soos, he is so sweet—he reminds me of Soth when we were little."

"You really like little ones."

"Soos, why?"

"I think, if you still want to petition the Conclave, to try once more, for Solot, I think we might."

He hugged her tightly.

"I just worry for you, though."

"I'll be alright. But why, what changed your mind?"

"I just thought that you should have a least one child, that you needed to be a father, even it's only a Blood Child."

She couldn't see his smile in the dark, but she could feel his excitement.

The next morning early, they hitched the mare to the wagon and went to Solot's house before time for him to go to his fields. He and his wife both wept at having another chance to try for a child.

"You realize the Conclave must grant special permission, it does not happen just because you want it," Salmar said when they went to him.

"At least we can ask," Saan said.

"If it is granted, Saan, you know you will most likely be very sick this time, not like the other times."

"I understand, Uncle, but if…if it works, it will be worth it, true?"

"True," he said. He knew how his brother and sister-in-law wanted to have a child in their house.

He regretted daily persuading them against adopting Saan when he was younger.

"I will take your request for petition, then they will advise you when to appear and we will go. It may take time, but it is two years before Saan will be old enough to fulfill requirement."

Chapter Sixteen
The Petition

Salmar left to take the request the next morning.

That afternoon late, two Conclave Custodians arrived saying they would escort the four others to Conclave the next day.

"So soon?" Strella asked. "Salmar said it could take weeks to be heard."

The Custodian smiled.

"By special dispensation of the Chief Elder Salar, Milady."

Strella insisted that the Custodians overnight with them. Remembering the hospitality of their previous times being fed at Strella's table, they gladly accepted. While Strella prepared the meal for themselves and their guests, Saan accompanied the Custodians to the home of his aunt and uncle to tell them the news.

The next morning, after Strella was satisfied no one could eat another bite, a Custodian drove Strella's wagon with the women cushioned comfortably in the back of it and his horse following along on tether. Saan, Solot, and the other Custodian were mounted on their own horses. Of the four villagers, only Strella had been to Conclave once before, when Sisten had married her Elder.

They were all properly awed at the sight of the complex.

Salmar met them at the gates. He was in a heightened state.

"I have never heard of this before, you have been assigned rooms within the Complex. I have even been given a room inside! Chief Elder Salar arraigned all this as soon as he learned of your request."

The Custodians helped the women down from the wagon and handed their bags to the Apprentices assigned to show them to their rooms. The villagers were given promises that their horses would be well cared for in the Conclave stables and the animals were led away.

Summoned by a Junior Apprentice, Soth soon met up with them.

"The Chief Elder has given me permission to be in the Senior Elder corridor for your stay, and he has planned a meal in your honor in one of the banquet rooms! Everyone is excited to have you here."

"Why? I mean, why are we getting such special treatment, Soth?" Saan asked.

Soth smiled.

"Saan, at home, you are the Second Husband of my grandmother," he said and hugged Strella. "Here, in the Conclave, you are considered not only that, but also a Prince of the Torbraugh. You are the only second member of royalty to enter the Conclave in recorded history, the first being your father."

"Do you think that will help with our petition?" Saan asked.

Soth just smiled.

"I am not allowed to say."

He winked.

They had been walking behind the Apprentices with their bags and now reached their assigned quarters.

Two doors were opened across the hallway from one another. Sisten came from three doors up the corridor, smiling, her arms open.

"Mother, Saan!"

While they hugged and kissed, Saan's aunt and uncle were shown into their quarters. Salmar informed them his quarters were next to theirs.

Sisten led her mother and Saan to show them where they would stay. Their bags were carefully taken into their bedroom. The Apprentices were in awe of their royal guests. For truly, if Saan were a prince, his legal marriage partner would be a princess.

While they were inspecting where they would stay and finding the gracious supply of special provisions stocking the kitchen area, the Conclave's own version of royalty walked through the doorway.

"Well, my boy! You have come to see us at last! You and your lovely lady," he said and bowed to Strella.

"I finally get to meet the grandmother of my favorite Apprentice."

He leaned in to whisper loudly in her ear.

"Don't tell him I said he was my favorite, don't want him to get all full of himself, do we?"

Strella laughed and whispered back.

"Esoos!"

Salar linked his arm through Strella's and patted her hand.

"My dear Lady, you have given much to the Dragon, we so appreciate you."

"I?"

"Certainly, first you gave us your daughter to keep Sailk in line and happy, then we had the service of your son in the war, your precious grandson is a fine Apprentice, and now you come with your prince to grace our walls in a most unselfish manner."

Salar kissed her on the cheek as she reddened.

"Now!" he said, I will give you a bit to freshen up from your journey and then I will send Soth back to collect all of you to come to the little dinner I have ordered to welcome you. Tomorrow we will address your petition."

He winked and left. Salar was getting quite old, but was as spry as when he escaped the Song-hee when he was barely younger than Saan was now.

Saan and Strella made use of the wash basin, wiping away the dust of the road and donned their best.

Strella's beautiful, fine stitching adorned all their clothing, but what they put on was her very best work on carefully made garments.

"You are so beautiful," Saan said to her as he looked at her and smiled. "I am always so proud to walk beside you and let everyone know that you are mine to love."

"And the clothing you make for us, even the court of the king was not so finely dressed."

He turned to show off his handsome outfit and gave her a gracious bow.

"Come here, you," she said, holding her hands out to him.

He went to her and they kissed long and deep. It had been well worth it to him, losing his Dragon and all, to have Strella. He loved her, had never loved another. Would never want another, ever.

A knock at the door to their quarters preceded Soth coming to collect them. Together they went to get the others. Sisten and her family joined them. The quiet attitude of her children made Saan think that they had all been freshly warned of the consequences should they embarrass their parents at this event.

Her eldest son, Stilk, gave the other children knowing older brother looks. He, himself, felt resplendent in his new Junior Elder robes, his fairly new bride walking on his arm, just beginning to show he would be a father soon.

They entered the banquet hall, larger than the home Strella and Saan shared, but still imbued with the intimacy of a small dinner party. Salar had invited the six High Elders and their families, which included assorted sizes of children, plus Tay and his wife. None of Tay's children had stayed with the Conclave, most were healers like him and were busy with patients. At the end of the main table, where Salar, his wife Sheelta and their special guests sat, one place setting at the end held no implements, but a bouquet of wildflowers, the favorites of Shela.

Soth had been consulted, as well as Sed and his wife, to make certain it would not be too painful for them. All agreed that they would want her remembered.

Salar relished the opportunity to tell some of his own old war stories to ears that had never heard them before. For the younger set, it was hard to believe that the Song-hee had once been enemies.

"Perhaps one day, we will think the same of the Torbraugh," he said. "Perhaps one day the war with the White Eagles will be forgotten forever—that will be a good day, soos, my young prince?"

"Soos," Saan answered. He felt a little odd with Salar continuously calling attention to King Maikel's being his father, but one did not correct or chide the Chief Elder.

Children were getting sleepy and tired of being on their best behavior for so long. The party began to break up as young mothers herded their broods home and to bed.

Salar decided it was time to speak of tomorrow.

"In the morning, when the High Council is ready to hear your petition, I will send Soth to you again to bring you to the meeting room. We will not be in the Great Hall," he said and laughed lightly. "We would get lost in there with so few, but we will meet in the smaller, Council Hall. It is much more intimate and less intimidating. There we will hear your petition and give you our decision. So, until the morning my friends, sleep well. Soth will make sure you make it back to your quarters."

With that, the Chief Elder rose, and accepting Sheelta's arm on his, they made their way to their own quarters.

Soth lay claim to Shela's flowers and held them tightly in his hands until after he had escorted his grandmother and the others to their quarters, and retired to his own.

There, he pressed the flowers between two of his heaviest volumes to keep as a remembrance. Then he allowed himself one last cry over his loss. He knew that tomorrow, after the High Council had heard Saan's petition and ruled, and all of them left for home again, he could finally, truly bring it to an end.

Tomorrow, when there were no visitors, and only members of the Conclave, then, it would be over. Shela's killer would face his execution, tomorrow.

And his executioner would be a half Song-hee Apprentice of the Black Dragon Tribe.

The next morning Soth was at his grandmother's door as the sun rose. She and Saan were up and eating from the generous supplies left for them. She did not have to work on her grandson long to convince him to eat with them.

"I have to confess, I was hoping you would ask me."

"When are we expected to go to the Council Chambers?" Saan asked him.

"Whenever you and all the others are ready. The Chief Elder and the High Elders are already there, but there are several things they are going over. Chief Elder said to come any time, no rush."

"Still, I don't want to keep them waiting," Strella said, and started putting things away. "Saan, why don't you go check to see if your uncles are about ready? Tell them they may come over here as soon as they are ready to go."

"Soos," he said and started for the door only to be met by Salmar with the other two in tow.

"Are we ready?" Salmar asked and clapped his nephew on the shoulder.

"I believe so, Uncle Salmar."

"I've got everything put away," Strella said, and took Saan's arm.

Saan gestured toward the door.

"Lead on, Mighty One," he said and laughed with Soth.

They went down the corridor, Soth beside his grandmother and Saan, followed by Salmar and Solot with Sheroma.

The parade had to stop by Sisten's door as she gave her mother and her two escorts kisses and hugs.

They continued on.

Soth led them through several corridors."

"How do you remember where everything is?" Saan asked him.

"You get lost a lot at first," he confessed. "But then you just know."

He stopped at last before a very ornate wooden door and knocked.

Sed came to the door.

"Good, we had just dispensed with the last of our other business, come in."

Soth kissed his grandmother and Saan on their cheeks.

"I am not allowed in this room yet. No Apprentice is unless he is in deep trouble and has proceedings against him."

"Will we see you again, Soth?" Saan asked.

"Soos, there is a room to the side where I will wait for you to take you back to your quarters before you leave, then I may take you to the gates before you leave for home."

Saan entered, Strella on his arm, next came his aunt and uncle and then his Uncle Salmar, Chieftain of the Black Dragon Tribe.

Inside, they saw a large, ornate wooden table with twelve chairs carved in the same motifs of Dragons.

At the far end of the table stood Salar, to his immediate right was an empty place to which Sed went after closing and bolting the door. Beside him stood two more High Elders. To Salar's left stood the other three High Elders.

The near end of the table was empty. The five chairs there waiting for the visitors.

"Please be seated, my friends. Prince Saan, please take the place of honor at the end with your lovely lady to your right. On her right, Chieftain Salmar, and to your left, your aunt and uncle."

Saan seated Strella and Solot seated his dearest,

Salmar waited for the others to be seated and then sat as the Chief Elder and the High Elders did.

Salar referred to a parchment in front of him.

"We have before the High Council a request for a fifth Ritual of Seeds Rights to the benefit of Solot and his wife, Sheroma, of the Black Dragon Tribe, the first four Rituals producing no issue, is this correct, Solot?"

"Soos, Chief Elder, it is correct."

"Sheroma, wife of Solot, are you willing to accept a fifth attempt of the Ritual to conceive a Blood Child by Saan, Second Husband to Strella?"

"Soos, Chief Elder, I am willing."

"Salmar, Chieftain of the Black Dragon Tribe, do you concur that to the best of your knowledge, there has been no issue to this marriage, neither natural nor by Ritual?"

"Soos, Chief Elder, this marriage has had no issue."

"Strella, Claimant of the Second Husband, Saan, do you grant your permission for a fifth Ritual after he obtains the age of manhood, knowing of the increased portion and resulting illness and unlikely but possible death?"

Strella hesitated for several moments.

"Soos, Chief Elder, I grant permission."

Saan lay his hand over hers and gently squeezed it.

"Prince Saan Maikel of the Torbraugh, son of King Maikel Railen of the Torbraugh and his wife Queen Slia, of the Torbraugh, Daughter of the Dragon, and you as the Second Husband of the Claimant Strella of the Black Dragon Tribe, are you, as subject of the Ritual, willing to give of yourself to a fifth Ritual once you reach the age of manhood, knowing of the increased portion and resulting illness and unlikely but possible death?"

"Soos, Chief Elder, I am willing."

"High Elders of the High Council of the Conclave of the People of the Dragon, having heard the affirmative answers given by these parties involved in this petition, how say you? Shall this petition be granted or denied?"

All six High Elders placed their right hands on the table, palm upwards, hand open—affirmative. No one lay his hand palm downward.

"The petition for a fifth Ritual once Prince Saan, Second Husband of Claimant Strella, reaches the age of manhood has been granted by the High Council of the Conclave of the People of the Dragon."

Salar smiled.

"We will now all sign the parchment, and it will remain in the archives of the Conclave. Saan, after we are finished here and before Soth takes you back to your quarters to prepare to return home, I would like to show you the archives, where your mother's ashes rest beside the certification of your birth. My Grandfather Kaul-Leb's works are there, too."

"I would be honored to see the archives, Sir."

The document made its way around the table, guided by Sed with the inkpot and stylus in hand, presenting it to each signer.

The whole group, High Elders and Soth included, walked down to the archives, below ground level.

"It's beautiful," Saan said, holding the jeweled box sent to his grandfather. He gently lifted the lid and saw the small pouch of his mother's ashes. He surprised himself with tears running down his face.

"I had something made for you, I was going to wait until you came to see Soth rise to Junior Elder, but I think now is the time. A long time ago, when I was an Apprentice, I lost someone very special to me. His father had this made for me."

Salar pulled the glass orb holding Sareen's ashes up from under his tunic.

"I took some of your mother's ashes and had one made for you. Sed?"

Sed handed his father another glass pendant filled with ash.

Salar held it up, allowing the lamp light to illuminate it.

He placed it over Saan's head.

Saan held the glass pendant up and kissed it.

"Thank you, Sir."

Salar hugged him and kissed him.

"Let me show you the certificate of your birth—I think Strella saw it the day you came, didn't you?"

"Soos, I did, but I couldn't read it."

"Nor can I, but I have some very smart young men who can."

They examined the document, just to see it. The markings meant nothing to them.

"Now, I hate to send you off, but I would prefer you arrive home in the light. It is only mid-morning, so I have had all the foods in your quarters you didn't eat packed up to eat along the way."

"Thank you, Chief Elder," Salmar said. "You have been very kind."

"It has been my pleasure to help you," he said and kissed both ladies on the cheek and winked at their men.

When the group emerged into the main corridor, the Chief Elder and his High Elders turned to go back to their work, and Soth took the rest back to retrieve their belongings.

Junior Apprentices appeared to carry baggage and food baskets to the waiting wagon and saddled horses. Sisten came to bid her farewells. Soth led them to the gates, their Custodians were ready to take them home. The group left for the Black Dragon village.

Chapter Seventeen
Soth Kills

Soth returned to his quarters to prepare himself.

Today, he would take a life. The life of the man who had devastated his plans for the future.

The other Senior Apprentice, Sekor, who shared quarters with Soth was waiting for him, along with three others. They would assist Soth as he readied for his new role. Ceremoniously, they removed his Apprentice robes and boots and redressed him in total black, the color worn throughout the People of the Dragon by executioners. After the death of his beloved, and the recovery of his senses, Soth had chosen the path of Fulfiller of the Law within the Conclave.

With the advent of Tay's Healers, Conclave Executioners no longer studied the healing arts, only those of punishment and death. He was still an Apprentice, still an Apprentice Executioner, but for this, Salar and the High Council had granted him special privilege.

After making his choice of service, Salar and Sed had given him the best knives to be found among the People. The knife he would use today had special meaning, for it had been one Salar carried during his time as a Song-hee warrior in his youth.

Soth took it from the black bag where it was kept with the others and once again tested the keen blade. He carefully rested his thumb on it, feeling the sharp edge. He gently pushed against it, exerting almost no pressure, and was satisfied with the thin line of red that appeared.

Without his desire to closely adhere to the Law, he would have chosen a duller blade, one that would linger the pain and suffering.

After carefully repacking his chosen knife away with the others in his black cloth bag, Soth handed the bag to Sekor, who had also dressed in black to act as one of Soth's assistants. His other assistant would be the Senior Executioner, acting as an Apprentice.

Selum was getting old and had had no Apprentice for several years. He was relieved when Soth chose his service, but sad for the boy's reason.

By tradition, no execution would take place within the Conclave buildings proper. Soth and his crew made their way down into the underground section, close to the Archives he had visited earlier in the day to the prisoner holding area.

There he entered the cell that had housed Seadol since the day of Shela's death.

His trial had taken place in closed Conclave, with no outsiders, during Soth's illness. The chief witness had been her father, Sed, who had found Seadol only moments after he killed Sed's youngest child.

The man had nearly died that day as Sed laid hold with a father's ire and nearly beat him to death before Custodians intervened.

The other witness against him had been Shela's Uncle Tay, testifying how his niece had died of a broken neck and that she had been savagely raped, as well.

The man himself had been the only witness for the defense. With his hands on the Dragon's Tooth of Truth, he had testified that he had no memory of the attack, that a demon must have been responsible for it, and he should be released, both from custody and from the Conclave.

He was found guilty and sentenced to death. When news arrived at the time of the court from Tay that Soth was improving, it was decided that sentence should be delayed. Soth had the right to witness it. But he had decided to carry it out.

"Salar."

"Soos, Grandfather?" Salar answered. He had not had a visitation from his Spirit Warrior in many years. Salar was not dreaming, he was awake, reading in his official study.

"Salar, be cautious, my child, for Soth."

"Soth? Why, Grandfather? He is an apt student, so the Elders say."

"Apt, soos, but remember his heritage."

"His heritage, Grandfather?"

"Soos. Soth's mother is full-blooded Song-hee. The pedigree of her line was lost in the migration. She is a direct descendant of my brother, the older of the twins. Although her brother Sturl never exhibited the Blood Fever, within her, the tendency is strong. She has given this tendency to her son Soth."

"Are you saying, Grandfather, that Soth should be forbidden to apprentice with the Executioner?"

"Esoos. Do not forbid him, but he must be told so he may guard himself from allowing the Beast to arise and overcome him."

"Is it safe to allow him to conduct the execution of Shela's killer?"

"Soos, if he is aware so that he may guard his emotion. And if you allow him some joy in his heart."

"Joy? How do I give him joy, Grandfather?"

"Today the Chieftain of the Black Dragon, Salmar, arrives with a request for petition for a fifth ritual for Soth's brother of the heart. Send for Saan and the others to allow Soth the joy of Saan's company. When the time of execution is upon him, his heart will still be warmed by the visit with this brother and the Beast and the Blood Fever avoided.

Otherwise, when Soth takes a knife to Seadol, and smells the blood, and feels the deep hate, his heart will feel it, and there will be no stopping the Blood Fever of the Song-hee."

"Soos, Grandfather. When should I tell him?"

"Now. Send for him now, while I am still with you."

"Will you speak with him yourself?"

"Soos."

Salar went to the door of his chamber, opened it, and sent one of the Custodians outside it to bring him Soth.

Grandfather Kaul-Leb, in full battle dress of the Song-hee Black Lions stood to the side, not to be seen by any but his grandson and soon, his great-great grandnephew.

Before long, a gentle knock was heard at the door.

"Enter," Salar called out.

The door opened and Soth appeared.

"You sent for me Chief Elder?"

"Soos, Apprentice Soth, come in and please shut the door behind you."

Soth slipped in and quietly pushed the ornate wooden door closed. As he turned from the door, Salar knew the moment the boy saw Kaul-Leb.

Soth froze in mid turn and his mouth and eyes opened wide. Only his eyes moved, cutting to Salar, questioning.

"Soth, who you see before you now is my Grandfather Kaul-Leb, and my Spirit Warrior."

Soth began to breathe again and bowed slightly to both.

"Chief Elder, and...and..."

Kaul-Leb smiled as he removed the Lion Head helmet from his head.

"Soth, you may call me Uncle, for one of my brothers was your forefather, in your mother's line."

"Uncle...Kaul-Leb."

"I know, child, that you worry your illness is returning. I assure you that it is not. I come to give you a warning, or cautious advice."

"Sir?"

"You, child, being half Song-hee and of a line manifesting the Blood Fever, must learn to guard yourself against it."

"The Blood Fever, Sir? I have it?"

"You could, child. Extreme anger triggered by the smell of blood can bring it on. And once it has you, you cannot control yourself and will strike out at any and all who come near you."

"Should I resign from service of Executioner?"

"Esoos, child, your Dragon half gives you more ability to hold it off. My son Lart was able to feel it coming and avoid it by allowing himself to calm.

You are able to do so, as well. Being warned, you may now recognize it and master the Beast."

"Thank you, Uncle Kaul-Leb."

Kaul-Leb pulled the Lion Head helmet back over his head and face and went to stand directly in front of Soth, staring at him with his emerald-green eyes, the same eyes Soth saw when he gazed into Saan's face.

"I was Blood Grandfather to Saan's grandfather Shalim, his is my child, and a Child of the Dragon, as you are a Child of the Dragon. It was no accident the two of you were born the same day or that you love him more than your heart can understand. The two of you are destined to stand together until the day you both die."

He smiled.

"Many years from now."

Kaul-Leb was gone.

Soth continued to stare where Kaul-Leb's face had been.

"Chief Elder? Did I really see who I think I saw?"

"Soos, Soth, you saw him. I've seen him many times over my life. This is the first time he has asked for anyone else, though. And now, he tells us that you and I are cousins."

Soth stood impassively while the charges were read and the sentence pronounced. There was no wall here to tie the condemned man against, not in a Conclave execution.

He and his assistants and the condemned were standing outdoors in the middle of a circle of all the Conclave. Chief Elder Salar and his High Elders stood barely inches away in the first concentric circle.

The next ring was made up of the Senior Elders, the following layer was Junior Elders, then the Apprentices, junior and senior mixed.

The man to die was tied between two posts, the white cloth wrapped around him to catch what blood it could. The man had not yet been gagged and was whimpering, begging, and cursing, each in turn.

"My wife, my children, think of them! How will they survive? I meant her no harm, she screamed. It was not my fault, she led me on. She was a wanton, a whore. It's not my fault!"

As the man defamed Shela, Soth looked him in the face and the cold vault he saw in his Executioner's eyes silenced him at last.

Soth held out his hand and the gag was placed in it. He walked to the man and forced the wooden block into his mouth, tying it tightly behind his head. Soth worked quickly despite the man's writhing to avoid it.

No room for the usual table used in the village squares, his assistants held his implements. His bag was unfolded and his blades revealed. First, Soth chose a short blade and with the man's eyes on him stood beside him and cut away the hair tied at the nape of his neck. This he put in a small drawstring bag held open for him.

He followed with what was left of the man's braids, shaving them off close to the skin. He wasn't worried about scraping the skin, and small beads of blood rose where the braids had grown from his temples. These went into the bag also.

Then Soth stepped around to the man's back and exchanged the blade he held for the very sharp one Salar had used when he was young. There was no salve spread over the man's Dragon mark—a Green Dragon, to alleviate pain or keep down infection.

Soth did not care if the man felt pain, and he would not live long enough to develop infection.

His blade tip cut a circular pattern around the tribal Dragon and blood began to flow down to the white loincloth.

Having gone all the way around it, Soth eased the blade under the edge of the skin and lifted, pulling it away as he cut the connecting tissue. At last, it came free in his hand.

He could not be executed as a citizen. Now he bore no marks of citizenship and could be put to death.

Soth placed the bit of removed back skin into the bag and the bag was pulled closed. It and his blood on the cloth around him were all of the man that would ever be sent to the Dragon in fire.

The man began screaming as soon as Soth's blades had pricked his skin and he continued as Soth walked back in front of him. His blood had overwhelmed the ability of the white loincloth to absorb it and pooled around his bare feet. He was crying, nearly choking on the gag.

Soth looked him straight in the eyes again and drew the knife across the side of his neck on the man's left. Every beat of his heart created a fountain of blood. Soth cut the artery on the man's right.
The man's eyes began to droop closed, but before he could die from bleeding out, the knife blade was rammed into his heart, slicing it open within the chest.

While taking the skin from the man's back, Soth had caught the stirring of the Blood Fever and purposely recalled his happiness of earlier in the day seeing his best friend.

As he heard the man screaming and smelled his blood, Soth made himself think of how bravely he had been told Saan walked up on the platform to lose his mark, and he just a boy.

He would not let himself think of Shela, for that would have fueled his anger, and possibly brought the Beast. He controlled himself and meticulously aimed his blade and finished his assignment.

The task done, he wiped his bloody blades against the few spots on the loincloth not already soaked. The cloth and the bodily contents of the bag would be sent to the Dragon—burned.

The body would be buried like the undeserving animal that he was.

Soth had not spoken during the whole ceremony, neither had he allowed himself to even breathe hard. He had forced himself back close to that place he had been before Saan pulled him out, the Beast could not reach him there.

He washed his hands and soiled blades in a basin brought to him and held by a Senior Apprentice. He was given a clean cloth to dry himself and his knives. The knives he used were packed away, he would go over them again later to make certain they were completely cleansed.

The crowd was gone by the time he finished, the dead man handing between the posts.

"Very immaculate, Soth," his mentor said and handed him back the folded bag with his blades.

"Sekor and I will now go send this to the Dragon, you go change." He had held up the bag to be burned.

Back in his quarters, Soth had the help of three Apprentices, since Sekor was elsewhere, changing back to his normal robes. One of them gathered up the black robes to take them to the Conclave laundry. There was most likely blood, even if it could not be seen.

The other two left, leaving Soth alone with his thoughts. He sat on the edge of his study chair, finally allowing himself to think of Shela and their future that had died with her. He felt a hand firmly grasp his shoulder and looked up to see Sed, who would have been his father-in-law in a little over a year. Soth started to rise to show respect for the High Elder, but Sed's hand held him still.

Sed leaned down and kissed him on top of his head, patted his shoulder, and turned and walked out without a word.

Chapter Eighteen
The Fifth Ritual

The day came that Saan and Soth were men. The Conclave was in session and would hold Soth's rise to Elder in the ancient ceremony the next day.

No one was prouder than His Highness, Prince Saan Maikel, the title Saan had to allow to be pinned upon him to attend his friend's greatest moment.

"Elder Soth," Saan said and bowed to his "twin" brother, then hugged him, showering his face with mock, passionate kisses, when all the ceremonial stiffness was over.

The loudest laughter came from Chief Elder Salar.

"At first, I had hoped you might come to us, my prince, but now I can see it would have been the end of the Conclave as we know it!"

Salar did not tell everything he knew that Grandfather Kaul-Leb told him. The path of these two young men would change the Conclave, but it was time.

Not many days later, Saan would undergo his fifth, and final, Ritual.

"Are you certain? If you aren't feeling well, this can be put off."

"Esoos, Saan. Please go on. I will feel better soon, most likely it is just anxiety over my boy."

Saan held Strella in his arms and held her against him.

"When I go to Stell's I will ask Tinka to look in, to make sure."

"If you must, I know I am fine, I wish you wouldn't worry so much."

"But I do worry, I love you, my girl."

Strella kissed him lightly and pushed him away.

"Go before Stell comes looking for you."

Saan kissed her nose and climbed up on his horse. He no longer rode in a wagon to Solot's for the Ritual. If he did become ill this time, Solot would bring him home.

He rode the short distance to Stell's house. Again, Stell would be with him for the Ritual. Getting to Stell and Tinka's, Saan dismounted and tied his horse to a post beside Stell's waiting animal.

He knocked and went through the door. Stell was sitting at the table bouncing one of his grandchildren on his lap.

"Ready, Saan? I had a little business to take care of here," he said, kissed the little one and set him on the floor.

"Are you sure you don't want the wagon?" Tinka asked, checking the child to see if his britches were dry or not. Satisfied, she kissed the little one's head.

"Esoos, I won't need it, and Solot can lend us his if needed. But could you check on Strella while I'm gone, she has seemed tired the last few days and I don't think she feels well today, but she insists I go."

"Certainly, the children and I can go over later— though if she's tired, she may tell us to leave!"

They all smiled, and the men left to mount their horses and go, each with a bag hooked to the saddle.

Salmar, Stant, and Stol met them on the edge of the village. Their trip to Solot's home was short and uneventful. After they got there, instead of just sitting around, the men went to the field to look at Solot's new colts. That evening, they ate well, especially Saan, he knew tomorrow he would have very little to eat or drink.

When the others ate the next day, he busied himself outside, watching the animals and clouds.

That night he drank the mixture that would help him sleep and went to bed. The next morning, he noticed that there were extra bindings on the bed, more than before.

"Do you really think I will get violent this time?"

"Soos, I do," Stol answered and handed Saan the cup of straight Dragon Fire. "Drink it quickly, or you may start getting sleepy and unable to finish it."

Saan took a deep breath and drank it down.

"Phew, it's bitter!"

"Soos, that's it's real taste, now lay back and let us get you strapped down."

As the other times, Saan had taken off his drawers before sitting down. He lay down, getting drowsy.

They began strapping him down, pulling all the bindings snuggly against him to prevent injury to themselves and Saan. His arms and legs began twitching as they finished.

He tried to sit up and jerked at the bindings when he found he couldn't. His head moved from side to side then he pulled with his legs and arms. His fingers arched against the bed linens, scratching wildly. His back twisted wildly as he fought the bindings across his body.

"Let me go! Untie me, let me up!"

"Saan, you know we can't," Stol said and brushed an errant hair from Saan's face. Saan jerked his head away from Stol's touch.

"Let me up, I said!" he shouted and bit at Stol's hand. He got nothing but air.

"He's really feeling it this time, be careful," Stol warned.

Saan pulled hard with each limb in turn and began to scream, great ear-splitting screeches. His long legs gathered and bunched, trying to kick. The muscles of his arms flexed against the bindings as he attempted to pull free.

The Receptacle was readied and placed on him, Stol thinking it would be needed soon.

Saan's breathing became hard and rapid, his hips ground into the bed, he fought every imaginable foe he could to free himself.

Then his back arched acutely and he screamed again, a long, high-pitched howl. The release came and he whimpered with the pain in his loins.

Saan was in agony. Fire burned within him, the muscles around his groin cramped, and a sickness began to rage in his gut. As the bile rose, he began to choke.

Rapidly, the bindings were torn from him to allow him to be rolled to his side. He began to heave violently, what little his body could find to bring up, it did. Gastric fluids burned his throat as his stomach emptied. His abdominal muscles pumped and pumped, causing him to heave over and over.

Tears rolled from his eyes with the pain of his mid-section and lower down. He grabbed at the bed linens and pulled himself into a tight fetal position, crying out.

"Strella, Strella, Strella," he called over and over, softer and softer as he lost consciousness.

The men wiped all around him, cleaning the vomit away from the bed linens and his mouth. A cool, wet cloth wiped his face and down his sweaty torso.

He began shivering violently and warm covers were placed around him. The fire in the already warm room was stoked. Saan began to dry heave again, his body straining to bring out what wasn't there. He was actively sick most of the day and into the night.

"Keep the candles burning," Stol advised. "We have to make sure he doesn't start bringing up blood. I have to be able to see what comes out of him."

"What do we do if he does start bleeding?" Salmar asked.

"Tay sent me a vial of his making to use if Saan does."

"And that will stop the bleeding?"

"Tay said that sometimes it stops bleeding from the stomach, sometimes it does not."

"What happens if the bleeding doesn't stop?"

Stol looked at Saan and wiped his forehead with a cool, damp cloth.

"If he does start to bleed and it can't be stopped, he could bleed to death."

After a rough time of heaving later, Stol ordered Saan held up in a sitting position. The cloth under his head was tinged in red.

Stol climbed in the bed and sat beside Saan, holding the vial to his lips and gently coaxing him to sip it.

"Saan, drink it, swallow it down, just a little, please," Stol asked him in quiet tones.

Saan shook his head, trying to avoid the fluid. Stol got some into the young man's mouth and spoke to him firmly.

"Strella said to drink it, all of it or she will be upset with you. Drink it, that's it, drink all of it."

Saan slowly consumed all the contents of Tay's vial and went back to sleep in Stol's arms.

"Do you want to put him down on the bed?" Stell asked.

"Esoos, I think it would be better to have him sit up for a while."

They all sat around him, watching him sleep. Stol rubbed and patted Saan's back, holding him against his chest.

A loud burp erupted from Saan's mouth.

The men all smiled and then began to laugh softly.

"Well, you burped the baby, Stol!" Salmar said as he rubbed his nephew's cheek tenderly.

When morning came, they considered him out of danger, there had been no more blood. But he was in agony.

Before he woke, soft groans signaled the intense pain. His eyes opened to mere slits as he grabbed at his midsection and doubled over. He cried out as they moved him around, trying to give him comfort.

Stol mixed a concoction from his bag with a weak broth and held the warm contents of the mug to his mouth.

"Please, Saan, try to drink this, it will help with your pain."

Saan leaned heavily against Stol's shoulder and obediently sipped at the broth. He was in so much pain, his eyes could not focus, but he could hear his voice, a voice he had trusted for most of his life.

Gradually, the cramping muscles relaxed and the sharp edge of the knife he thought of in his groin eased. He slipped into an oblivious slumber.

"Why didn't you give him that before?" Solot asked.

"Tay's mixture for the bleeding could not be mixed with anything else, it would be too diluted to work effectively."

"Our precious prince," Solot said and leaned over Saan asleep on Stol's shoulder and kissed his nephew's sweaty forehead.

Then he turned to his older brother.

"Salmar, why did the Chief Elder refer to Saan so frequently as being a prince? I know he was born to a king, but here..."

"Because in the Law of the Dragon, only for the petition for a fifth Ritual would he be allowed to enter the Conclave Complex. He would have been brought in and swiftly taken out after his business was conducted. As a royal dignitary, he is not under obligation to be a citizen to enter and enjoy the hospitality of the Conclave."

Stol stroked Saan's arm, thoughtfully and spoke softly.

"So, if the Ritual is successful this time, would the child be considered Torbraugh royalty, since this is considered a legitimate conception?"

"Soos, I would think so," Salmar answered. "But the Conclave would probably need to rule on that, I'm just a Chieftain, not a student of the Law."

Saan slept on and off during the course of the day. Each time he woke, he was in pain, usually slightly less than the time before. Stol dosed him with the herbal broth and kept him sleeping. Eventually,

Saan was returned to lie in the bed, being held upright only to sip the broth. There was no more retching, no more blood, only pain and sleep.

He roused once asking for the privy and was helped to use a clay pot. He was too sore to attempt walking.

Saan was never left alone over the course of the next night and day. Usually, all the men were arranged around him, tending to him, watching him, speaking to one another in subdued tones.

Stell wondered that his mother had not come to see how Saan was faring. He became slightly anxious, knowing that she had not felt well the day they left.

He voiced his worry to Stol and the others.

"Would you feel better if I rode over to see?" Stol asked. "Since Saan has just gone back to sleep, I could be gone for a while, and if Strella is feeling ill, maybe leave some herbs for her."

"Could you? I would go, but I don't think I would be any help."

Stol was gone longer than Stell expected, and Stell didn't like the way the Executioner looked when he returned.

Stell stood as Stol entered the room, ready to go himself if his mother were truly ill.

"Sit, Stell. You will need to be sitting down. Esoos, your mother is not ill, exactly."

"What then? What is wrong with her? Should I return home? Does she need me?"

"Esoos, she does not need you, and your returning home would not help. Tinka is with her, not that she really needs her, but..."

"What?"

"It is generally believed by the women of the village, and I have to agree after speaking with Strella and examining her that, well...that she is pregnant."

Everyone stared at Stol. Every mouth fell open. Only Saan did not react, still deep in his drugged sleep.

The men looked at him as he slept.

"But Mother is way beyond the age...she is...she is..."

"She is having a baby," Stol said.

"How?"

Stol opened his eyes widely and looked at Stell as if he could not believe the man did not understand about how to have babies. Then he cut his eyes toward Saan.

"I know she's been bedding with Saan, he's her Second Husband, but isn't she too...old?"

"It appears she is not."

"She has great-grandchildren!"

"I know, Stell, I've known your mother all my life, remember? We were boys together, we both have grandchildren, and I would be just as shocked as you are if someone told me that my mother was to have another baby. I've sent for Tay, just to be sure."

"Tay, the Chief Elder's son? You've sent all the way to the Conclave for him?"

Stell had stood, but now sat back down. For a few moments he could not speak.

"Soos, I've sent for Tay. When he sent a Custodian to me with the herbs medicine for a bleeding stomach should Saan have trouble with it, he requested, esoos, ordered that if anything unusual occurred involving Saan, I was to report it."

He looked at Saan, still sleeping.

"You must admit, siring a child with a woman well beyond child-bearing years is unusual."

Stol sat down beside the sleeping Saan and lightly touched his forehead.

"No fever, and he's not moaning any, that's good." He turned back to Stell.

"The verse we all sang as children, I've been thinking about it. Remember, the last prophecy of Kaul-Leb. I'm sure you remember it," he said, looking at Saan's three uncles. "It's recited by the children every year at the Remembrance."

"Soos, Stol," Salmar said. "But no one has any idea what it means. He wrote it just as he was about to die, it may mean nothing."

"I wonder, though," Stol said. "Say it, think about it. Think about it looking at Saan."

To satisfy Stol, Salmar repeated the old verse.

"Come the King
On Dragon Wing
With Eagle spread
Of Lion bred.
Seed once spurned,
The stones returned.
From his back, the Dragon torn,"

Salmar hesitated after saying 'torn." Then he continued on.

"Two of Blood and Three of Bed--one day born.
Sons, One of Each and One More--
One More and The Tribal Four.
But come again the Dragon Sign
White Dragon draws the final line.
Glory upon Glory and Woven In."

"Who do you know is a cross between Dragon, Lion, and Eagle? Who do you know has had the Dragon taken from his back? And who do you know," Stol asked, almost afraid to speak the last. "Who do you know is the son of a king, and could, however remote the possibility, be a king one day?"

Stol stood and walked across the room. He stared at a blank place on the wall and spoke more to himself than to the others.

"Now we've had another Ritual, and there may be a Blood Rights child, or maybe two."

Stell stood again and stepped toward Stol.

"Are you saying that my mother may be about to have THREE babies, three sons?"

Stol turned to face his old friend.

"I just don't know, Stell, but, but...the first part...it makes me wonder."

Tay was there before dark, his horse and the horses of his accompanying Conclave Custodians lathered with sweat from being pushed to get there quickly.

When the five started asking him questions about the prophesy, he raised his hand for silence. He shut the door and spoke barely above a whisper.

"Have you spoken of this to anyone outside this room?"

"Esoos," they said.

"Have you spoken of this with Saan?"

"Esoos," Stol said. "But he is here, he may have heard, though asleep."

"Did he need the vial I sent?"

"Soos."

"Did he drink it all?"

"Soos."

"Then he will not remember."

Salmar spoke.

"Is he the one of the prophesy?"

Tay pressed his lips together for several moments, then answered.

"Father thinks he may be, but is not for certain. He believes it best not to tell Saan—or anyone. If Saan is the One, it will happen, and happen best without our interference. If he is NOT the One...well, it is best it goes no further than this room."

Tay opened the door and started out, then turned back.

"Wait here, no talking."

He went out the door and was back in a few moments with four Custodians. Two stood outside the room guarding the door after Tay closed it again. Two stood inside the door, blocking the way out.

In his hands, Tay carried a golden box, He opened it and revealed a large tooth resting on a cloth of gold.

"I need all five of you to swear on the True Dragon's Tooth of Truth that you will speak no more of this to anyone, that you will never utter a word, even to one another, not even talk it over with only yourself, even if you think yourselves alone, and that you will say nothing of it to Saan."

He held the precious relic in front of him.

"Come place your hands on the Tooth and utter the words, 'I so swear.'"

Stell felt that as the father of an Elder of the Conclave and possibly the half-brother to children of the prophesy, he was obligated to comply and went first.

He stepped up to Tay, placed his hands on top of the tooth and took the oath of silence on the matter.

"I so swear."

He removed his hands from the tooth and backed away in awe of what he had touched.

Stol went next. He touched the tooth and said, "I so swear."

Salmar and his brothers went next, in order of their births. They each, in turn, touched the tooth and said the solemn words: "I so swear."

"Remember, your oaths include Saan, Strella, and Sotol's wife, Sheroma, as well."

"Soos." They all agreed.

Tay reverently shut the golden box.

"My father and brother usually handle these things, but it draws less attention for me to come here instead of either of them."

"Now, Stell, your son Junior Elder Soth is doing well, as are your sister and her family. In fact, Soth has risen to full Conclave Executioner."

Stol smiled at the thought of "little" Soth being a full Executioner, at the Conclave, no less.

Soth would keep records of all those sentenced to death within the People of the Dragon, and could come witness any execution carried out by a village executioner, if he so chose. Village executioners were also minor healers, Soth dealt only with the Law and punishments.

"Also," Tay continued. "I shall go see Strella to see to her suspected pregnancy. It will not be out of place as it is unusual in itself. As far as is to be known by anyone, that is my reason for coming. I came here first to consult the matter with Stol."

He looked them over.

"Any questions?"

No one spoke.

"Good, take care of our young man. Will you be taking him home tomorrow?"

"Soos," Stol answered.

"Very well, I'll tell Strella. Citizens, I will see you another time."

Holding the golden box snug in his hand, he turned to the door, and a Custodian opened it for him. As he walked down the hall, the Custodians fell in behind him. The sound could be heard as the door to the house opened and closed.

The men looked at one another, but said nothing. In their own minds, each wondered what the Custodians would have done if they had not sworn as Tay instructed.

The next morning Saan was carefully helped into the back of Solot's well padded wagon bed. Stol had dosed him liberally with his herbal broth, putting Saan into a deep sleep.

Salmar sat with Saan, both their horses tied to the wagon's rear. They progressed slowly, not wanting to jar his body, even if he were sleeping.

As they neared the village proper, Stell trotted his horse ahead of the others to let his mother know Saan was almost home.

He found her in her chair sewing tiny garments, humming to herself.

"Mother? Are you doing alright?"

"Soos, Stell."

She stood, her hand across her abdomen.

"Is Saan here?"

"He'll be here soon, but Stol has him asleep. He's had a hard time of it."

"That's what Tay said when he was here, so sweet of him to worry over me, don't you think?"

"Mother, you are awfully calm, considering."

"I've had babies before."

"But, Mother..."

"Stell, if the Dragon has seen fit to give me a child by Saan, I am not going to worry over it. Worry never changed a thing. Except to cause an upset stomach. Do I hear a wagon?"

Saan was carried in, still asleep.

Stol checked him out, that he was resting comfortably.

"I will be back after midday to check how he is doing, but for now, I think I shall go see my family. He won't need any more herbal broth until then." He kissed Strella on the cheek and left.

"Saan's had a rough time, Stol's herbs have kept him knocked out since..."

"Since what?"

"Nothing, Mother."

"Since he got over his bleeding stomach? Is that it, Stell?"

"Soos, Mother, how did you know."

"When Stol came to see about me, I made him tell me everything about Saan and how he was doing—I forced him to, I started crying about him and Stol couldn't handle that."

She laughed.

"I still have a few tricks."

"That wasn't fair, was it?"

"Esoos, but considering everything..."

"Everything—like the fact that I am going to be a big brother?"

"That, too. Sit down, or do you need to get home?"

Salmar and his brothers came in through the stable's connecting doorway.

"We've got Saan's horse settled in his stall and mucked out around the mare," Salmar said. "Do you need anything else before we leave? I don't think Saan is going to be up to doing much for a few days."

"Esoos, we will be fine, but thank you. Stol said he would be in to check on Saan after while and Stell's house it just over the way. Thank you, though," she said and smiled.

"If you do need something, please send for me, and Strella, thank you for letting Saan try once more for Solot."

Salmar and his brothers left. Solot was hoping that he was heading home to a wife as happily with child as Strella seemed to be.

Stell left for his home, too, with promises to be back before long. He retrieved his horse and walked in front of it to his own home and stable.

Strella went into the bedroom to check on Saan.

Stol's herbs were still working.

She stroked his hair.

"So much better than the old days," she said to him, knowing he could not hear. "When the pain just stayed and stayed."

She could not stop smiling as she sat beside him.

"I am having your baby, Saan," she said and ran her finger down the line of relaxed muscle of his arm. "I don't know what caused this miracle, but I don't care."

Knowing it would be a while yet before Stol would check with them again, she kicked off her short boots and pulled her feet up onto the bed. She lay beside him and dozed, her arm around his bare shoulders.

When Saan awoke, he discovered he was home again and that Strella lay beside him, curled up, her arm across him. He stretched slightly and felt a dull ache in his lower abdominal area. He moved to put his arm across her and hurt a little, but it was much better than the last time he was awake.

His touch roused her.

He smiled as she opened her eyes.

Her hand reached to his upper lip and smoothed the hairs down, then she kissed him.

"I've missed you," she said and kissed him again.

"I am so glad to be home and back to you where I belong. I don't ever want to be away from you again. Just you and me, that's all I need."

"You haven't heard, then?"

"Heard what?"

"About the...baby?"

"What? Solot and Sheroma's baby?"

"No, our baby."

"OUR baby? What do you mean, our baby?"

Strella sat up and patted her belly.

"This baby. I'm pregnant."

Saan sat up, wincing at the movement.

"You? You are pregnant? But... I thought..."

"So did I. But it seems that somehow it has happened. Do you mind?" Strella asked. For the first time, she wasn't so sure it was a happy event.

"Mind?" he asked and placed his hand on her belly.

"I never thought it possible we could have our own! I'm, I'm, I'm beyond happy!"

He put his head down by his hand, wincing again, but laughing.

"Hello in there, this is your father talking!"

Strella pulled his face up to hers and kissed him hard.

"Is it safe to come in?" Slot's voice called from the hallway.

"Soos, come in," Saan said as Strella retrieved her boots, slipped them on, and stood.

"Have you heard the big news? We're going to have a baby!"

"Stol was one of the first to know," Strella said. "Stell sent him over to check on me after the Ritual."

"And you didn't tell me?"

"I told it to Stell in front of you, but you were in no condition to listen. You had a very hard time of it."

"Soos, I did," Saan admitted. "Does that mean that the Ritual will be successful?"

"It remains to be seen, but I am guessing it was."

Stol thought how he wished he could mention the prophesy, that he was sure there would not only be a baby in Solot's house, but most likely two. And that he feared Strella would carry three. But he had sworn on the Tooth.

"How are you feeling? Do you want to have any more herbs for pain?"

"Esoos, I want to be able to stay awake—I can stand the pain that there is."

"Good. I do need to give my attention to a few others now."

"Thank you, Stol, I know I've kept you awfully busy."

Stol patted him on the head and winked at him.

"You have always been one of my favorite children."

The three of them laughed and Stol left to go home again, wondering how the next few months would go.

Chapter Nineteen
Babies

Strella eased herself over the edge of the bed and felt around for her boots with her toes.

"Strella, let me get those for you," Saan said and knelt down at her feet, slipping her boots over her feet, one at a time.

The boots she wore were new, much larger than what she usually wore. Her feet, ankles, and calves were swollen. She hadn't seen them in weeks, she couldn't bend over far enough to even know if she still had feet.

She held her hands out and Saan gently pulled her up and onto her swollen feet. He took her right hand in his and wrapped his left arm around her waist, guiding her carefully into the front of the house toward the kitchen. Walking was not easy for her, her large belly impeded her balance and prevented her back from proper alignment.

Everyone had first been baffled and amazed that a woman of Strella's age was with child, then they thought she must be carrying twins. Now it was wondered just how many babies she was harboring within her.

Solot's wife, Sheroma, was also quite large with child, but not quite as large as Strella. It was rumored that barren women touching Strella, or even Sheroma were now expecting. Women with large families tended to avoid close contact with either one of them.

Once Saan had Strella settled at the table in the kitchen, he first poured her a large mug of hot tea with honey to sweeten. She took a small sip, then sat it down.

"Is something wrong? Did I mix it wrong?" he asked, anxious over everything involving her.

"Esoos, it tastes fine, but I think—I think I just had a birth pain."

"Let me see," a voice said from behind Saan. Tay's voice. He had insisted that he stay with them for the last two weeks, thinking he might be needed at any time.

He gently placed a hand on her rounded belly. Under his touch, he felt the muscles move and grow hard, then ease. Another contraction followed. Then another.

"The pains are coming fast," she said. "Before, it was much longer between them at first."

She groaned lightly.

"I think it's nearly time, I feel like the baby is coming. NOW!"

Between them, Saan and Tay practically carried Strella back into the bedroom. Tay quickly spread the several pieces of tanned hides over the bed to protect it from the fluids that would come with birth, then spread soft cloths. Saan helped her back up to the bed and lie down, slipping off her boots and doing what he could to make her comfortable.

"Tell the Custodians to get the women," Tay said to Saan as the Healer felt again the rapidly increasing contractions with his hand on Strella.

Saan ran to the front of the house and burst through the door to the Custodians stationed outside.

"Tay said to get the women, the baby...the babies are coming."

There had been four Custodians at the door ever since Tay had moved in. As others had realized the similarities between Saan and Kaul-Leb's prophesy, Salar began to fear interference and had sent a large detail of his Custodians to protect Strella and Sheroma.

Several women were notified and came quickly to Strella's home. Others, following the prophesy climbed into a wagon and started for the home of Solot. If the prophesy were true, there would be babies born at his house today, as well.

As soon as Tinka arrived and went into the room with Strella, Tay, and the other women who came in with Tinka, Saan was banished to the front of the house. He moved restlessly around, unable to focus his attention on any one thing. Stell was almost as bad. Stol, Salmar, and Stant soon joined them. It wasn't long before the cry of a newborn child was heard.

Saan went to his bedroom, met by Tay at the door.

"Esoos, Saan, not now. The next one is almost here."

Tay shut the door.

Stol and Stell took him by the hands and pulled him back into the front of the house. They made him sit in a chair and gave him tea with orders to drink. He tried, but just sat and held the mug in his lap.

They heard other cries.

"Is that the same, or another?" Saan asked.

No one answered. They didn't know.

He set his tea mug on the floor and rose. He stood, looking down the hallway, listening. Saan could hear muffled voices coming from the room, but could not understand.

Another cry.

Saan's breathing became hard and deep.

"I've got to know!" he said softly. "I've got to know!"

After a long forever to Saan, the door opened, and Tay came out. He closed it behind himself and came to Saan.

Saan clasped his hands together tightly, the knuckles going white with the pressure.

Tay smiled.

"How? How is Strella?"

"I have never seen an easier birth, or should I say births? Saan, you have three sons."
Saan leaned against the wall, pale.

"Three? Are they, are they?"

"Soos, all three healthy looking and robust."

Tay took Saan by the arm and led him toward the closed door. It opened and Tinka and the other women filed out, Tinka kissed his cheek as she passed by him.

Saan looked at Tay and Tay pushed the younger man ahead of him into the room. Strella sat propped up in the bed, looking tired but happy and satisfied.

Three little naked newborn boys lay in a wad on her lap, snuggled up together, their coverings off to one side.

"It is time for you to name your sons, Saan," Strella said to him as he gaped at the abundance before him.

She took a white covering from beside herself and wrapped the child nearest her belly loosely, handing him to his young father.

"This one is your firstborn."

"What?" he swallowed hard, looking at his child. "What name should I give him?"

"What does your heart tell you?"

He said the first name that came to his mind.

"Shalim, for my grandfather,"

He wrapped little Shalim snuggly and kissed him, cradling the little one in his arms protectively.

Secure in his father's arms, Shalim slept. Tay gently took the baby and kissed him himself before placing him in the empty crib by the bed.

Strella had the second baby with a red covering ready for Saan.

"This little fellow is your second son. What will you name him?"

"For my father, Maikel."

Saan held his father's namesake close and snuggled his face against the little belly, then wrapped him securely in his covering. He held the infant close in his arms and watched him sleep, then handed him to Tay. Tay kissed the little forehead and put him in the crib next to his brother.

The third baby had a blue covering wrapped loosely around him as Saan took him. Saan noticed a mark on the bottom of the little right foot.

"What are the three black dots on his foot?"

"Tay marked each one as he was born," Strella said. "So we would not confuse who was who."

"Shalim has one mark, Maikel has two, now who is this little one with three marks?" Tay asked.

Saan held his third son up against his chest, stroking the baby's back. He hesitated for a bit.

"For the grandfather I never knew, Railen."

Railen was securely wrapped and only went to sleep after seeming to stare at his father for several moments.

Tay chuckled.

"He's keeping a watch over you, Saan."

After Tay took possession of Railen, Saan carefully sat down next to Strella and kissed her lightly on the lips.

"How is my girl?" he asked. "You have done very fine work today."

"A little tired, but very, very, VERY happy. Aren't they beautiful?"

"Almost as beautiful as their mother," Saan said and kissed her again.

A knock sounded at the door and Tinka pushed it open

"Tay, a Custodian has come with a message for you."

"Thank you, Tinka," he said and left the room.

Tinka let him pass then came in, holding a mug of steaming tea.

She handed it to Strella and turned to Saan.

"Now, it is time for all new fathers to let new mothers drink their tea and get some rest."

"Soos," Tay said, returning. "And Saan, you are needed elsewhere. Solot's wife, Sheroma, is in active labor and about to deliver."

"But she is not as far along as Strella was."

"Tell the babies, not me."

"But they are Solot's children now, not mine."

Saan looked Tay straight in the eye.

"Or are you believing Kaul-Leb's prophesy, do you think it meant my babies?"

"Has someone spoken to you of it?"

"I learned that verse as a child like everyone else. And it seems the Conclave and its Healer have been more than interested in the lives of a simple Second Husband and the babies he fathered."

"Saan, there has never been anything simple about your life. Not one day of it."

Saan just looked at Tay for a while, thinking. He bent down and kissed Strella softly and smiled at her.

"You rest like Tinka said, get something to eat, and I'll be home as soon as I can."

Strella took his face in her hands and kissed him hard.

"I love you, Saan, never forget, no matter what, I love you."

He gazed into her eyes, mirroring the love, stood, and left with Tay.

As they mounted their horses and rode to Solot's house, Saan wondered if there were any Custodians left at the Conclave. A full detail accompanied them, and their village had them everywhere. He saw many more at Solot's home.

They entered the dwelling and Tay walked quicky into the bedroom, passing by Solot. He, like Saan had been, was ordered away and confined to the main room of the house. After learning that Strella's children had been well born and healthy, Solot's brothers and Stol had ridden over to keep him company. Stell remained in his mother's house should Tinka need him.

Saan sat with them. Or fidgeted about.

No one spoke, listening for a baby to announce himself.

It was midday when they heard the first cry of an infant, not long after, another. With the second cry, Saan grabbed at his back, gasping. He stood, his eyes wide, and fell to his knees, pulling at his tunic.

"What is it?" Stol asked, pulling the back of Saan's tunic up to see what bothered him so.

Stol froze, the tunic hem in his hand as he held it up and away from the flesh of Saan's back. Then he pulled the cloth up to Saan's shoulders.

"Come look," was all he could say.

Saan was now on his hands and knees, almost panting.

His uncles went to him, and looked as Stol said.

From the top of his shoulders down nearly to the top of his britches was an exquisite White Dragon, its wings spread out from its body, filling almost all the skin of his back. Its two front "hands" were open, the one on his left seeming to hold the Black Dragon mark of his joining with Strella, the right held out as if holding the eagle-looking scar gently within its grasp. Its magnificent head turned upwards as if looking to the heavens. Its hindquarters were as the mighty, muscular legs and tail of a lion.

By the time Tay came to retrieve Solot and Saan to see the babies, the men had Saan stripped to the waist sitting on a short stool.

His breathing had returned to normal, but he looked bewildered.

Tay could not see Saan's back when he first entered the room. He walked around to look. His mouth dropped open and he went to the door.

He came back in after speaking with the Custodians.

"I have sent for my father. He will need to see for himself. He may already be on his way as I sent word earlier this morning that the babies were coming."

Tay came back and looked again at Saan's back, touching the beautiful White Dragon.

Then, remembering why he had entered the room. He spoke to Solot and Saan.

"We have two more healthy boys awaiting their names. Come, both of you."

Saan retrieved his tunic and slipped it on, buttoning it.

Obediently, they followed Tay into the room with the babies and their mother. Aware of how Tay made sure of the identity, Saan took note of the bottoms of the babies' feet. He said nothing when he saw that one baby had four marks on his foot, the other five. He thought he would have to ask Tay later why it wasn't one and two. He also saw the cloths provided for Sooo to use for her little boys to wrap them were a black one and a green one.

"Why am I here?" Saan asked. "These are Solot's children, he names them."

"Wouldn't you wish to be among the first to hear their names? You are their Blood Father."

Saan shrugged his shoulders, smiling. They were as much his own by bloodline as the three Strella had given him earlier, but legally, that was a different matter.

Solot had heard as they waited the names given to the triplets. He would not be naming either of these for his own father. He held the baby in the black wrap and watched the child stretch and pull his little legs back up in the fetal position. How long I have waited, he thought.

Days gone by rushed through his thoughts and the name that imprinted upon his heart came to his lips.

"This child shall be named for Stell," he said. "He never became my brother, but he is one of the most honorable men I have ever known."

Tay took the child from his legal father and placed him in the crib. Sheroma handed her second son to Solot, wrapped in green.

"And this one, this precious little boy shall be named for the one who has given the most solace to Saan, he shall be named Soth."

"Thank you, Uncle Solot," Saan said, his eyes swimming in tears. He kissed the baby's head and then bent over the crib to kiss little Stell as Tay placed little Soth beside him.

A noise came to them from the hallway. The door opened and Salar entered, carrying an object wrapped in a golden cloth. He spoke to his son Tay.

"Your second messenger intercepted my coach as it neared the village. I stopped briefly to see the first three, then came here."

The Chief Elder stepped over to the crib to gaze upon the little twins.

"They are boys, soos?"

"Soos, Father. Solot has named them Stell and Soth."

Salar turned and beckoned toward the door.

"Soth, come see the little prince named for you."

Soth came from the hallway, pausing briefly to place his hand on Saan's shoulder, then advanced to the crib. Around Soth's waist over his Elder robes, was a leather belt with a scabbard and sword.

"Which one is my namesake?"

"The one in green," Tay answered. "Now, we should all leave and let Sheroma rest. Being on exhibit is not an activity for a new mother."

"Certainly," Salar said and led the way out, leaving only Solot to stay with his wife.

Once in the main room with Salmar and Stol and several of the Chief Elder's personal Custodians, Salar turned to Saan and addressed him.

"Now, my young prince, may I see your back?"

Saan removed his tunic, holding it in his hand, he turned to allow Salar to see.

"Soos," he said thoughtfully. "That is it."

"Sir?" Saan asked.

Salar beckoned to a Custodian by the door, The man advanced holding a volume that looked very, very old. Salar handed the cloth covered bundle in his hand to Soth.

The Custodian held the old book up as Salar carefully opened the ancient tome to a page marked with a ribbon of gold.

The hand painted page made all the villagers in the room that had seen Saan's back gasp.

"What?" Saan asked. "What is it?"

"Look at the page in my book, Prince Saan."

Saan turned and saw the page.

"This is the White Dragon that now resides on your back. Even down to the Black Dragon marriage mark

and the Eagle scar."

"How?"

"It is from the prophesy of the last king of the People of the Dragon. Over one thousand years ago. This is the first time since the building of the Conclave it has been out of the archives."

Saan could not speak for several moments.

"The king? A thousand years ago?" he finally was able to ask.

"Soos, King Seraclek the Law Giver, the Writer of the Law of the Dragon. He renounced his throne and became the first Chief Elder of the Conclave."

Salar gently closed the book and the Custodian carefully carried it out. He walked between two others, ready to catch him should he trip.

"The king's crown had lain in the Archives since his abdication. He pulled all the jewels off and sold them to pay for the building of the Conclave buildings. He told his people that when the gems returned, it would be time for the next king."

He beckoned to another Custodian. The man produced the box King Maikel had used to send Slia's ashes home. There were no longer jewels on it.

"All Seraclek's jewels returned to us but one."

Salar took the bundle back from Soth and stripped away the cloth. In his hand was a jeweled crown. In the front was a diamond on what looked like some sort of stem sticking out. Around it was emptiness. Something was missing.

"But we know where it is hidden. Soth, please bring me the jewel."

Soth advanced to Saan, reached to his friend's neck, and grabbed Slia's pendant. He cut the cord with his sword, handing the stone to Salar.

Salar turned the stone, looking at it closely, then slipped the hole that had been for the cord over the diamond and onto the mounting. It snapped in tightly.

"Your Majesty, your crown."

Salar held the restored crown out in both hands.

Saan just stared at him and dropped his tunic to the floor.

"Quite right, Your Majesty, something needs to be done before you may accept your crown. High Council? Shall Saan, Son of Maikel, Son of Railen, all of royal birth in the Torbraugh be returned to Citizenship among the People of the Dragon?"

Sed's right hand was held out, palm up. One by one the other members of the High Council did the same.

Soth stepped forward and did the honors, untying Saan's hair from behind his neck, then weaving the braids from the hair of his temples. He gathered braids and loose hair behind Saan's neck and retied it.

Salar walked up to Saan and settled the crown on Saan's head, smiling.

"Your Majesty," he said, and bowed. The Chief Elder had just bowed to him. The Chief Elder!

Saan's mouth fell open, but he could not speak.

"We will have your official coronation at your home in the Conclave when your children are a few weeks older and better able to travel. For now, due to the tender nature of newborns, they will be left as they are. But there is one here who needs to swear his allegiance to you today, for he and your guards will never kneel again in your presence as they will be ever watchful, defending your life and the lives of those you love."

Saan still stood silently but was able to close his mouth as Soth stood in front of him, sword in hand, holding it out. Soth dropped to his knees and raised the sword above his head and bowed down.

"My King, I am yours. I pledge my life to protecting yours, Always and Forever."

With Soth, every Conclave Custodian in the room knelt before Saan, his sword raised in subjection.

The enormity of the proceedings struck Saan. The Chief Elder had just declared him a king. Not just any king, but the King of the People of the Dragon. His best friend and a whole detail of Conclave Custodians had just pledged their lives to protect him.

He stood in the midst of the crowd around him, half-naked with an ancient crown on his head. He felt the Dragon speaking through him.

"Arise, Soth, Defender of the Dragon, rise also my Custodians of the Dragon."

Swords found their scabbards. Saan reached his hands out to Soth and they clasped forearms, looking into one another's eyes.

"I thought you only wanted to study the Law. I thought I was the one who liked to play with weapons."

"I thought so, too. But who can I trust you to? My heart beats with yours, it always has."

Saan pulled Soth into his arms and they embraced as true brothers. When they released their holds, Saan reached to his crown, now skewed on his head and lifted it off, turning to Salar.

"Perhaps you should take care of this for me, Chief Elder, I am not accustomed to caring for ancient treasures. Save this one."

He kissed the prominent red stone that he had worn around his neck for most of his life and handed the crown back to Salar. Only the glass pendant with Slia's ashes remained hanging below his collar bone.

One of the Custodians lifted Saan's tunic from the floor and handed it to Soth. The Custodian himself was too intimidated to touch the new king standing before him and help him on with his clothing.

Soth eased the sleeves over Saan's arms and buttoned the front.

"Remember the day I came and you put those boots on my feet?"

"Soos." They both laughed.

Saan regained his composure thinking of Strella.

"What do I tell your grandmother? How is she going to take this?"

Salar answered.

"Remember, my King, I went first to your home in the village and saw your queen and children. She knows."

"You told her?"

"She knew before I arrived. As she rested from giving birth and you had gone to be near for the twins, she had a visitor, your mother, Queen Slia. She appeared to your mother and told her of your destiny."

"That must have been strange, Mother was to have been Strella's daughter-in-law, and now Strella has given her grandchildren."

"Soos, but only as we see things. To the spirit world, there is no strangeness, only what is and what is to be."

"Chief Elder, you said I and my children would live in the Conclave Complex?"

"Soos?"

"I won't be taking these two from Solot, will I?"

"Esoos, my King, only if you commanded. They are only of the prophesy; they are not your heirs. But having served the prophesy, Solot and his wife will be rewarded. Not only will they both live to see grandchildren and great-grandchildren, but their house will also be full of more of their own now."

"We will have more?" Solot asked, astounded, from the hallway. "Forgive me for eavesdropping, but I heard words, words I didn't fully understand, so came in here."

He looked fully at his nephew.

"Have I heard correctly? It is the prophesy? It has come to pass?"

"Soos, Uncle, so the Chief Elder has said."

Salmar stood with his face in his hands.

Saan went to him and pulled his hands away to look at him.

"What is wrong, Uncle Salmar?"

"When I think of how miserable I made your early life, it breaks my heart, and you were only fulfilling the prophesy. I could have harmed you."

"Esoos, Uncle. You made it come to pass. Soos, you did. If you had not kept me from adoption, if I had been less drawn to Soth and Strella......Why do you think Mother did not come to you in your dreams until it was too late to change my fate?"

Salmar started to hug Saan, but hesitated.

"I will always be your nephew, no matter what else I may become."

Chapter Twenty
The Coronation

"You will come to us in the Conclave, won't you, Stell? You and Tinka and your whole houseful of youngsters are always welcome. Anytime, not just for the wedding and crowning."

"I suppose we could just send all of them with you now," Stell answered, laughing.

"Not without Mother to make them behave," Soth said, holding his mother in a big hug.

Their little group was surrounded by Saan's Custodians as they bid their farewells to the village.

Strella and the three little baby boys were comfortably settled in the coach sent by Salar.

The twins were in Solot's arms and Saan kissed them each good-bye before he boarded the coach to leave.

The residents of the village were gathered at a respectful distance to watch their new king leave them. At the periphery, a wave of disruption caught the attention of not only the detail of Custodians, but Soth. Hands went to hilts, ready to begin defending, if necessary.

Soth stood with his back to the coach after closing the door and signaling its being surrounded by Custodians. He motioned with his eyes toward Saan's uncle holding the twins and Custodians quickly bunched around him and Saan's Blood Sons.

The cause for the distress neared. It was a detail of Torbraugh. Sixteen wore the royal livery, last seen when a similar detail brought Saan. Two others rode in their midst, wearing the well-cut dress clothing of the Torbraugh King's Court.

Soth, hand on the hilt of his sword, advanced toward them, Custodians filling the gap by the coach when he left it.

The two not in military dress dismounted, handing their horses' reins to others. Seeing Soth step forward, the men went to him and bowed.

The older of the two spoke in heavily accented Dragon.

"We come from the court of the Torbraugh seeking the one sent here years ago by King Rondol."

"For what purpose?" Soth asked. "Why, after all this time?"

The man looked greatly pained, as if what he had to say physically hurt to utter.

"Three weeks ago, King Rondol ordered all within the royal family to assemble in the palace. His sons, his grandsons, uncles, nephews, and all, all their wives. His wife, his daughters, and granddaughters-- every member who could possibly lay claim to the royal house, and even his children born bastard and their families. He had them all murdered before his eyes. He commanded his royal guard to slaughter them all. Then he retired to his own chambers and, and taking a dagger that had belonged to his father, he cut his own throat."

Sweat poured from the man's forehead and he licked his dry lips.

"We come seeking what remains of the royal house of the Torbraugh. We come asking, esoos, begging for the return of Prince Saan."

The coach door opened and Saan stood in the breach. A powerful dread fell over the Torbraugh, as if at any moment they expected to be destroyed by the same force that had maddened this young man's oldest brother.

"I am Saan, son of Maikel and Slia. According to the prophesy of the White Dragon, I have been declared King of the People of the Dragon. I go now to take residency in the Conclave with my sons and their mother."

The Torbraugh detail dismounted and knelt, following the actions of the officials, who had gone to their knees.

"Your Majesty, we beg you accept as well the crown of the Torbraugh," the official said. His body trembled. In his mind, he knew that those were not the words he had intended to say, but that those words had come out of his mouth and were the ones that a force outside himself had wanted.

The official stood and from a stout box attached to his saddle withdrew a golden crown that glinted in the sunlight.

"This, Your Majesty, is the crown worn by your father, King Maikel, and by his father, King Railen, and the kings before them."

He went back to his knees as Soth advanced to accept the crown for Saan. Carrying it both hands, Soth took it to Saan. As the floor of the coach was only knee height from the ground, Saan bowed slightly to allow his brother of the heart to place the Torbraugh emblem of power on his head. Only Soth could see the wink given him by Saan as the crown nestled in his hair.

Saan unbuttoned his tunic and allowed it to slip down. Behind him, reaching across the children, Strella caught it before it reached the floor. Saan turned to face her to allow the Torbraugh and any others who wanted to see the White Dragon on his back.

Saan stood tall with Soth facing the Torbraugh in front of him.

Beyond his reasoning, Saan found he could remember the words of his early childhood.

He spoke to the Men of the Eagle behind him.

"Do you see, men of the Torbraugh, the mark of the Prophecy upon my back? You see on my right shoulder, the Torbraugh Eagle in the gentle grasp of the hands of the Dragon with the hind quarters of the Lion?"

He turned back to face them.

"I accept the crown of my father and grandfather. With this, the People of the Torbraugh, The People of the Song-hee, and the People of the Dragon are united into One People, as predicted in the Prophecy of the Poet Kaul-Leb."

He thought for a moment.

"Please stand and get back on your horses. Follow my coach to the Conclave. You will be given food, a place to rest, and stabling for your horses. After you are rested, I will send the detail back to the Palace of my father with my orders. You men of the court will remain to observe my coronation as King of the One People."

He turned to Strella and reclaimed his tunic, put his arms through the sleeves and sat down facing her.

Soth closed the door and mounted his horse, staying close to the side of the coach.

He reached to the top of his head and lifted off the golden crown. He turned it this way and that and set it on the cushioned seat. The coach began moving, the sound of hoof falls surrounding them.

"The last time I saw that, it was on Rondol's head." Strella smiled at him, reached forward, and patted his knee next to hers.

"And now it's yours."

She glanced at their sons to her right on the seat, sleeping.

"Your sons slept through all of it."

"Our sons, Your Majesty," he said to her.

"Our sons," she said and looked at them again.

"Their father is feeling neglected," he said, patting the seat beside himself.

He held her hands as she rose and moved across to sit beside him. He moved the golden crown to where she had been sitting. Saan put his arms around her and they kissed. Then they snuggled and she went to sleep in the crook of his arm.

Strella was wide awake early the morning of the coronation. She wore a new dress she had not made herself. Not since her childhood when her mother sewed for her had that happened. Her Saan would also be wearing clothing she had not sewn.

To satisfy the nobles of the Torbraugh, they had accepted the royal garb from them. As soon as the detail had arrived home, the nobles readied to come as instructed by their new king, managing to acquire gifts before leaving. The Torbraugh guests had made it to the Conclave in record time, wanting to show their delight in their young king. The men of the detail had been lush in praising him and his generosity.

They were also consumed with curiosity about the Conclave Complex and their new queen who had given birth so easily so late in life. That their king already had children born and healthy was a boon. The Great Hall was packed with members of the Conclave from Apprentices to High Elders, Village Elders, Tribal Chieftains, Torbraugh Nobles, and every known person of the bloodline of Kaul-Leb.

Saan's and Strella's families sat in honored places with Salar and Sheelta. Tinka and her older children held the triplets. Solot and his wife sat by them with their twins.

All rose as Saan and Soth entered and walked to the center of the raised platform. Soth motioned for them to sit.

Saan had only the britches to his new outfit. On his shoulders was the golden marriage cape used by generations of Elders of the Conclave. Strella entered on the arm of her son Stell and advanced to the steps leading to the platform.

Soth turned Saan away from the gathered crowd and lifted the hem of the cape, revealing to all the assembly his White Dragon. He dropped the hem and turned his beloved friend around and went to collect his grandmother from his father to present her to his king. Stell went to sit with his family as his son gave Strella to Saan. He was in his seat as Saan lifted the right hem of the cape and surrounded Strella with it, touching his left shoulder.

Three Custodians advanced to Stell and Tinka and took the triplets in their arms, carrying them to their parents. Strella held one in each arm, Saan took one in his left, the cape covering their whole family.

Saan kissed his bride and cheers rose across the Hall. He was no longer a Second Husband, but her true husband and she his true wife. And their sons heirs of prophesy come to pass.

The Custodians reclaimed the babies and took them again to Tinka and Stell. Soth helped Saan off with the marriage cape, handing it to a Senior Elder, and taking the grand tunic given by the Torbraugh nobles. He helped Saan to dress, taking care of the pendant of Slia's ashes still hanging to her son's neck.

Salar left his seat accompanied by Sed. In Sed's hands were the two crowns. Reading in the old prophesy of a term, Glory upon Glory, Sed had discovered a groove in the ancient Dragon crown that the Torbraugh crown fit into perfectly as if made to fit together. Today, they were together. Laced through the dual crown was fragrant lion's tooth laurel, used as ceremonial crowns among the Song-hee for generations.

Salar and Sed mounted the steps to the platform and stood before a golden cushion placed there by an Apprentice. On this cushion, Saan knelt, his head bowed, demonstrating his own humility before the Law of the Dragon. The crown, imbued with the history of the three peoples made one was placed on his head by Salar.

For several moments, nothing was said, none moved. Then Salar spoke.

"Arise, my King."

Sed and Soth were on either side of him to steady him as he stood, no one wanted the king's crown to slide off because he stumbled. Saan stayed by the golden cushion as Strella was led to it by Soth and helped to kneel.

An Apprentice coming from the back of the platform carefully carried a thin golden circle with one large white stone, the queen's crown, made especially for the new queen. It was white for the White Dragon, it held one stone for the One People.

Strella had been the primary designer, wanting nothing ornate, but simple and meaningful. Sed took the crown and handed it to his father, who handed it to Saan. Saan kissed the stone and placed the crown gently on Strella's bowed head.

Again, for several moments, nothing was said until Saan spoke.

"Arise, my Queen."

He alone helped Strella to her feet and placed his arm around her waist before turning together to face the crowd. He raised his hand in tribute to his people and they showered him with their vocal praise.

That night, alone in their quarters in the High Elder corridor, Salar and his wife Sheelta lay in one another's arms. And so they were found the next day. They had walked the dark corridor together, neither one having to go on living without the other.

His one desire had been to see his grandfather's last prophesy come to life and it had been granted. The next night, Salar made his first visit to Saan as his Spirit Warrior.

"Saan, child."

Saan looked up from the copy of the Law Soth had given him.

"Chief Elder?"

"Esoos, not Chief Elder any more, just Salar," he said and winked.

Saan stood.

"Sit, child, you ARE the king."

Saan sat.

"I won't come to you often, child, you won't need me."

"What message do you have for me, Chief El— Salar?"

"Only that your people will have peace, a long peace. A peace that will last five hundred years, one hundred years for each of your sons of prophesy."

"What will happen, then, Salar?"

"The same that happens with all kingdoms of men, Saan."

"My distant children will not be good kings?"

"Esoos, my child, no kingdom made by man, no matter how well it starts, no matter how wonderful it is, will last. Men become greedy and only love themselves and their pleasures. Remember your brother Rondol?"

"Soos," Saan said softly.

"But do not be sad, child. Five hundred years of peace is a goodly amount. Many good and righteous people will live out their lives because of you."

"Will there ever be a kingdom that doesn't fail, Salar?"

"Soos, there will be one, my child. There will be one and it will last forever. At first, it will seem to fall, and its king will die, but He will return, and He will rule forever."

"I don't understand, Salar."

"You are not meant to, my child. Just trust that it is so. Just as you must trust that there will be five hundred years of peace for the One People of the White Dragon. It grows late and you are not an Apprentice studying to please an Elder. Go to bed, a king needs a clear head."

"Soos, Salar. Will you come to me, when I don't know what to do? When I need advice?"

Salar grinned, winked, and spoke to him before he left.

"Always and forever."

Chapter Twenty-one
The Final Chapter

"Are you going to release this one around Easter, then?" LB asked his brother, Stahl.

"I think so, it ends with hope, and I think people need that, don't you?"

"How did it work out, not having Ted as Kaul-Leb's voice over?"

"Not bad, his brother worked out fine, and seems to enjoy it. Ted just wanted to let his brother have it all to himself, said Bob makes a better young Kaul-Leb now, anyway."

"Guess so, have you seen the latest pictures of the twins?" LB said and turned a frame around to show his brother. "Maikel has three teeth, Railen has two."

"My nephews get their good looks from their uncle, that's for sure. Do you have room to work on that desk? So many pictures!"

"A little, I may have to get a bigger desk, though," LB said and laughed.

"The kids and Taylor, they are my life, not all this," he said, gesturing around his office filled with the workings of the publishing part of their family business.

"I know, I know," Stahl said. "Same here, but I have to deal with teenagers now, too."

"Teenagers and toddlers," LB said. "Brave man."

"Don't forget it, little bro, family first."

LB turned to his big brother, the producer known for dropping production negotiations flat if one of his kids needed him, no matter what.

"Always and forever."

They laughed and toasted one another with their diet sodas, then turned out the lights, and went home to their families.